ALSO BY LISA ZUMPANO

THE LILLIE MEAD HISTORICAL MYSTERY SERIES

An Unfortunate End

A Willful Grievance

A Fine Duplicity

A FINE DUPLICITY

A LILLIE MEAD HISTORICAL MYSTERY

LISA ZUMPANO

FIELDING HOUSE PRESS

For my boys

1

STEFANIE

CORNWALL, SUMMER 1922

The Cornish coast was steeped with the smell of stale and rotting fish. Perhaps it was the weather—a hot and humid late July morning without much of a breeze. Or her particular location—on the crest of a curved black cliff high above a swirling bay where the fishermen were laying out their catch on the dark rocks below. Basket after bountiful basket of silvery pilchards, flopping about in the morning sun, the rays catching their scales and flicking their glinting bodies with an ultraviolet spectrum that in turn changed them from grey to gold and back again. Their aroma was making her feel slightly ill as she watched the men without any envy, and contemplated her trajectory.

She glanced back at the house, wondering if the duke's guest was still there—a man who appeared, at least visually, to be his own uncanny doppelgänger. If it weren't for the slight difference in accent and mannerism, the two could quite conceivably be related. The thought caused her to shiver. She preferred her privacy, and decided to walk along the cliff's edge to the mouth of the bay instead of making her way back to the house to indulge in idle chit chat inside the house.

She rounded the corner of the bay and faced the lonely solitude of the open sea, feeling its melancholy mist on her face as it swelled like laundry on the line. A textured linen sheet rolling in and out. It was a better angle, to be sure, safer and less dependent on the tide, and although she had never tried that location before, she was astute enough to know where she should and should not jump.

Thirty feet was her limit, although this looked more like forty. Perhaps even greater than that. Her dive in Antwerp had been thirty feet. It was her speciality. 1920. She remembered it like it was yesterday, and yet two years had already passed.

Alek had been there, although thankfully she hadn't known until after the competition. She had spotted him at the medal ceremony as she had leaned down from the podium so the steward could put the gold around her neck and a bouquet of hypericum berries in her hands, their burlap ribbon chafing her waterlogged palms. She brushed the medal, sliding her fingers over the athlete's naked metal body and laurel crown. It was rougher than she had expected, and she reflected then on her lack of surprise at winning it. She had always known she was a good diver, and at the Olympics she knew she was the best in the world.

Her hair had still been wet from the pool, she reminisced, and she had braided it quickly and wound it around into a bun at the nape of her neck. She could feel the wisps of hair around her face drying, escaping their confines and caressing her skin as she smiled, the band playing the Swedish *Du gamla, du fria* ever so slightly out of tune. Having lived the past few years in England, the anthem sounded oddly foreign to her.

Alek. She could pick him out of any crowd. She had wished then that she had taken more time with her appearance. His soft, strawberry blonde hair was turning white with the summer sun. It was always just a little bit too long and she remembered how it touched the back of his neck as she wound her fingers into it, feeling it slip through her hands like silk. He had stood there watching her and she wondered why he had come, without his wife, to watch her compete. But it was the Olympics, after all, and Alek always enjoyed an event.

Just for spite, Stefanie locked eyes with him. Willing herself in that moment, *her moment,* to remember every inch of his body, his skin stretched smoothly over his muscular thighs, his arms wrapped around her waist, his shoulders flexed, as he lay on top of her. The smell of his hair like woodland oak, the curve of his neck, the touch of his fingers on her flesh, his eyes —as pure as the waves below her now...

She caught her breath as a spray of ocean lashed violently at the base of the cliff, bringing her back to the present. Alek was gone. Married was the same as gone, wasn't it? Perfectly arranged, neatly tied up. His father now in union with his wife's father. A shipping conglomerate in the making. A profitable arrangement indeed.

And *she*...well...she was nothing. The daughter of a deceased cobbler who had been shipped off to live with her aunt in England after her mother had taken her own life. An orphan. All she had was an Olympic medal and a dream to leave Cornwall forever. Back to Sweden, perhaps? Or somewhere new. America?

She looked back at The Headland in the distance, its limestone and brick facade blurring together from the distance of the cliffs. Would the man never leave? The duke would still be in his leisure clothes, no doubt. His ivory, ankle-length trousers and the striped navy jumper he favoured the most; its elbows now threadbare, its wide V-neck allowing a sprout of pale chest hair to peek out the top. His pencil moustache would still be unwaxed, its haphazard bristles undeniably askew as he puttered around the staff-less house in search of another cup of tea for his guest.

The duke couldn't very well have staff in the house when

his mistress was staying with him, could he? She'd always disliked his summer house. It was too large for its surroundings: a great monolith rudely towering over the whitewashed cottages of the town, its menacing stature a reminder of those who have, and those who have not.

Sometimes, when she lay with the duke, she wondered if she could ever really love him. He didn't have the Nordic physique she'd loved from her youth. *Alek's physique*, if she were honest with herself. He was nearly twenty years older than her and of the English variety: thin, soft and weak, his flesh flaccid and pale. He adored her figure; its strength and vigour. He said it was nothing like an English girl's—*she wondered how many he had had*—and that she reminded him of a voyager sea maiden, strong and determined, hailing from the North Atlantic and bearing down on England with the ferocity of a Viking princess. He was always lyrical. Fantastical really, and hardly set in reality. Which, she supposed, was why he thought he could have a Cornish mistress and get away with it.

She let him do what he wanted with her. He was kind and gentle, and madly in love with her. She saw him in the summers and rarely in the winter months, although of late he was finding excuses to leave his ancestral home in Oxfordshire to travel to Cornwall with alarming regularity. She always wondered what his wife must think. He probably lied and said he had business in London. Stefanie never asked.

They had first been introduced at the bank, where, when Stefanie had first come to live in Cornwall, her aunt had somehow managed to find her a job. The bank was a small subsidiary of a much larger entity based in London with branches in New York, Boston, Dublin and the West Country. He was her superior, and subsequent to their first meeting she had been given a substantial raise. She had been uncomfortable with being paid more handsomely than her counterparts ever since. It was the duke's doing, no doubt, and so when he asked for something at the bank she obliged him without question, even if it caused her discomfort.

If she tried to put her finger on it, to really analyze what she felt for the duke, she supposed it would be gratitude. And, if she were brutally honest, he provided her with opportunity. She wanted out and he was her road to the world beyond. She could have done far worse. At least the duke loved and cared for her. And she was fond of him in return, if not in love. She felt about him as she would a brother, even though she knew when he touched her his feelings ran far deeper.

She put her hands above her head and stretched her body out, carefully putting her toes over the edge of the cliff, the wet moss giving way to slippery rock. Despite the calmness of the day, the sea came in and out, thrashing around, churning, and amusingly it reminded her of Alek between her sheets, the sensuousness of his skin, the hardness of his body.

Would she ever see him again?

He had come to her that night after she won her medal in Antwerp, to her hotel room, her bed. He knew where to find her somehow. Like a homing pigeon. And she hadn't been able to resist him; she had never been able to resist him. After a torrid, sleepless night he had crept from her room and slinked back to his English wife.

She hadn't set eyes on him since. She knew he was here in England now. He had left Sweden and made his way to London about a year ago to join his wife and work for their fathers. Belgravia, apparently, or so said Anneka, her friend back in Sweden. She had written that they had had a going-away party for him and he had got so drunk he'd wept like a baby and said he didn't want to go.

It didn't matter. They were finished. He lived only in her heart and in her head now. It had taken time, but eventually, as is true of everything, the wretchedness began to subside.

She pulled her arms down from the sky and stretched them

out and forward, filling her lungs with the fresh morning air, feeling her Nordic hair caress her bare shoulders, listening to the crash of waves below and the sound of gulls at her back.

A scream splintered her thoughts, followed by the pop pop of a gunshot. It was as blood-curdling as death itself and she swung around in the direction of the house. She could see the duke on the doorstep, he was staggering this way and that, holding his chest and weaving dangerously. His ivory trousers were stained with something dark. Eventually he fell, tumbling down the last few steps and lying with unnatural stillness at the bottom. A crumpled heap of summer clothes amongst a freshly weeded garden.

A figure dressed in dark clothes and a low-slung cap was running towards her, his face half covered by the collar of a coat too warm for the day, its mottled greys blurring. It, along with the figure's darkness, was a horrific foil to the lightening day. She wondered for a moment how the person had managed to almost reach her already, and for a fleeting moment she thought of the duke's guest. Her pursuer was covering the dry, mossy ground with enormous speed and Stefanie felt herself shudder as he came nearer and nearer, the sound of his panting and exertion chilling her spine.

Where was the duke's houseguest? Had he gone? Been shot? Was he the one who had done the shooting? Or was he an accomplice to the man rushing towards her?

This man's clothes were bulky, as if he had layers underneath his coat, and she found it bizarre that he would dress in such a manner on such a day. Her legs were weak, their usual strength overtaken by the raising of her pulse and the steady chorusing of blood as it pumped faster and faster throughout her body. It was circling at a dizzying rate.

She frantically searched for a way to escape, glancing left and right as she backed up quickly, not wanting to take her eyes of the figure as he came closer and closer. Owing to her location on the crest of the inlet cliffs she hadn't anywhere to go. To the left was a craggy section of rock that would be impossible to navigate, let alone dive from, so she made for the right. The same topography existed this way but it was the lesser of the two evils and while in front of her was The Headland, beyond it was nothing but bramble and fields. Judging by the speed he was coming, her pursuer was likely to catch her if she attempted to make for the open terrain. Knowledge of the probable gunshot wound to the duke's chest meant being in the open was hardly an option.

She could hear the change in her own breath as she tripped and stumbled over the cliff's sharp edge. She was scrambling for a rock about fifteen feet below her that she had seen earlier and could use for a platform. If she slipped, she thought miserably, it would be lights out. The rocks were still wet from an overnight rain and she lost her footing momentarily, slicing the bottom of her foot along a sharp piece of slate as she caught herself. Crying out in pain and frustration, she looked up to see the figure standing above her on the grass. He slowly raised a small gun, cradling it between his fingers and Stefanie noticed his gloved hands quivered slightly, as though he were unsure. There was something familiar about the stance. The way he held his arms, the curvature of the shoulders—but it was fleeting, and her mind wasn't in a state to take much in.

He fired once, missing her, as she ducked and scrambled. The sun was in their eyes. And then he fired again, also missing. The echo of the shots rang across the bay and a flock of gulls registered their alarm—the wings of a hundred birds coursing through the ether.

Reaching the platform on her hands and knees she stood up and took one last, long look at her pursuer. He seemed to be fiddling with the gun as he had it cradled over his knees. Then she turned her back to him, praying he wouldn't have time to aim again, and faced the ocean. She gave a quick prayer that she would land at the right time—on an incoming wave rather than a bare rock. And then, just as she did almost daily in Cornwall, although never from such a terrific height, she jumped and executed a perfect dive into the icy waters below.

~

WHEN SHE SURFACED AGAIN she was as far down the coast as her body would take her. She couldn't see the fishermen anymore, nor the bay outside of which she had landed, and the sky had changed—the brilliant blue of the morning chased off by advancing rain clouds. Her immediate relief was short-lived. The sickening scene of the duke falling from his front steps, his blood seeping through the cotton of his trousers, and the dread that she was going to be next, flooded her consciousness and permeated every stroke she took. She continued to swim as far out from shore as was possible to avoid being tossed around in the surf near the shoreline. The Headland was no longer visible and she realized she could move much faster along the coast swimming than the man could move on land.

And she was a good swimmer. The salt water had numbed the cut on the bottom of her foot and whatever pain she had felt from it was gone for the moment. She altered her usual stroke, favouring a low-in-the-water side stroke over a front crawl to reduce the chance of her being seen from the shore. She focused on her breathing, the swish in and out of her lungs, the swift scissor-kick of her legs, the reach up and through, up and through, of her arms. Just as she had done thousands of time in the pool. It helped her from descending into an anxious abyss. From time to time she stopped to gather her breath, treading for a few minutes while the cold crept in, but finding relief in the knowledge that, at least for now, she was alone. Eventually, the vast remoteness of the cliffs gave way to small villages and a smattering of farms. Initially she recognized some of them, but familiarity soon gave way to new land-scapes and the panic that inevitably came with being lost and hunted.

She pushed the image of the duke toppling down the stairs out of her mind. Was he dead? A wave of nausea washed over her as she imagined his face. Who would want him dead? A kind man like that? And a duke, no less. He had just made her breakfast in bed. Soggy toast with far too much butter...she fought the urge to give up and let the sea take her. Her stroke slowed as her mind flooded with memories and a sickening fear that whoever wanted the duke dead had been about to kill her too.

She could see a wide swath of empty beach stretching out to her right where the cliffs gave way to a secluded bay. Where was she now? How long had she been swimming? Twenty minutes? An hour? Two? The surface rolled and rocked her body this way and that, and she ducked under the water to avoid it. It was cold but she barely felt it. Was there a road to that beach? If there was, she would pass it by and carry on swimming. She searched and searched, her seawater-blurred eyes scanning the coastline for any sign of the man. Perhaps he thought she was dead from the fall. If this was the case, she would try to keep it that way.

Dead.

It was then that she realized something utterly life altering. An epiphany of sorts—with her body floating on the huge swells, the beach a glimmer that was lost and then found again. A watershed moment, if you will, the kind of opportunity that rarely presents itself but cannot be ignored when it does.

She reflected on her time in England. She had had affairs with two married men. The duke, of course, and a junior detec-tive in the Newquay police department. The last had been fleet-ing, a stolen evening here and there. It had meant nothing to her, although she had quickly realized the same couldn't be said for him. His experience had been much more meaningful and when she had delicately tried to extract herself, he had been angry—and once, even violent with her.

She took stock. For all the killer knew, she was dead. She couldn't very well contact the same department where her ex-lover sat pushing paper around. She was the current mistress of a man who had just been shot. Even worse, she had been at the house when it happened. She could just as easily be a suspect as a victim. She would be hunted on a number of different fronts. Even more unsettling was the work she had done at the bank at the request of the duke—transfers that didn't have the proper authorization—she was in the thick of it all, any way she turned, she was in the thick of it.

Being dead was the perfect opportunity to disappear.

2

LILLIE

"Are you sure you haven't been a little rash in your decision-making?" Lillie lifted her teacup and frowned into it, realizing it was empty.

She reached across the little round table for the teapot and poured herself another cup. There was never any shortage of tea in England. It was ubiquitous—something that could hardly be said in America. Superintendent Felix Petters pushed the sugar dish towards her but she waved it away.

"Only the milk, please. Thanks."

He watched her with interest while she stirred the liquid in and carefully put the spoon on the table.

"You know," he began carefully, "everyone who comes into this cafe puts their hands on that table. It is a cesspool of germs, mark my words. I sincerely hope you will not be using that spoon again."

Lillie gave him a stern look. "And I hope you aren't like this with Jeremiah. Poor boy will develop a psychological condition with you hammering away at him about this stuff all the time."

Petters had recently adopted a boy from an orphanage in Chipping Norton and moved to a small cottage in Oxford in time for the boy's school enrolment for the following September.

Petters smiled back at her. He was completely disarming: his pinched face pleasantly clean-shaven, his hair cropped perfectly short, the smell of his soap on his immaculate but inexpensive clothes—he was on a policeman's salary after all. Or had been.

"Back to my initial question: are you sure this is what you want to do? Quit the constabulary?"

"I want to be a father, and at the moment I am a single father. I need to be there when Jeremiah gets home from school. I want to take him to cricket practice. I want to visit London more often."

He gave her a shy smile.

"To see Calista?" Jeremiah's aunt had recently come back into the boy's life and it was plain to see she had stolen Petters' heart. From what Lillie understood, Calista didn't want to leave her job in the city to relocate to Oxford. Or not yet, anyway. Although Lillie felt Petters was ignoring the obvious: that an engagement ring might solve that particular dilemma.

Petters ignored the question.

Lillie continued. "But a private detective? Really? What if you don't get any clients? What then? Starvation? Living off your wits?"

"Let's hope not. But, contrary to your belief, I already have a client. It didn't take long."

"Do tell. A woman who has lost her cat?" Lillie teased, screwing up her face in mock horror.

"I can tell you, and as head of the crime section at the *Oxford Daily Press* you should know this, people get murdered with some regularity in this fine country of ours."

"Yours," Lillie corrected. She was, after all, American.

"Right, mine. Well, anyway, people die, the police investigate, as do you, but things don't always get solved. Manpower hours, budgets, politics—it's limiting, as you well know. And the wealthy don't mind paying for a little added service."

"I see." She took a careful sip of her tea. "So who is this client of yours?"

"A duchess, actually. Her husband turned up dead at their summer home in Cornwall. Shot, as it were."

"Terrible."

"Mmm, it certainly is. No suspects yet, and there isn't likely to be, by the looks of it. A friend of mine down in Newquay says the police are calling it a cold trail. I'm heading there tomorrow."

"So much for the single father being present for cricket practice."

"It's the end of the school year, if you must know, and the team wrapped up their dismal season a few weeks ago with an astonishing win. Anyway, Calista is taking Jeremiah for a few days," he said, ignoring the barb. "She wants to introduce him to some extended family in Surrey."

"I'll come with you, shall I?"

"To Cornwall?" he asked, to which she nodded. "A bit of a way for a day at the beach."

"I haven't anything much here to report on; summer is slow. I wouldn't mind covering something a little further afield. If we are going to thrive as a newspaper we need a more national focus. I'm sure Jeremy wouldn't mind."

Jeremy Winston was her boss and owner of the *Oxford Daily Press*. He gave her enough creative licence for her to know that she could cover just about anything she liked. He was fond of her, and she of him, although this camaraderie had a tendency to cause Lillie some trouble in other spheres of her world.

"I'd be happy for the company, as long as you don't interfere with my apprehending a criminal. I still haven't forgotten how you let that last one get away—quite literally—with murder."

Petters' last major case before his retirement from the

constabulary had involved a remorseful murderer who had avenged the death of his dear friend and mentor. Lillie hadn't actually done anything other than take pity on the man after he helped save an entire wedding party from perishing at the hands of a political vigilante.

"I did no such thing," she answered shakily.

Even she had to admit to herself that Petters did have a point.

"He is probably living on a beach somewhere in the South of France, sipping champagne and celebrating his slipperiness."

Petters scanned Lillie's face. She, knowing full well Petters' escapee was back in New York and nowhere near France, concentrated on making her face as neutral as was humanly possible. Lying wasn't her strong suit.

She changed the subject. "So, Cornwall then. When do we leave?"

3

LILLIE

"Well, this is exciting. I've been needing a change of scene. I'll just head up and pack a bag, shall I?"

Lillie looked at her friend Harry, incredulous.

"Harry, I am just here to let you know I am going so you can relay the message to Jack if he comes back from whatever assignment he is on now. I haven't been in touch with him for weeks. Talk about an absentee fiancé."

Lillie had finally agreed to marry her long-term, on-again off-again boyfriend Jack, despite her reservations about his job in the foreign intelligence office. It irked her that no sooner had he put a ring on her finger than he had disappeared again. From what she could piece together, Russia was causing the British government an enormous amount of angst and although he wouldn't confirm it, she had a sneaking suspicion her fiancé could be found somewhere in the urban wilds of Petrograd or Moscow.

She continued, "And what about Primrose? You are a married man now, you can't just be jaunting around the country like a debutante."

"Debutantes hardly 'jaunt around the country', my dear.

They do *the season* in London. Sometimes you are glaringly American. And Primrose has gone north to visit her parents. She won't be back until next month and it is terribly dull here, me rambling about in this ramshackle old place with a brute of a butler in this stifling heat."

Lillie glanced around the enormous Tynesmore drawing room in which they were now seated. It had been recently remodelled and was lavishly appointed in spring-green and pink chintz, its herringbone floor polished to a rich, oaky shine, its newly painted shell-white French doors thrown open to reveal an immaculate boxwood and grass garden, beyond which a herd of dappled horses grazed. A breeze fluttered the gauzy linen drapes.

"Hardly ramshackle, Harry. My goodness, you should see how the other ninety-nine per cent of the world lives. And besides which, I will be working while I am away, it isn't a vacation. Most people don't bring their friends on business trips."

He pointedly ignored her. "I won't be in the way, I promise. I'll have Rumple take us to the station, shall I?"

Harry's manservant, or butler, depending on the day, upon hearing his name, entered the drawing room as though he had been cued from the wing of a stage.

"Ah, Rumple, there you are, theatrical as always. I'll be taking a little trip with Miss Mead. Cornwall. Would you pack some things for me? Obviously leisurewear, old sport. It's summer after all."

"Yes, sir." Rumple attempted a ridiculous bow that threatened to slit his rather too-tight trousers. There was the distinct sound of the fabric giving way.

Lillie raised an eyebrow at Harry as Rumple departed. "New fashion, I suppose?"

"He isn't happy about it but he has gained a considerable amount of weight since I have been married. I thought I was supposed to be the one to gain the weight. Anyway, he refuses to wear his livery a size larger on the grounds that it admits defeat."

"I see. So long as you know *that* is an accident waiting to happen."

"Mm yes, I know. How terribly mortifying. Now, Cornwall, shall I pack a dinner jacket? I know the most charming little inn we could stay at, been in the same family for generations, I hear it's been recently refurbished..."

Lillie stood up, hoping he would cease his prattling on but it did little to diminish his enthusiasm.

"...there is this very modern beach club there, just below the cliffs on which the inn sits, now...what is the name of it again? Let me think, Doncaster or something or other. No, no, that isn't it. Somercast, I think that might be it?" He trailed off.

Lillie moved towards the door.

"Boncaster—that's it. No that wasn't it..."

She had her hand on the doorknob. "Goodbye, Harry. Train leaves at one o'clock. I'll meet you at the station, shall I?"

"Lancaster! That's it."

4

STEFANIE

As the train rattled down the tracks spewing its steam into the warm night air, its firemen no doubt sweating as they shunted enough coal to keep them moving, Stefanie put her head back on the seat and closed her eyes—the duke's words swirling through her mind were as whimsical and fleeting as he was. Poems he used to recite to her late into the night, silly things he used to say.

Who would be, a mermaid fair, singing alone, combing her hair, under the sea, in a golden curl, with a comb of pearl, on a throne? Tennyson, she believed, although she never really paid enough attention.

Love was a tricky thing. One of two people could feel so much attraction and affection—and the other? Well, sometimes the other just couldn't. How she wished she could have loved him. She wondered, not for the first time, if she would ever love anyone as she had loved...Anyway, it didn't matter. She would do better to not spend any more time on the futility of nostalgia.

She thought back to the past few days—her escape from the water had certainly complicated things.

∾

SHE HAD NEEDED CLOTHES. *And money.*

Tired and shaking from the length of time in the water, Stefanie had stumbled onto a beach she didn't recognize and taken a minute to recover from her exertions. Now she was walking on it, the slash on her foot began to bleed again so she stopped and pressed her hand against it while she surveyed her surroundings and fought to catch her breath. She was a good athlete, but that amount of swimming would test even the most Herculean of Olympians. She lay down on the warm sand and breathed deeply.

The duke was more than likely dead and someone she didn't know was gunning for her also. His wife? Had she found out? Hired an assassin? It was the only answer she could come up with. Having never met the woman it was easy to let her imagination run rampant. The duke rarely spoke of her, preferring when he was with Stefanie to pretend he wasn't a married man. They had children, this she knew. Two sons, both grown now. Maybe one of them? Or both together, in conjunction with their mother? It wasn't unheard of.

She wracked her brain. Who knew of their affair? Friends of his? She had been at the house once when an acquaintance of his had shown up, but that had been ages ago. She had pretended to be a housemaid. Fairly unconvincingly, as it turned out. The man had looked her up and down knowingly, letting a disgusting little smile creep across his late-middle-aged face. Perhaps he had told the duchess? He was certainly the type that would.

There was a tiny fisherman's cottage in the distance, painted in the palest robin's-egg blue, and Stefanie started towards it, shaking the sand from her hair as she limped along and adjusted her swimsuit. By the time she reached it, she had had enough time to scout out her surroundings. By the looks of it, there wasn't another living soul anywhere and the cottage chimney didn't have smoke. Ideally, the fisherman who inhabited it was still out on the water.

She knocked tentatively. Then a little louder, brushing the sand from her legs as she did so while attempting to keep her injured foot off the ground. It was beginning to cause her some agony and she longed to wrap it with something to stem the bleeding. She tried the handle. The door was unlocked, as many cottages were in Cornwall, and she quietly entered.

It was as tiny inside as it looked from the outside, with ceilings not more than six feet and considerably lower through the doorways. She instantly disliked the feeling of being a thief and a trespasser although she didn't see she had much of a choice. She passed quickly into the kitchen where she searched the cupboards for something to wrap her foot with. Finding an old towel she set about shredding it into long strips. Hunched over she rested her elbows on her bare thighs and carefully started to wrap it, beginning on the top of the foot and pulling the fabric tight as she wound it down around the sole of her foot and back up again. She had just finished and was tying off the extra fabric when she felt a hand on the back of her head, it grabbed at her hair and held it in a tight fist so she couldn't move.

"And just what do you think you are doing?" said the voice behind her.

The smell of stale whiskey wafted into her nose and she held her breath, feeling the man push his body into the back of hers, her wet suit cold and damp against her back.

"I...I can explain, truly, if you would just let go of my hair, please..." She was begging him but his hold on her, along with the pain in her foot and the monumental exhaustion from her swim, was beginning to make her eyes water.

The man relaxed his hold slightly and she breathed in relief.

"I'm injured and lost," she continued. "I was swimming and the current took me further and further away from where I was. I'm a weak swimmer you see, and I just washed up here and I'm separated from my party. I'm not trying to burgle you. I promise. Perhaps you might be able to point me in the right direction?"

The man let go of her and she turned to face him. He didn't look much like a fisherman, more like a hermit. Unwashed, unshaven and vile-faced. His mottled skin reminded her of a reptile, as did the lecherous way his eyes roved over her. She sized him up—no taller than she was—possibly an inch shorter. Fatter, to be sure, with a waist that hadn't seen physical exercise in the last decade. He would weigh much more than she did and could possibly out-muscle her with sheer gravity, but it was doubtful he would be quick enough to do so, even in her exhausted state she believed she could get away.

She raised her foot to show him. "I hurt it, and I wasn't thinking clearly. I was hoping you were here because I need some help," she lied, optimistic she could talk her way out of the situation she had stupidly put herself in.

He smiled in a way that let her know exactly what unsavoury thoughts he was thinking. He wasn't going to be a receptive audience, she realized with some dread, and began searching the room in her peripheral vision for something to hit him with. There were open shelves in the kitchen, over-flowing with Cornish pottery and any piece of it would do the trick.

"May I?" She motioned towards a row of mugs near a grimy sink.

The reptile nodded his scaly head and she moved carefully away from him and turned towards the sink. She could feel him moving with her even with her back turned, and his breath let her know his proximity. Did he really think he could overpower her? Fool. It was her experience that men always thought they were more physically capable than they actually were.

She reached up as though for a mug but instead grabbed the largest pottery bowl she could find, spun and smashed it across his face with every bit of strength she had. He stumbled back, his depraved eyes shocked but very much conscious and without the slightest remorse or hesitation she kicked him with her good foot squarely in the stomach, ensuring he hit the floor. The obese snake took a chair down with him and slithered around on the floor, shouting at her as he tried to get his feet under him.

"Whore! Bitch!"

Stefanie picked up the chair that had toppled and hit him with it again and again, incensed by his words, causing him to fall back on his tailbone. Bleeding from his forehead he sat there holding his lizard-like head and glared at her, wheezing for breath. With any luck the vile, foul-mouthed slob would also have a heart condition, she thought meanly.

She grabbed a raincoat off a hook as she exited the kitchen at an awkward sprint and managed to locate a small bowl of coins on a console table beside the front door. Grabbing both she headed outside, doubling back for a split second to grab a pair of his old shoes and then half hobbled, half sprinted up a dry grass hill behind the house. He would never catch her, not with his physique. But he *was* the type to report the intrusion to the police, which put her at a disadvantage. She needed to disappear. And quickly.

~

THE GUARD WAS HEADING down the aisle calling for their stubs. Stefanie fumbled around in her stolen bag and held it out for him as he passed. He gave her a nod, punched it, and carried on, leaving her to her thoughts.

After the incident with the licentious hermit she had walked for what seemed like hours to get from the beach to Padstow. Her bandaged foot ached, but it wasn't enough to stop her moving forward. Realizing she looked more like a hobo than a woman who worked at a bank, she used some of the money she had stolen to buy herself a cotton dress. After that, there wasn't much money left so she stole some proper shoes from the back of a cobbler's shop. They were too tight and rubbed her heels when she walked but at least they looked presentable. While she was in the changing room at the dress shop she had put her hair back with some pins she had nicked from a chemist.

She then set off to find a pub. She needed to eat and rest and figure out a plan. She reviewed her decision not to call the police. If the duke's death had anything to do with the bank surely she was in the thick of it. But did it? Messages, transfers, balances that didn't add up—could that be it? Or was it just their affair? Her being his mistress. No, she decided, the police weren't an option at this moment. And regardless, whoever had killed him would surely get to her. She didn't need to draw them a map.

Now, two days later, she was on an express train bound for London. The easiest place to disappear was in a city. Everyone knew that. And she planned to disappear. In the dim lighting of the passenger car she looked at the stranger in the seat across from her. The woman was eighty if she was a day. Her rheumy eyes met Stefanie's and she smiled a smile that would make the Mona Lisa envious.

Surely everyone had secrets, didn't they?

5

LILLIE

The duchess motioned to their waiter by holding up a thin, veined hand heavy with rings. After attracting his attention she placed it back on the table with precision and glanced out of the hotel window at the bay, its shale and granite cliffs curving dramatically east and west before giving way to the gentler white sand beach and its accompanying gorse and bramble, their yellow flowers fading against the heat of the July sun. Holidaymakers littered the bay. Locals were easily identified by their rolled-up trousers, on a break from whatever occupation employed them, wading into the surf with all the carefulness of a surgeon, forgetting the now wet and sea-salted caps in their hands.

Former Superintendent Felix Petters gave Lillie a knowing look. Was it a look to tell her that there was more to the duchess than met the eye? Something Lillie had already deduced. Or was it a look to tell her how he had been right all along? That everyone under the sun put their hands on restaurant tables leaving life-threatening germs in their wake.

Lillie made a conscious effort not to be distracted. "Tell us, was there anything left at the summer house to make you think that perhaps the duke was entertaining? Or wasn't alone while he was there?"

"I didn't know he *was* there." She looked down her nose at Lillie with barely concealed disdain.

The woman was off-topic. Again.

Lillie attempted to bring her back. "Yes, we do understand that. He told you he was going to London."

"That is correct."

"But now we know he did, in fact, go to Cornwall. Either after London or instead of London. Do you know why he would go to Cornwall?"

"Well, we have a home here of course, as you very well know." She looked out the window again, as if to confirm it.

Was she trying to be deliberately obtuse?

"Yes." Lillie consulted her notes. "The Headland."

"That is correct."

This was becoming her favourite response.

"And at The Headland, did the police think that the duke had been entertaining?"

The duchess remained silent. She glanced around the room, searching for something. Perhaps for someone she knew, or some other distraction to take her mind off her problems. Lillie would have felt sorry for her if she didn't dislike her so much.

"Your grace?" Lillie prompted.

"Perhaps."

"Such as?"

"A few things. In the…the…uh"—she cleared her throat —"the bedroom."

"I see. And what were these things?"

"A negligee of some sort. And dishes. Two cups. Two plates. Breakfast for two."

"And the police didn't think this was of any consequence? Is that correct?"

"I'm sure they did, Miss Mead, but not having found anything with which to trace the woman they aren't able to pursue it."

The duchess's eyes glazed over and she reached up and fiddled with her pearl necklace, her shaking hands entwining the white strands around her aging fingers, then letting them drop back against her chest.

Petters gave Lillie a hard look to suggest they really weren't getting anything useful from the woman. They already knew there had been someone with the duke from the police report. Petters had managed to get access to it through an old friend of his in the Truro City Police who had leaned on a young officer in Newquay to send it his way.

"Perhaps we should look at another angle," Petters suggested gently, and the woman gave a visible sigh of relief. "Tell us about what the duke did when he travelled to London."

"Oh." She smiled at Petters, obviously preferring either him or his line of questioning. Probably both. "He spent time at his club, visited friends, one of our sons lives in London..."

"Did he do any business there?"

"Some. He is...*was*...on the board of a bank. A figurehead really, he didn't actually do anything other than attend meetings, once a quarter or so."

"Oh? Which bank?"

Petters took out his notebook and pen. There hadn't been any mention of it in the police file.

"Ainsworth Capital. But as I said, he wasn't really involved in any meaningful way."

"I see. Any other business ventures? Companies?"

"No, only horses. He loved the racing."

"And did he have any enemies? Anyone who might want to see him harmed in any way?"

"Not that I know of."

The duchess shifted slightly in her seat and let her eyes wander.

"Well, thank you for this. Are you staying here in Cornwall?"

"Yes, I suppose I have to, at least until the police are finished. I have taken a room here. The Headland isn't a home to me anymore." She looked down at her hands. "I suppose it will have to be sold. Although who would want a buy a house where a man was murdered..." A sob caught in her throat.

Lillie contemplated reaching across the table to hold her hand but decided the duchess wouldn't welcome the affection.

The duchess dabbed her eyes and stood up. She wore a dress made fashionable before the war: a white blouse-like bodice over an hourglass, ankle-length Edwardian-style skirt. Lillie didn't envy the corset and wondered briefly at the household budget for new, more fashionable clothing. "I will head to my room. Please let me know if you require anything further."

Lillie and Petters watched her depart before either of them spoke.

"It is entirely possible she had him killed." Petters whispered, taking a sip of his coffee. "Hiring me would be the perfect cover."

"It's a theory, to be sure. Or one of the sons? Found out about the affair."

"Perhaps. Or maybe he's a gambler, she said he liked horse racing. Many an aristocrat has lost the farm betting on horses."

Lillie rubbed at a faint scar above her eyebrow.

"Now what?" Petters exhaled, pushing back in his chair and staring out at the arresting view of the water.

Lillie gave him a scheming look. "Now we send in Harry."

STEFANIE

I t had rained overnight in London. A good, long, cleansing summer rain that smelled of grass and dirt and the Streatham pavements steamed as Stefanie's feet hit them, step after step, not entirely sure where she was going to end up for breakfast, but moving all the same.

She had found a job at Tooting Bathing Lake her first day in London, and it was here in the south west of the city Stefanie had found a noisy bedsit in a terraced house that she could rent by the week. It was in a dismal place, built in the mid-1860s as part of a larger, futile, attempt to house at least some of the lower middle classes, and it reeked of desperation and damp. She wondered how bad it would feel in the winter months given that in the summer heat the walls were still oozing with moisture and rot. She didn't plan to stay long enough to find out.

She found a bakery near the pool and ordered a bun with jam and butter and a small pot of tea. Today was her second shift at the pool, but it didn't start until nine thirty so she had plenty of time. As she waited for her tea, she picked up a newspaper from an agent outside and slid twopence across the narrow wooden counter.

"Thanks."

"Aye, have a good day, girl." The man winked, causing Stefanie to force a polite smile in return.

At her table she did as she did every morning when she got the paper, and flicked through it quickly looking for any information on the duke. There had been a brief notice of his death in yesterday's edition but nothing to suggest he had been murdered. Nothing today either, by the looks of it. She turned to the classified ads at the rear of the paper to see if there was any mention of her, the scent of ink and paper mixing with that of her over-steeped tea. She hurriedly poured a cup while she scanned the newsprint for the missing and wanted. And there, as she had expected, was a picture of her buried on the next-to-last page, beneath that of two other men who were also reported as missing. It was a grainy photo, thankfully. Her hair loose, falling over one shoulder and obscuring one eye. She must remember to always wear it back now. The photo had been taken two years ago just after her first Olympic heat, at a party for the competitors in an ancient but beautiful Flemish house on the banks of the River Scheldt. It had had a view of the twin steeples of the Cathedral of our Lady and the persistent smell of cow dung from the farms across the water. Not even a room full of perfume had dampened the earthy odour of bovine.

Folding the paper she started in on her jam-filled bun, ravenous, even with the memory of the smell of the cows still in her nostrils. She wondered what she was *really* doing here in London. Half of her thought she should hightail it back to Sweden, but if someone was after her they would certainly think to look there. London was temporary. Just a place to make a bit of money so she could have choices, but she would have to tread carefully. She kept telling herself that, anyway. She thought about getting word to her aunt that she was alive, and perhaps if they had had a better relationship it might have been more of a priority. The two women were never really more than lodger and landlady, and she'd been even more ornery than usual lately. This she mulled over as she chewed. *London was temporary*, she repeated to herself.

Which didn't explain why she'd journeyed to Belgravia yesterday evening after work in order to stroll around and stare up at the white townhouses, the curved streets, the glossy black window boxes, and wonder which was his. Or why she had found a new cafe in the area where she ordered a small dinner and a glass of wine and sat amongst the evening dog walkers and strolling couples, all the while searching for a face she knew well and a body she knew even better. Perhaps she was misinformed, perhaps it wasn't Belgravia he lived in after all. It could have been Knightsbridge, or Regent's Park, or any number of other places, and Anneka may have been mistaken. In reality, London was an enormous city and the chances of running in to anyone you knew were slim at best. But why was she even looking for him? It wasn't like he was going to save her, or run away with her.

She pushed her empty plate away and gulped the last of her tea. The women's swimming team would be arriving at the pool and it was her job to run them through their paces before the male coaches arrived and she went back to cleaning the toilets. Not that the coaches were any better than she was, far from it— after all, none of them had ever won an Olympic medal, she thought miserably as she got to her feet. To them she was just the hired help and no one knew Anabel Graybel wasn't really her name.

Tonight she would resume her silent watch over the city. And maybe...just maybe, she would see Alek.

LILLIE

"Have you seen this?" Lillie turned the newspaper she was reading towards Petters and watched his sharp eyes skim the page.

She glanced towards the hotel bar and noticed Harry seemed to be making good progress with the duchess. She was smiling at him and Harry had the gleam in his eye that he often got when he knew his audience was enthralled by him. Perhaps he would be useful after all.

"Which one in particular? There are three of them here."

"Well, the woman obviously, since she is the only one from Cornwall. Unless of course the duke was having extra-marital relations with another man from"—she leaned over and peered at the print—"North Yorkshire. And he left his negligee behind." Lillie gave him an exasperated look.

"And remind me why we are looking at the missing and wanted persons of Cornwall in order to ascertain who the duke was having an affair with?" Petters had lowered his voice so they wouldn't be overheard. The hotel bar wasn't overly busy but there were enough holidaymakers around to hear them.

"Because if it were me, and I saw my beloved get murdered

before my very eyes, I would make a run for it and I bet this girl did the same thing."

"But why wouldn't she just run back to where she came from? Her home, her family, whatever life she had?"

"Because she is a target now too? Because someone saw her face? Because she knows who the killer is? Or very well might be able to identify him and if she returns home she is a dead woman? It could be any one of these things."

Lillie looked at the photograph of the missing woman again. She was attractive, although not in an overly traditional way. She looked...athletic, strong, determined. Her hair was very light, her cheekbones high and defined, she couldn't have been more than twenty-two or twenty-three years old. Surely she should disregard her. Why would she have been with a man as middle-aged as the duke? She read the paragraph under the photo again.

"It says she was an Olympic medallist. Did you see that part? A diver. The high dive."

"So maybe she died jumping off these horrendous cliffs and they haven't found her body yet and she has nothing to do with this mess."

"Either way I think we should track down her family, don't you?"

"I think you are off on a wild goose chase and your goose is long gone."

Lillie smiled. "I would agree with you actually, if it weren't for this little detail in the small print here..." she pointed to the text under the woman's picture. "It says she worked at a bank in Newquay."

Petters looked as though his interest was piqued. "Ainsworth Capital by any chance—the duke's bank?"

"It doesn't say."

"Hmm. Except I don't think you have considered another scenario—maybe *she* is the one who actually killed him."

"Why would she leave behind a negligee if she were the killer?"

"You have a point, although I hasten to enlighten you—when it comes to murder things don't often go as planned. But, either way, this is one goose we should look into, I suppose."

"Speaking of gooses"—Lillie nodded her head towards the bar—"Harry seems to be having all the success of a snake charmer over there. I think that is their third drink together. I hope he can remember what he is supposed to be there for."

"He does tend to get carried away," Petters agreed.

They both watched as Harry leaned forward and whispered something in the duchess's ear that caused her to quite uncharacteristically break out in giggles as he signalled the bartender for another round. She hardly looked like the same woman they had interviewed that morning. Her cheeks were flushed and she had the look of a schoolgirl beneath the wrinkles and heavy make-up.

Lillie shot Petters an exasperated look. "Shall we leave him to it? I'm not sure I can watch anymore."

"Lead on. Let's find this aunt who posted the missing person's ad, it says she is just outside Newquay."

～

"It isn't like her to just disappear for days without saying a thing—well, not usually, anyway."

The woman before them looked as though she hadn't slept in days. Her hair was a frizzled mess of bleached curls, her eyes rimmed in dark shadows. The missing girl's aunt looked at them as though she expected them to contradict her. "And the bank hasn't seen her either. She never misses work."

"Which bank did Stefanie work for? It doesn't say here..." Lillie motioned to the open newspaper on the table.

"Ainsworth Capital. Well, a branch of it anyway; they have

branches all over the place." She waved her hand, dangling a cigarette precariously between her fingers. Inhaling, she added, "She was a clerk."

Lillie didn't need to look at Petters to know he would quietly keep his reaction under wraps.

"And did she ever spend the weekend away from home?"

"Sometimes, yes." She turned, grinding out her cigarette, and began to fuss with the edges of a blue and white floral table cloth. She smoothed at its creases, over and over. "But she always told me when she was going to be away. And she did this past weekend as well, she just didn't come back on Sunday night like she usually would. She's dead, isn't she? Otherwise you wouldn't be here. You think she is dead." She had turned back to face them, but her watery eyes did little to hold their gaze. Instead they roamed the room as if seeing it for the first time.

"Not necessarily," Lillie said gently. "How was your relationship with Stefanie?"

The woman shrugged. "Don't know what you mean. I'm her aunt, she came here after my sister died. We are family."

"I think what I meant was would Stefanie confide in you, do you think? About matters of the heart? Or perhaps what was going on at the bank?"

The woman shrugged again.

By now Lillie was getting the gist of it. The two women weren't particularly close. She held up a picture of the duke for the woman. "Do you recognize this man?"

The woman visibly stiffened, then—willfully it seemed—relaxed somewhat. "Yes. He owns that big house there on the edge of the cliffs. The Headland."

"Do you know if Stefanie knew him?"

"She never spoke of him—but I'm sure their paths must have crossed. Why are you asking me this? I know he was killed a few days ago. Do you think that is why Stefanie didn't come home?"

"Not necessarily. One may have absolutely nothing to do with the other."

"You'll tell me if you find out anything, won't you?"

"Of course we will."

"Did she have any friends here? Good friends who she might confide in?"

"Acquaintances mostly. Her best friend is back in Sweden, Anneka something-or-other. I've never met her. They write from time to time. And there was a young man, also from Sweden. He lives in London now, apparently, but they don't keep in touch that I know of."

"I see. Do you think we might be able to have a look at her room?"

∼

THE HOTEL WASN'T FAR from Stefanie's aunt's cottage and as they walked back along the sun-drenched road, the smell of the ocean in their noses and dust on their shoes, Lillie let herself muse.

"So if you were Stefanie, assuming she is alive, where would you go? Back to Sweden?"

"Possibly, although with no money it would be difficult." Petters kicked at a stone on the road, and they watched as it rolled into the dry grass.

"London perhaps? Track down the old boyfriend."

"Again, possible, but don't forget he is married now. That complicates things and according to the aunt they didn't keep in touch."

"Not that she would have a clue. Did you notice her reaction to the picture of the duke?"

"Mm. A little uncomfortable, to be sure."

"Practiced, more like. No wonder Stefanie disappeared. Living with a chameleon like that can't have been easy."

"You think she's hiding something?"

"Perhaps. Or, she is just acting as any one of us would if someone came to our house and began asking a whole slew of questions." They walked in silence for a few moments. "Of course, the letters we found in her room tell us Stefanie and her old boyfriend were in touch around the time of the games. He was there in Antwerp when she won her medal—that attests to his love for her. And he was married then, too. I wonder how much the wife knows...although none of this has to do with our victim. All we know about that is that they both worked in the same bank."

"Yes." Petters shaded his eyes from the sun. It was low in the sky and the sharp angle of its rays cut through the atmosphere like swords.

"But there was nothing in her room to suggest she was into anything illegal, or that she knew the duke, yet the duke is dead and Stefanie is missing."

"Yes."

"It could be a coincidence."

"It could," Petters replied. "It could also be that the duchess knows all about them working together and didn't tell us."

"True, although according to her the duke only attended quarterly meetings for the bank. Theoretically he wouldn't have anything to do with someone in a position as lowly as Stefanie's." Lillie wound her hair around her finger as she walked. "I don't suppose we can march into the branch here in Newquay and demand access to everything Stefanie worked on."

"No. Only the local police could do that."

"But presumably Stefanie worked with other clerks in the bank and we might be able to get to one of them. Outside of work?"

"Good thinking. You will make an exceptional detective one day."

"Or a good reporter today." She winked.

"Shall we surveil the branch at closing and see what shakes out?"

8

ALEK

He couldn't believe what he was seeing. It felt as though he had been kicked in the stomach—*hard*—and he was desperately struggling for air. He looked around the club, at the room he frequented every day after work, finding comfort in its leather chairs, their caramel, tanned hides infused with vanilla and tobacco from member after member doing precisely what he was doing now. Escaping his marriage. It was a large room, with high ceilings and polished walnut panelling. The carpets were Persian, hand-knotted wool, worn from years of men treading across them, pipe and whiskey in hand. It was a room better suited for winter nights and today the summer air was heavy and heated, causing him to perspire. He loosened his tie and undid the top button of his shirt. Putting down the newspaper he signalled the barman for another drink.

Stefanie.

Missing.

He knew more than he should have about her. He knew she was involved with that duke who had turned up dead. He knew she worked at his bank. He knew she still lived with her aunt in

Cornwall. Surely the dead duke and her disappearance were linked. He would never admit it, not to anyone, but he kept in touch with Anneka in Sweden who told him everything Stefanie wrote in her letters. He still dreamed of her, imagined her long hair and sinewy body draped over his own, the way she looked at him and stared directly into his soul. No short-cuts, no games. He couldn't deny the disgust and jealousy he felt when he imagined her with another man. He fought back the urge to vomit.

His wife had found out about his infatuation unfortunately, and he wondered now if she didn't also know about the night of lovemaking after Stefanie won her medal in Antwerp. He had said he was in Brussels on business, but over the past two years he had realized something about his wife he hadn't previously known—she was a smart, conniving bitch of a woman who seemed to have an endless supply of resources with which to follow him. He was under her constant scrutiny. At least now he knew it and could be more careful. He wondered if she could actually see inside his head? See his turmoil and fantasy, see his imaginings, see what he saw—his beautiful Stefanie, his hands on her body, the tickle of her hair on his face and his chest. The shape of her hands, her chiselled stomach, the arch of her back, the lean strength of her legs as she wound them around his. She belonged there, in his mind, part of his body, forever. She was his first love, his home, his safe place.

No, his wife couldn't see inside his head—at least he had the privacy of his thoughts. It was what was written all over his face that he worried about.

~

BY THE TIME he left the club it was well after nine o'clock and he was a good deal drunker than when he had arrived. He would walk home, he decided, and set out reluctantly at a slow pace along the heated pavement, weaving slightly, feeling its warmth radiate up his legs. There was no need to hurry and he hoped his wife would be in bed when he arrived. Preferably asleep. He didn't feel like facing her tonight; his grief would be all too apparent. It was a fault of his to be sure, the inability to hide his feelings, wearing them like a badge.

He had thought of disappearing himself. Just leaving one day, heading off into the modern abyss of the world, leaving nothing to trace him by. Back to Sweden perhaps, he had always fancied himself holed up on an ocean-swept inlet, the forest and meadows at his back, a faded red cottage in which to lay his head. He didn't need this life he was part of. He disliked the shipping business. He had never liked it. It was his father's calling, not his. He didn't need to be successful or urban; although rich was nice. It gave one options. But rich in his own right, rich without his wife, now that was something to strive for. His home in Belgravia made him uncomfortable with its glossy surfaces, precious fabrics and icy acquaintances. He wasn't long for that world.

He was ashamed of it, but over the past few years he'd sought out women that looked like Stefanie. Searching for them had become so engrained in his daily consciousness that he didn't even realize he was doing it anymore. Sometimes he had dalliances with them, discarding them all eventually, one by one, when he realized time and again that just because someone looked like her it didn't make them so. He often wondered what was wrong with him. He no longer recognized, or even liked himself. He had always known where she was. Cornwall. And yet he had never once gone to see her to tell her how he couldn't get over her. And now she was gone. He stifled a sob. It wasn't supposed to be like this.

The sun was setting, casting long, low shadows over Belgravia, darkening the facades of white townhouses and making them appear ghostly. Reaching his street Alek surveyed his surroundings attempting to snuff out the creeping loneliness he was beginning to feel. He decided it was too early to go home after all and turned in the opposite direction instead. He would find a restaurant and have some dinner first.

Finding a suitable dining patio three streets from his house he settled into a small table on a shadowed edge of the pavement, wedged between an iron fence and a planter of cypress. He picked up a tattered paper menu and searched it, not really hungry but trying all the same. The restaurant was full and the conversations around him hummed with all the annoyance of a wasp's nest, grating on him; the tinny laughter contrived, the stories too loud for their surroundings. He thought about leaving and put his menu down.

"May I?" It was a woman's voice and he recognized it immediately. The hand on the chair across the table was comfortingly familiar. Of course it wasn't possible. He was intoxicated and building castles in the air. He looked up into the most beautiful blue eyes, white-blonde hair falling over one perfect cheek. Surely this was a dream and the woman standing before him just a mirage?

"Stefanie?" He breathed.

It was but an optimistic whisper.

9

LILLIE

T hey had been there for the better part of an hour, sitting on the sand, watching the sun disappear on the horizon, leaving streaks of rose rubbed across a twilight sky. The air was still warm on their skin and Lillie realized how much she liked Cornwall, its easy-going nature and hard-working inhabitants. It was no wonder artists flocked to the West Country like bees to pollen. Only a week had passed and already Lillie was beginning to feel like a local.

Petters had commandeered three deck chairs from a kiosk that had closed for the day, with the promise of returning them that evening. Lillie settled back into hers, watching the salt water lap at the beach and listening to the fiddling of the young man beside her. They had all but coerced Angus Braithwaite, Stefanie's colleague from the bank, to join them but he was as jumpy as a stick of dynamite. She glanced over at him and silently willed him to relax.

"I'll just pop back to the pub and get us some food, shall I? Fish and chips alright with everyone?" Petters asked.

Lillie nodded. "Please. I am ravenous. And beer. Or something stronger?" Looking at Angus she thought a drink might help loosen his tongue.

"I really should be getting home," he was saying now and Lillie placed a hand on his arm.

"Just stay and have something to eat. The least we can do is feed you."

With Petters gone she decided she would have another go at the young man.

"Stefanie was very pretty, wasn't she?" Lillie watched the retreating back of Petters as he walked back across the sand to the pub in the distance, his figure getting smaller and smaller.

Angus smiled nervously. "Oh yes."

"And did she have a boyfriend that you knew of?"

"I really couldn't say." He was giving their surroundings darting glances, as though they were about to be eaten by a pack of wolves. "One of our clerks fancied her," he continued, "but she wouldn't give him the time of day. She would sometimes go to lunch with one of our directors, the one who just died, but I think they were just friends. He was married."

"The duke of Wells," Lillie stated flatly. "That was very tragic. Was he at the bank often?"

"Not really, no. Summers, more than winters, and often on Fridays, before a weekend."

"What was Stefanie working on before she disappeared, do you know?"

"She was just a clerk. Like me. We do what we are told but for the most part she was involved with the overseas files."

"Meaning what exactly?"

"Handling anything originating from our New York or Boston branches. Or Dublin." he added.

"Money transfers? Deposits? That sort of thing?"

"Yes."

"And who was her supervisor?"

"Same as mine, the branch manager, although she also took her orders from the directors if necessary."

"Do you take orders from the directors?"

"I suppose I would if I were asked but I haven't been asked."

"Why do you think Stefanie was asked?"

"I am not sure. Different files, I suppose." He searched the horizon as though he were looking for something he'd lost.

"So if she were asked by a director of the bank to do something, would the branch manager also be involved?"

"I don't really know. I suppose he should be but he is a busy man so it's possible he would let a director handle whatever it was without him."

"When Stefanie transferred money from the United States, let's say, where would it go?"

"To various accounts. Sometimes it would get sent on, transferred again to somewhere else."

"Such as?"

"Oh, London perhaps, or our Dublin branch."

Lillie looked up to see Petters coming back, negotiating the sand while attempting to carry three plates of fish and chips without dropping them. She hopped up to help him and relieved him of a corked bottle of wine he had adeptly tucked under one arm along with three pewter mugs.

"I figured glass wouldn't have a chance with me carrying it. These looked a little more robust." Petters handed each of them a mug and a plate of food while Lillie poured the wine.

"Angus and I were just discussing some files Stefanie was working on. Angus, do you think you might be able to get us what Stefanie was working on in the last, oh...month or so?"

"Certainly not. That is confidential bank business. I could be sacked for that."

"I understand." She realized she would have to tread more carefully. "Angus, you liked Stefanie, didn't you?"

He nodded solemnly.

"She is a missing person now and her life is at stake. There is a very good chance that she is missing because of something that happened at the bank. We can get a search warrant if need be. Mr Petters here has friends in the police department, but that takes time and time isn't something Stefanie has if she is still alive. One of your directors is already dead. How long do you think it will take for them to find her if they haven't already?"

The young man resumed his stare at the horizon, his food growing cold.

"Do you think she is dead?" he asked finally, taking a long drink of wine.

"No. I don't. But I think she is in some trouble."

He appeared to be holding his breath and exhaled deeply through his nose, swallowing. "I'll see what I can find tomorrow but I can't remove any paperwork from the bank. That would be illegal."

"Of course not..."

"And I don't want to be seen with either of you. I will meet you here tomorrow night, around dusk after the beachgoers all head home for the day."

"Thank you..."

"I'm not promising anything, don't thank me yet." As though it were contaminated, he put his half-eaten dinner down on the sand and walked away.

10

STEFANIE

S he couldn't see him in the darkness. The shape of his body was but an imagining conjured up by the tips of her fingers as she traced his outline, shoulder to arm, arm to stomach, between his legs, down his thighs and back up again. Neither of them were sleeping, not wanting to waste what little time they had. He groaned, pulling her on top of him and she began to move slowly, rubbing him with her body, feeling him lose control.

His hair felt the same, although he smelled different. The woodland boy replaced by the scent of a married man. She didn't care. He would always be her boy.

He was clutching her, hands on her hips, controlling her movement and she let him, imagining his face, feeling him beneath her.

"God, I love you..." he exhaled, and she smiled into the darkness, moving faster, listening to him cry out and then become silent.

She rolled off and lay still beside him. He reached out and touched her hand while they both stared at the ceiling of the hotel room.

It was some time before either of them spoke.

"I think someone is trying to kill me," she said eventually, realizing that until that moment she hadn't even admitted it to herself.

She felt Alek stir beside her. He reached up and switched on a bedside lamp and she rolled over to face him, still somewhat startled that she had finally found him.

"I don't understand...you said they murdered the duke and you escaped..."

"Yes. But here's the thing—I couldn't see them, not really. I was too far away to make an identification so I would hardly have been a loose thread for them to tie up. The man chased me to the very edge of the cliff, he even fired twice, obviously not expecting me to jump. He wanted me dead, I'm sure of it."

Alek had pulled on his undershorts and was pacing around the room now, obviously agitated. He ran his fingers through his hair. It was shorter than she remembered.

"But why?"

"That part I am not so sure of. Of course, I have hardly been a lily-white example of moral fortitude..."

"Nor I, but that doesn't mean someone should murder us for it."

"It could be I was involved with the wrong person. Or did something, something I am not aware of. At first I thought it could be a jealous wife, or an angry son, or any number of things. A jilted lover, a double-crossed friend. But I didn't know the duke well enough to know if any of those things really exist. He seemed, for the most part, a fairly simple and straightforward man. A little whimsical perhaps, but not evil."

Alek's face looked pained. She knew him well enough to know the thought of her with the duke bothered him.

"You must have some idea, something that didn't feel right?"

"There were a great many things that weren't right. Our

affair, for one. Maybe something at the bank. Although I can't think what. It was just a small branch, one of many."

"Usually people are murdered for personal reasons— revenge, passion, treachery, theft."

"I suppose it could be any of those things."

Alek had stopped pacing and sat on the side of the bed.

"At least you are safe. No one knows where you are and for all the killer knows you jumped off that cliff to your death."

Stefanie sighed. "Except for one little detail." She fiddled with the sheet, pulling it over her body. "I was seen, after I jumped, by a horrible man whose cottage I broke into to find money and clothes. As soon as he sees that picture of me in the paper he will report it, I'm sure of it."

"Well ..." Alek leaned down to kiss her, then stood back up and frowned. "Let's just hope he doesn't read the newspaper."

11

LILLIE

"I don't bloody feel well. There must be some sort of a flu going around."

Harry's skin had taken on a greenish pallor and he appeared to be sweating across his brow.

Lillie watched as he reached across the table and poured himself a third glass of water.

"Have you seen this?" He held up his glass to the light. "They put cucumber in the water, it's brilliant. Yesterday it was lemon and strawberry. I am going to ask Rumple to start doing this at Tynesmore. It's wonderfully refreshing." He took a long drink and wiped at his forehead. "It's terribly warm out here. Do you think perhaps we should hire an umbrella?" He searched around him for an attendant, while abandoning his ivory linen blazer to the back of his chair and waving a napkin at his face.

They were having lunch on a patio overlooking the ocean and waiting for Petters to return from the police department. He had gone to review the file on the duke's murder and suggest they issue a search warrant for the bank on the chance that the young Angus Braithwaite wasn't successful with finding Stefanie's files. The

Cornish police seemed a great deal more open to outsiders than the Oxfordshire constabulary was and through his introduction by his chum in Truro, Petters had become a regular fixture at the station. Lillie wondered if he wasn't missing it all just a little. Being an investigator was a great deal different to being part of a police force. Rather like being lone wolf when one is used to a pack.

"It isn't the flu." Lillie gave him a hard stare.

"I beg your pardon?"

"Harry Green. You are hungover. After an entire afternoon *and* evening at the hotel bar entertaining the duchess, I am hardly surprised."

"I was working! And incidentally, I have never been hungover in my life. I am hardly a neophyte. Honestly, Lillie, how terribly bourgeois."

Harry resumed his search for an umbrella.

"Speaking of *working*, did you find out anything useful amidst the endless stream of martinis?" she asked, raising one dark eyebrow.

Harry shot her a dirty look. "Actually, I did. Were you aware the duke and duchess are effectively bankrupt?"

"Really? I did wonder..." She thought of the duchess's dress again.

"Yes. He inherited his title but the bulk of the fortune was unfortunately lost in the late 1890s. The family has been selling off bits of land here and there in order to keep their heads above water ever since, but there isn't much left to speak of and the war was the final nail in the coffin. They still retain the main seat in Oxfordshire, although without any surrounding farmland, and a small townhouse in London, but that has to be put up for sale now."

"Of course they still own their summer home here, The Headland."

"They do, but with a very large mortgage. The duchess

wanted to sell it years ago but the duke seemed so fond of it that they never actually got around to it—although good luck finding a buyer now; not only is it architecturally hideous— Rococo in Cornwall, what *were* they thinking—but it's got blood splashed across the front steps. Ah, there he is..." Harry had spotted an attendant and waved him over as though he were signalling for a lifeboat on the *Titanic*.

"Hm. That does put a different lens on things, doesn't it?"

"Broke people do desperate things. So I hear..." Harry adjusted his seat so the attendant could erect the umbrella he had brought over from an abandoned table. "So much better, thank you, old sport." Harry slipped the man some coins while he resumed his conversation. "Did you know he was also having an affair?"

"Yes, I think we are up to speed on that one."

"And that he disliked apples?"

"I'm not sure how that is relevant to his death..."

"He said they gave him gas," Harry prattled on. "Also, he didn't wear undergarments most of the time."

"How very interesting, but I'm not sure..."

"He loved poetry and the violin and...something else...the bagpipes, yes that was it, said they were 'melancholy'..."

"Yes, well, who doesn't really..."

"And he refused to travel to Ireland. Ever."

"Really?"

"It was the cause of a number of rows between them apparently. The duchess has relatives there and enjoys visiting... Cork, I believe, or was it County Mayo, I honestly can't remember. Anyway, he absolutely dug in and refused to go."

"That is strange. But he liked travelling in general?"

"Oh yes, loved it, apparently. Scotland, Wales, Austria-Hungary—before the war, of course—Northern Africa, France, Spain, America. Everywhere but Ireland. In fact, they were married abroad—somewhere no one actually ever visits... Switzerland, I think it was."

Lillie took some time processing all this. Why would someone not want to visit a specific country, and one as close as Ireland?

Harry interrupted her thoughts.

"You know, I have the strongest craving for fried food, it's the oddest thing. Shall we order?"

12

STEFANIE

After a night spent at the hotel with Alek, the bedsit Stefanie had rented looked abysmal by comparison. Its filthy windows faced an even filthier street and the front steps were smudged with decades-old grime as owner after owner failed to comprehend the importance of first impressions.

There were the vaguely mixed smells of a lavatory and frying sausages as she entered the foyer, removed her shoes, and contemplated climbing the stairs to her bedroom. She looked up the worn, wooden steps and sighed exhaustedly. Up all night, she wondered how she would get through her shift at the pool that morning. Perhaps if she just closed her eyes for a few minutes.

"It is you! Out all night?" Her landlady came around the corner, wiping her hands on her apron and eyed her not unkindly, giving her a conspiratorial wink. "Someone's come by looking for you last night. I told him you weren't here but he waited anyway. After an hour he gave up and left. Wouldn't leave a name but said he'd be back today. A friend of yours?" She busied herself with tidying the coat rack, with hopeless results, and retrieving the mail from a hallway table. "Didn't know you knew anyone in the city," she said absently, flipping through the envelopes.

Stefanie felt her stomach turn. "I'm not really sure, I..." What else could she say? Who would have any idea she was here, of all places? "What did he look like?"

"Oh, sort of short and squat, a little round over the middle. Now that I think of it, not very attractive. His skin was sort of reddish, marked. But can't judge a book by its cover, I am sure he is a very nice fellow. Good manners anyway...in a slick sort of way." The landlady slapped the envelopes back onto the table.

Stefanie would have to leave immediately.

"Thank you, Mrs Fitz. I'll just run upstairs now and wash." Her mind racing, she was thankful she hadn't told the landlady where she worked but she wondered now if she was still safe or had they followed her there as well? It would only be a matter of time before they figured it out. She wondered if she could go into the pool today and collect her pay—she hadn't been at her job for more than five days but it was clear she would have to move on, and quickly.

"Will you be joining us for breakfast?"

"Not today, thanks, I am in a bit of a hurry."

Her mind was going in a thousand different directions and she was having trouble focusing. She would need to get in touch with Alek, at least now they had a plan on how to do that. She would leave word for him with the hotel concierge. Next, she would gather what was owing to her at the pool and never go back. Alek had offered her money and she would take him up on it. In some fantastical version of reality she had actually thought she could keep her job as an anonymous entity; she liked being around diving and swimming, it made her feel like herself, but now this, too, was unachievable.

She reached her room and began stuffing her bag with

what little she had—clothes, shoes, a few little bottles, some laundry that needed washing—when something dawned on her. She realized she wasn't going to be content on the run. The constant disappearing, living the life of a nomad. She was an Olympian and she wanted to train and compete and have a family and have Alek.

Perhaps this was a turning point for her, where the hunted doubles back and becomes the hunter. Whoever this man was who had found her had prompted in her a desire to fight back or die trying. They had murdered her friend and they were coming for her too.

Well, she thought angrily, *do your worst.*

She imagined the duke's face, his mouth whispering to her, the ghost of his faith in her. She was, after all, a voyager sea maiden, a Viking princess bearing down on England and today, inside her, she realized, was a wrath as deep and as violent as the North Sea.

~

THE FAT MAN came back just after lunch time. Stefanie had missed her shift at the pool and chosen to wait for him instead, her bag packed and stashed under a wilting laurel bush on the north side of the house. She watched from the street as he climbed the filthy steps and knocked at the door while her landlady, still in the same apron from that morning and now covered in cooking grease, shook her head at something he said. The fat man tipped his hat and turned away from the house, heading north up the street, hands shoved in his pockets.

Stefanie waited only a few seconds before she retrieved her things and followed, keeping him at a safe distance. She realized something about people who are hired to follow someone else; they don't realize that someone might actually be following *them*. The man didn't turn around once and unless he was outrageously good at using peripheral vision or had eyes in the back of his head, it became clear to her that the man had absolutely no idea he was being tracked.

He made his way through the streets, faded and parched from an unrelenting sun, stopping only to buy a newspaper and smoke a cigarette. Depressed neighbourhoods gave way to commercial ones, commercial ones to shopping districts, markets to slums and then, after a time, they were wandering through the industrial bustle somewhere along the river. When he finally stopped outside a low block of storage buildings, their haphazard facades a riot of competing materials—steel, wood, and wire mesh—they had covered at least half of the city on foot. The fat man wiped at his face with his sleeve and even from a distance Stefanie could see his shirt was soaked through with perspiration. He pushed through a peeling green door at the end of the block, above which were three filthy, broken windows and a lifetime of pigeon excrement. There was little she could do now but wait.

When he didn't re-emerge she made herself comfortable across the alleyway and a few buildings down. Here she found an old wooden crate to sit on in the shade and she passed the time watching the ships on the river.

"I follow you across the entire length of the city and find you here, eh..."

The voice startled her and she looked up to see the fat man standing in front of her. How had she missed him?

"Pretty thing, aren't you?" He was chewing on something as he spoke and a bit of whatever it was clung to the whiskers around his mouth. "Well, they said you were anyway."

"And just who might that be?" Stefanie stood up so she didn't feel so intimidated. He wasn't tall but she didn't like the feeling of someone standing over her.

"Not sure really. I just get my orders and do as I am hired to do."

"Follow me."

"Ay."

"And then what?"

"Give you a message."

"Which is?"

He paused and exhaled, having swallowed whatever was in his mouth. Garlic wafted on the air between them and she fought the urge to screw up her face in disgust. A flock of gulls flew overhead, piercing a sky which had grown hazy with the heat of the day.

"You have something my employer needs. He needs you to get it back."

"I don't understand...what have I got?"

"Access to his stolen money. And he isn't a man to be trifled with."

"How could I possibly have that?" Stefanie knew it had to have something to do with the bank and the duke—neither of which she could access now. She straightened up her shoulders and looked directly at him. "I suppose your employer is the man who killed the director of the bank, in Cornwall?"

The man laughed. "Don't think he'd be too likely to kill a man who holds his cash now, do you?" He wiped his mouth with the back of his hand. "No. That was an inconvenience, to be sure. Which is why you're here." His smile was more of a leer.

"And just who is your employer?"

"Someone more unpleasant than I am, I can tell you."

"English?"

"Not pertinent." The man concluded.

"But there isn't anything I can do. I don't even work there anymore and even if I did, I wouldn't have a clue where to look for it. Presumably if your employer's money was stolen through that branch, it would have to have been done in such a way as to be untraceable. How could I possibly figure that out from the outside?"

"Better figure it out quick, girl. Guys like me are easy hires. And the next guy won't just be talking. He will be a great deal more unpleasant, I can assure you."

Stefanie didn't doubt it.

"You have two weeks," he summed up neatly. Then he turned on his heel, effectively dismissing her, and retreated back through the door of the warehouse, thankfully taking the stench of garlic and body odour with him.

13

LILLIE

The wind had swept through Cornwall late that afternoon, taking with it the heat and stickiness Lillie and Harry had suffered through with their luncheon. Great dark clouds lingered out over the water, the occasional ray of light escaping through the swaths and illuminating a frothy, mermaid-green ocean as it reached its fingers across the sand. The beach was littered with brambles from the nearby hills, brought there on great, gusting waves of air, the same air that now diffused the cold smell of seaweed across the bay.

Lillie and Petters picked their way across the sand to the closed beach hut in the distance. Lillie could make out the shape of a man sitting on one of the chairs in front of it. Angus was already there waiting for them. She could see the back of his head, leaning forward as though he were dozing and decided she better talk quickly to Petters before they reached him.

"So, she is alive. I thought she was," she said hurriedly in a low voice.

"Apparently." Petters tripped on the sand and caught his balance. "The chaps at the station said a man came in, an old recluse, from a village up the coast. Apparently he saw her picture and said it was the woman who had robbed him on the afternoon of the day she disappeared. So, you were right. She is on the run, probably frightened and trying to disappear."

"She saw something. Or knows something. Or both."

"Very likely. I'm working on getting that search warrant for the bank but it is going to take a few days."

"They seem to like you there, at the station." Lillie winked at him. "Missing it?"

"I haven't had time to miss anything yet."

"So where do you think she went?"

"I doubt she is around here, if she was we would have had another sighting. It isn't a very big area and with that picture of her in the newspaper it would be sure to shake her out. I would bet London. At least initially—perhaps as a step to getting to Sweden, but she would need money and papers. It isn't going to be easy for her to disappear."

"No, I shouldn't think so."

They had almost reached the beach kiosk, its shuttered windows closed for the night, great drifts of blown sand littering the wood flooring under its eaves. Angus hadn't yet heard them, his position unchanged from minutes before, and Lillie wondered if he wouldn't have sore neck from sitting in that awkward, slumped position. She noticed a dark pool of something at his feet and wondered if he had spilled a drink.

Immediately Petters put out a hand, sensing something just as she did, and stopped her from moving any closer. She froze, realizing it wasn't Angus's drink on the sand. Petters carefully and slowly walked in a wide arc around his chair. Lillie followed in his footsteps, making the same large circle and coming to rest in front of the young man they had met the day before and gazed in horror at the sight before them.

Angus's eyes, large and surprised, stared down at his chest

and the one bloody gunshot wound through his heart that had taken his life.

～

"I STILL CAN'T BELIEVE IT."

Lillie was sitting on the same patio she and Harry had had lunch on that day, wrapped in a blanket provided by the hotel staff and drinking a cup of spiked tea. It tasted horrible.

Harry nodded.

Felix Petters was across the patio in a huddle with three police officers from the Newquay station. He was doing more listening than talking, nodding here and there and rubbing at the back of his neck. She could see the beach kiosk from where she sat, its fading paint a surreal backdrop to the covered body on the sand. It was surrounded now by police and ambulance staff. A photographer was taking pictures and a small crowd of onlookers had amassed on the edge of the sand. A canvas stretcher lay beside the body but they hadn't yet removed Angus from his resting place. Lillie wondered about his family.

"He is dead because of us."

"I hardly think we can hold ourselves responsible for the actions of murderers, my dear," Harry soothed and Lillie wished she could agree with him.

Petters finished with the officers and slowly made his way towards their little table. The sound of a chair scraping across the floor sounded like fingernails on a chalkboard. He sat down across from her and motioned to the waiting staff to bring him something to drink. He looked to Harry who nodded and Petters held up two fingers and tipped his hat in thanks.

"The police are at the bank now," he started quietly.

"A little late." Lillie realized she sounded bitter.

"Angus didn't have any files on him when they searched his body."

"He said he wouldn't. He wasn't going to remove anything from the bank."

"There is the possibility that Angus may not have been as innocent in the whole thing as we think," he said gently.

Lillie's eyes snapped up. "In what way?"

"Well," he began, waiting until the waiter had put their drinks down and left before he continued. "He may not have been being entirely truthful when he said he didn't know if the duke and Stefanie were having an affair."

"How do you know this?"

"An associate of his at the bank said that Angus and the duke were well acquainted."

"But Angus made it sound as though he barely knew any of the directors, much less the duke."

"Yes..." Petters didn't elaborate, leaving Lillie to draw her own conclusions.

"What did this associate witness to make him or her think that?"

"Her. And she overheard them in the duke's office about a month ago having quite a heated argument about some transfers coming in from America and moving through London. Angus said something about the duke having his little girlfriend do his dirty work."

"Presumably Stefanie?"

"That was the impression she got. But the police will get to the bottom of it."

"Not quickly, I'm sure."

Petters sighed. "No, probably not. There are the intricacies of national banking legislation to contend with, surely. The protected privacy of financial institutions has always been a thorn in our sides."

"Well, I don't see any point sitting here and waiting for the police to cut through reams of bureaucratic red tape, do you?"

"What are you suggesting?"

"This little backwater bank is just that. A point of entry for funds. Ultimately, the real story originates in America and terminates elsewhere—or so we think. But absolutely everything must first flow through the main branch in London. In the meantime, we have someone on the run who is either very involved or a complete patsy—and she is likely in London. I say we jettison this place."

"Somebody did murder Angus. That person is presumably still here."

"Possibly, although unlikely. And it is a police matter at this point. There isn't anything we can help with."

Petters appeared to be thinking about this.

"Why do I get the feeling you are about to leave us?" Harry mused.

Petters' head snapped up in response, his eyes searching Lillie's.

"I am going to London," she stated bluntly.

"You are not!" Petters nearly spat back at her. "You are a reporter, not a police officer, nor a private investigator. And I can fairly reasonably assert that poking around in whatever unsavoury circles of organized crime you find will leave you very vulnerable indeed."

"I have to agree with Petters," Harry said, nodding. "But if you insist on going, at least be reasonable and take one of us with you."

Lillie stared out at the horizon, the early evening sun had vanished and swaths of musty purples and greys smeared the landscape.

She wouldn't be able to stop Harry from tagging along, this she knew, but the work she needed to do in London—and the person she needed help from—would require complete secrecy.

She stood up. "I need to go to the Post Office. I'll see you both later."

"I should think it would be well closed by now my dear, it's nearly seven o'clock." Harry glanced at his watch then eyed her suspiciously.

Lillie knew that while he was right about the general Post Office, as an essential service the telegram counter remained open until the general store closed at nine. "There is a drop box outside. I saw it earlier when I bought some stamps."

"I'll come with you," Harry said, pushing his chair away from the table.

"No, no. Really, I'm fine. I just want to send a few letters I've written," she lied, tacking a superficial smile to her face. "I could use the quiet." She hardly wanted Harry peering over her shoulder while she sent a telegram to New York.

She had a contact who might be able to help her—she only hoped she could still reach him using an address that was over a year old, having never tried it. Petters would be livid if he knew she was in contact with the very same fugitive his old department was still, for all intents and purposes, supposed to be looking for. With the passage of time, Lillie knew the search no longer took priority unless, of course, the man was daft enough to end up on English soil. She also knew that if she was to navigate the underworld, it was reasonable to assume he might be able to help draw her a map.

"Shall we meet for dinner, then?" Harry asked. "I'll make some reservations on the train for the morning."

"Please," she answered, and said her goodbyes.

As she left the patio and entered the large doors to the hotel lounge, she saw the duchess sitting at a small table on her own, sipping a cup of tea. She was reading a newspaper, her tepid eyes skimming it at a reading pace not even Woodrow Wilson could maintain and Lillie had the distinct impression the woman had pretended to not see her. *To hell with it*, she thought, not bothering to stop to say hello. For a brief moment she wondered what the woman was still doing here in Cornwall? Surely she would be more comfortable back home in Oxford?

Lillie glanced back at the patio where a small group of police were still gathered and studied them for a moment. The duchess, she noticed, seemed to be doing the same.

~

"Jack sent a letter."

Harry handed her a small envelope, dirty from its travels, one large smear across the return address. Lillie could make out a Russian postmark. He must have sent it to Oxford and Harry's household staff had sent it on to London.

She slipped it into her pocket.

"Aren't you going to read it?"

They were sitting in the lounge of Claridge's, Harry's favourite London hotel, having been in the city for the past four days. It had been two weeks since the Duke's murder, five days since Angus had been killed, and they were no closer to understanding who had killed either of them nor where Stefanie was hiding. Harry was planning on returning to Oxford the day after tomorrow—he was only staying because he wanted to go to the cinema for the final showing of *Foolish Wives*, and Lillie had reluctantly agreed to accompany him. Petters had opted to stay in Cornwall for the time being with the hopes of helping local law enforcement apprehend their murderer.

"Later."

Harry raised his eyebrows then frowned. He motioned to the bartender. "Two whiskeys please, Pete," he called.

Lillie felt suddenly terribly homesick for Oxford and her little cottage. She hoped Rumple had remembered to water her flowers.

Harry interrupted her thoughts. "Is there something you want to tell me?"

"What about?"

"Well, you have just decided to hunt down a woman no one seems to be able to find, *alone* I might add, and you aren't even going to read what must be a long-anticipated letter from your fiancé."

"Don't be silly, I'm just tired. It's a long trip from Cornwall."

"That was days ago; do try to come up with a better excuse."

They had been friends long enough that she was sure Harry could see her thoughts and feelings. She didn't want him to see what turmoil was wrenching around there. Engaged to be married but having second thoughts. What was wrong with her?

"Have you set a date?"

Harry was prodding her.

"Not yet. He isn't even in the country, how could we possibly?"

"Cold feet?"

Lillie willed her eyes not to fill and Harry's face softened. The bartender brought over their whiskeys and disappeared as quickly as he came.

"It's more than that. Did you always know Primrose was the girl for you? Was there ever anyone else?" she asked him.

Harry sighed and leaned back in his seat, taking his whiskey glass with him. "I see."

"What do you see?"

"There are always others, in answer to your question. That is what life brings you if you are lucky; and you are. Options. To go this way or that, to be here or there. It's what makes it all so terribly exciting, you see. It also makes it very difficult." He leaned forward. "Listen, old sport, Jack is a good man but if you don't want to be married to him that's another thing entirely."

"I just don't know…"

"Well"—he took a long sip— "the good news is you don't have to know right now. He is across the continent and you have time to figure this all out. Want to tell me anything? An old school love wound his way out of the woodwork and confessed his undying love to you?"

Lillie smiled at him. "Nothing like that."

"Ah, but something like that," he mused.

"No, it's just Jack's disappearance—during the war—well, I would be dishonest if I said it hadn't changed things for me. I'm not sure being married to a man who is in turn married to the government, and rarely present, is the surest route to happiness —that's all."

Harry nodded and sipped his whiskey. They sat in silence for a while, watching tourists laden with bags make their way through the lobby, a constant blur of mindless entertainment.

"He loves you, regardless of what he does for a living," Harry said finally.

"Yes, I know. And he is a spy for the British government. Do you ever wonder if it's possible to successfully be both of those people?"

"If anyone can do it, Jack can." Harry motioned for another whiskey while Lillie mulled this over.

She wasn't sure Harry was right.

14

LILLIE

The streets of London were in such contrast to the beaches of Cornwall that Lillie immediately felt claustrophobic and found her breath had hastened to match the pace of the city. It felt like the first day of school after spending the summer holidaying about the countryside, and being faced with the sharp crack of a ruler—the dizzying dash of people hurrying about their evening no different to a sudden pile of textbooks and the flutter of notepaper. It had begun to rain, giving the city a thorough soaking after what had been days of dry weather, and rivulets streamed down the pavement, washing a season of filth along with them.

It was a realization of sorts: to be back in a city she knew well and yet still feel like an outsider. She didn't plan to stay long. Just long enough to locate the source of the funds being funnelled through the West Country branch of the bank as they spiralled their way across the Irish Sea en route to Dublin, or London, or Geneva.

Her boss at the newspaper hadn't been best pleased when she told him she needed to track a thread in London.

"Tell me you are joking," he had said, exasperated. "You

work for the *Oxford Daily Press*, not the bloody *London Times*." The line they were sharing had a very good connection and his voice boomed down the receiver like a trumpet, causing her to hold the earpiece a good distance away from her head.

Perhaps she should be working for the *Times*, she though angrily, or even better, the *International Tribune*. "It's worthwhile, believe me. And if I don't have any leads by this time next week I will wrap it up and come home." She was placating him in an attempt to wind up the call. If there was anything she thoroughly disliked, it was being scolded.

"I'll come with you then, I can be on a train tonight. You can't go it alone, especially if you think all this mess is connected in some way to a criminal underworld."

Jeremy accompanying her in London would send her fiancé into a tailspin—*were he here*, she thought, not without bitterness. Jack was already jealous of their working relationship and had very little patience when it came to her boss. No. If she was going to work with anyone it would be Petters, but he was needed in Cornwall. And no one could know where she was getting her leads from. Although, having not yet received word back from New York she wondered if her on-the-lam contact had even received her telegram? She silently counted the days since she'd sent it. Five. Surely he would have made contact by now?

"That really isn't necessary. I have a friend who can accompany me if I need it." It wasn't entirely a lie, although labelling her contact a "friend" was dubious at best. And he wasn't anywhere near the city, being across the Atlantic.

"A week then," her boss had sighed, resignedly. "But I want reports along the way."

"It's a good story, Jeremy, you won't regret it." She hoped she wouldn't either, and she tried to shake the feeling that she was walking into a lion's den.

She had spent the last few days poring over what little

paperwork she had from the bank. What Petters had managed to glean from his contact in the police department he had secretly copied and slipped to her before she left Cornwall.

Accounts in and out, mostly numbered, some with names she would follow up on but which were no doubt legitimate, stared up at her from the pages. But one stood out: Flegenheimst. It was hardly a generic name. A great sum of money had trickled into the Cornwall bank through small deposits over the past six months from three American banks, all in New York City, into a number of accounts. It was quite a bit of work to trace the deposits but each account ultimately ended up with the same benefactor. Arthur Flegenheimst.

From here the money was sent onwards—some to Switzerland, some to Ireland and a large amount tracked back through the head branch in London where it was slowly and steadily withdrawn. What became increasingly clear, as she created her own charts and spreadsheets through which to track the funds, was that there seemed to be a slow but steady leak. The money that came into Cornwall left it—to be sure—but not all of it seemed to have a destination. From what she could see, a great sum of money seemed to have vanished into thin air. No routing bank, no numbered account, no benefactor. Just gone.

By the time her train had chuffed into Paddington station and Lillie had disembarked, she had known only two things. One, the man she needed help from may not even be reachable anymore. And, two, the stolen bank statements she had carefully hidden in the lining of her suitcase didn't balance. More money came into the Cornwall account than left it for elsewhere. By her calculations, over twenty per cent seemed to have been skimmed off the top—which was a small fortune considering the overall sum.

The sound of her feet on the pavement and the incessant noise of the streets catapulted her attention back to a city which felt nothing like home. Which was good. She had work to do.

15

DANIEL

He woke with a start.

He had been dreaming, thankfully. None of it was real. Not the dead girl in the river with the auburn hair and glassy green eyes. Not the sickness he felt even now as he swung his long legs over the side of the cot and sat with his head in his hands, his back bare to the chilled cabin, the tangled blankets a testament to his thrashing.

He inhaled deeply and stood up. It wasn't yet light but he wouldn't sleep anymore. He ran his hand through his short hair as he stalked to the tiny closet in his underwear and extracted an undershirt from his leather bag. He pulled it on over his lean frame. A sudden rocking of the ship took him by surprise and he grasped the cupboard door for a moment to steady himself. He needed coffee: strong, black and unforgiving, the way he liked it. He glanced around his compartment. Neat and tidy. Absolutely zero clutter. Nothing he didn't need and only the best of what he did.

He gathered up the last of his things, a first edition by Nietzsche—still in pristine condition, a Rolex Oyster watch, a pair of olive-coloured reading glasses which he tucked into their shell casing while he looked out the small port-hole window, now greasy with the salt and the weather of the past five days. Through the darkness of the early morning he could see the harbour lights in the distance. They would be in port in a few hours. Of course he was already packed and ready to go—he had been ready the moment he received her telegram.

She was here, he thought with anticipation. In this country that he was about to be delivered to—breathing the same air as he was, hearing the same sounds. It was intoxicating. And she needed him. *Him.* He caught sight of his reflection in the smoked glass of the mirrored cabin door. Tall, strong, and impossibly fit, even for him. Maybe too fit, he thought, noticing his face was bordering on gaunt, the lines on either side of his mouth becoming sharper with each passing day, his jaw and cheekbones three sides of a daunting triangle. It was no wonder his enemies took him seriously. Although there were less and less of them these days. He was out, and had been for some time now. There would always be those who would come for him, thinking that his guard would be down and the time ripe for whatever revenge or honour they wanted to take back from him. And so he had funded his latest project from afar. A school for orphaned youth. He their anonymous patron. He didn't want anyone from his past showing up there looking for him or harming any of his pupils.

And now she was looking for him. The American reporter he had met last year when he had been exacting the type of revenge his enemies wanted to take on him. Picking off members of a committee responsible for killing innocent people during the war. A committee responsible for killing his friend and mentor. She had been the reason he had stopped, job half finished, the police on his tail. Her involvement had led to her own disappearance and he had switched gears and hunted for her instead. Across the frozen Oxfordshire land- scape he had tracked her, and eventually tracked her kidnapper

—a half-crazed woman who would stop at nothing to expose the entire mess of that wartime cock-up. He had slipped away, slithered through the fingers of the law and boarded a ship back to America when it was all over. They hadn't come for him and he had thought, after watching his back every minute of every day for the past year, that they wouldn't.

And then there it was. That pale yellow piece of paper from Western Union—its circular logo at the top of the page a beacon of hope in a lonely world. He had sat in that smokey bar that night; the very same one he had told her about the last time he had seen her, never dreaming she would actually find him again. And yet there it was. He imagined her: the intelligent eyes that looked straight through him with their uncanny ability to reach inside his chest and grab out all the emotion and feeling he had always been so good at burying.

Why him? Of all the people she could ask for help, why him? But he knew. He was on the fringe. He knew the people and the intricacies of the underworld, and it would be there that she would find what she needed. He was her tour guide. That was all. Of course she was something else to him entirely. He would have to control that freight train once his ship docked.

This was business, nothing more.

He sat back down on his cot and watched the light slowly creep into his cabin, willing it to push away the shadows of his memories.

16

STEFANIE

A knock on the hotel room door woke Stefanie, and she rolled over groggily to find her watch. She held it up to what little light was coming through the curtains, straining her eyes to see the tiny hands in the shadows.

Six thirty.

Perhaps she could ignore whoever it was. She rolled back onto the bed. A sharp pain seared across her temples.

The knocking persisted.

Groaning, she pulled the sheet off, and reached down to find the clothes she had dropped on the floor the night before. She briefly thought of the man at the docks. It had been almost a week since their meeting and she wasn't any nearer to finding out where his employer's money had gone. Every morning since, she had woken up with a feeling of dread. She had come up with a few ideas and had even tried to approach a clerk from the bank's London branch, but she had lost her nerve when the diminutive clerk had questioned her identity. Stefanie had fled and not gone back, thinking that she would instead have to find a more back channel approach.

Her head felt thick and heavy and she realized when she

stood up that she was dizzy. She struggled to pull on her blouse and skirt. Her breasts felt tender and swollen.

The knocking continued, a little louder and with increasing haste.

An impatient irritant, and Stefanie wondered what had happened to Alek? He had been there when she had fallen asleep but as she glanced around the room she noticed his things were gone and the bed was empty. She ran her hand hesitantly across his pillow, feeling the depression where his head had been. She had told him of the man at the docks and he had urged her to leave London. As long as she was there, he had argued, she would be an easy target to find. She half-wondered if Alek was having second thoughts about their affair? He had become increasingly agitated over the past few days.

Another knock.

Her body felt as though it weighed twice what it usually did; her arms like pieces of lead. The room swayed as she stood up and attempted to make her way to the door. She stumbled, catching herself on a chair—what was wrong with her? She felt drunk.

She reached the door and hesitantly opened it, half thinking it would be Alek, for who else would be knocking at this early hour? He must have forgotten his key. Instead, she found herself staring into the face of a woman who would have been quite beautiful if it weren't for the miserable look etched on her face.

"Where is he, you treacherous harlot?" The woman spat with ferocity and Stephanie recoiled, stunned.

"I...I..."

"He is a married man. Does that mean nothing to a woman like you?" She was inside the room now and Stefanie stood awkwardly at the open door, her hand on the frame to steady herself, while she fought the urge to vomit. Something was terribly wrong.

"I don't know where he is," came her cautious answer, and she swallowed hard.

There wasn't any use pretending and so she took the moment to size up Alek's wife: short, thin, and very well dressed. Stefanie felt enormous next to her, which was a strange sensation given that the diminutive and hostile woman before her was vociferously intimidating, to say the least.

Alek's wife swung around to face her, scowling at the rumpled bed as she did so. "I've had him followed, you know. Watched all his disgusting antics. You two, carrying on like a couple of rabbits in heat... Don't think you have seen or heard the last of this."

Stefanie didn't think there was any point replying to this and every time she opened her mouth she risked throwing up. Where was he anyway? Surely he would have left her a note; her eyes cautiously took in the room but could see nothing.

His wife was back at the door now, having searched the adjoining bathroom and finding nothing. She stomped out into the hallway and Stefanie got a nauseating whiff of perfume as she went by. Shalimar in all likelihood, or Chanel. Neither of which she cared for.

Stefanie decided not to wait for Alek's wife to level any parting shots. She swiftly slammed the door shut behind the odious woman while simultaneously leaning over to vomit into an empty wastebasket.

17

DANIEL

He caught his breath, knowing it was her even before she turned around. He took the moment to study her: the curve of her back, the delicate line of her shoulders, the way her auburn hair caught the light and flicked its defiant gold highlights back at him. She was speaking to one of the doormen and he wondered if he should approach her, or wait? He felt the cool metal of the car door handle under his hand. He shifted his position and the leather seat beneath him groaned. He had waited this long, he decided, releasing it—what was a few more minutes?

He had been waiting outside Claridge's for an hour and a half, his driver keeping a steady eye on his watch and the rear-view mirror, while he kept his eye on the traffic progressing in and out of the lobby doors. When she had finally emerged, as he had hoped she would, they were ready. She had left the hotel and headed south-east into the city by taxi, although he had nearly lost track of her as his own driver was unable to negotiate a particularly crowded road near the Savoy. Eventually they had tracked the car once again, and it was only minutes later when it dropped her in front of a small, rather hidden, restaurant in an area of London he wasn't familiar with. He had carefully watched as she entered the building, noting a couple of men who leeringly admired her as she passed, ready to pounce if they did anything further, and then paid his driver handsomely for his efforts and followed her inside.

Now, standing awkwardly in the reception area, he glanced around the restaurant. Its white, linen-draped tables were reflected in the mirrored walls, their glass sharply outlined in a sleek and elegant Art Deco metal grid. Row upon row of triangular-shaped reflections cast the room as a hologram of brass and crystal, and he found himself growing dizzy as the image of her was thrust back at him, again and again, as she made her way to a table across the room.

Would she come here alone? Was she meeting someone? Did he dare make contact? Surely she must be waiting for someone, he deduced, taking another glance around. The restaurant was busy tonight, its smooth service edging towards the harried. The steady, floating dance of tailed and waist-coated waiters was becoming less of a waltz and more of a foxtrot. Why would a woman like her go anywhere alone, he wondered?

He continued to watch as she took her seat. Would she sell him out if he approached? Surely not. Not now, not after more than a year had already passed. After all, she had made contact with him. Not the other way around. He wondered if there was an extradition treaty between America and England, something he really should know.

The noise from the band was revving, its quartet hammering out 'I'm Always Chasing Rainbows', and he imagined the room as it would have looked a mere five years previous—when women would defiantly light up cigarettes and seek out the one or two French soldiers through the haze—the sparkle of a foreign blue uniform surely adding some wartime zest to a blossoming romance. Tonight the uniforms were noticeably absent, replaced by the robust and steadied march of modernity—short skirts, sex, and the glitter of Bolshevism. The initial exaltation of the post-war years had morphed into a Victorian mother's lament—petting parties and indecency were ruining the next generation.

A group of men sat at the curved onyx bar, their claret-coloured velvet stools gathered in a semi-circle so they could hear each other over the din of the music while they watched a few brave couples venture out to the nearly empty dance floor. An hysterical laugh from the pack told him they were already heavily into the cocktails. He knew their type. At home in New York, they would be tossing back Bronxes and bragging about their latest conquests—money, women, it was all the same—and he suspected, by the look of the them, that the same men existed in England. The only difference, perhaps, was their choice of drink. A few more couples got up, and then a few more, and soon the dance floor was full of hopping and jittering dancers.

He had that feeling in his chest again, he noted. That familiar tightness he remembered so well. Was it from the concern that he may be walking into a police sting—a trap to finally catch him for the murders he had regretfully committed in England? Possibly. Or, more likely, it was due to something else entirely and he was looking at the culprit. He slowed his breathing as he watched a waiter deliver a drink to her table. She murmured something to him, and when he left she pulled something out of her bag. A magazine of some sort, it appeared, and she took a sip of her drink and then absently began flipping through it. She glanced up at her surroundings from time to time, never seeing him, and then carried on reading. He was staring at the very woman he had thought he would never set eyes on again, he reflected, and he was alight.

He ran his hand through his short hair and toyed with the

idea of running, even as he knew his legs, like his mind, were fixated. He willed her to turn, knowing even as he did that he was exposed. A sitting duck.

The hostess saw him first, raising her kohl-rubbed eyes and spotting him, the glint of her sequinned headpiece catching the light as she sauntered towards him.

"A table for one?" She queried, giving him an approving peruse, her painted lips attempting a seductive pout.

He shook his head, immune. "I'm just looking for someone."

He realized that he couldn't stand there like a loiterer all night. The hostess nodded and, with some reluctance, moved on to the people behind him. He took a deep breath and started across the marble floor towards her table. He would take the chance.

As he got closer to her he could see what she was reading. *Punch* magazine, although he couldn't make out what the cover illustration was supposed to be satirizing. She had a mild smirk on her face as she read, and he wondered what it was that pleased her?

"Fancy seeing you here." His steady voice surprised even him, as did his choice of words.

She looked up abruptly, dropping the magazine onto the table, and he was treated to the full view of her face. Her green eyes dark in the light of the restaurant, her cheekbones casting a soft shadow under her eyes, her mouth in a full startle of recognition.

The kohl-eyed hostess was seating a couple at a table beside them and had he been the slightest bit interested, he would have seen a look of disappointment cross her face. The laughter, the music, the conversation, seemed to fade away instantly. Everything he needed to focus on was right in front of him and he was having just the easiest time concentrating on it.

"Are you here alone?" He realized she had yet to say anything, and he willed his eyes not to swallow her whole.

"Daniel?" She ignored his question, stupefied. "What are you doing here?"

"Are you?" he repeated, needing to know before they continued. She was wearing the most beautiful but simple silver necklace and he longed to bury his lips in her neck. He fought to control himself. "Alone?"

"Yes." She swallowed and he watched as her throat moved. "For now, anyway. I am only here for a quick bite before the cinema. I am supposed to be meeting...oh, never mind. What are you doing here? Are you here because of my telegram? You shouldn't be..."

"Shhh...never mind that." He pulled out a chair and sat down across from her.

She frowned at him. They had history, the two of them. He, an assassin on the run, her, a reporter who wouldn't turn him in.

"You really are the most infuriating man," she reprimanded, leaning in so they wouldn't be heard. He caught a whiff of her perfume and committed it to memory. Lily-of-the-valley, orange, something else he couldn't place.... "This is the absolute worst place for you."

"You wrote, so I thought you could use some help."

"I do need your help."

His stomach rolled. Although the look on her face told him it was business he let himself fantasize for a few seconds.

"Intriguing," he said finally, wishing he could order a drink. He signalled to the waiter for another of whatever she was having.

She watched him carefully, unsure perhaps, then glanced around the room. Was she nervous? Of him? Who was she going to the cinema with? Jesus, you idiot, get a grip on yourself.

The silence between them should have been filled with the din of their surroundings: broken conversations, jazz music, the laughter of an intoxicated girl, but it just deepened, and deepened. A monolithic chasm of unsaid words from two polar extremes of this world they inhabited together.

He noticed she was wearing an engagement ring. This was new, and he noted that it bothered him to a ridiculous extent. She was hardly privy to his private fantasy.

The dance floor was becoming a raucous display of the uninhibited. Waiting staff skirted it, careful not to get hit, trays of drinks held with both hands in the event of a jostle or two. Daniel gazed up at the bar, its liquor bottles ascending nearly two storeys, either side flanked by a spiralling staircase, their curving gold bannisters draped with flappers and young men in slim tweed pants, hands in pockets, bowties askew—two of whom were snorting cocaine off the bare back of a scantily clad woman who was bent over and fondling a third man. Lillie followed his gaze.

"Quite a place. I had no idea—Harry suggested it, of course. He wouldn't dream of letting me sit here alone. Something must have happened to hold him up." Was she apologizing? If she could have seen his world, then she would hardly feel the need to.

Daniel looked back at her, preferring the view across the table to any other, and not giving a damn if Harry walked in at that very moment and found them there. What was it that she stirred in him? Abandon, perhaps. A reckless abandon. That sounded about right.

"You remember Harry?" she continued, and he nodded. Her friend whose wedding they had interrupted last year while they had taken down a half-crazed woman intent on massacring a whole church full of guests. His help in that escapade was the only reason he had any currency with her now. This he knew.

Of course he remembered. He remembered anything and everything that had to do with her.

"So, Harry will be joining us?"

He waited for her to speak, not wanting to prompt her. He had all night and the longer she took, the longer he could sit across from her.

"He routinely shows up late, but yes, eventually. I do need some help," she continued. "I didn't know who to call."

He nodded for her to carry on.

"I'm working on a story about a man, a duke, who was murdered in Cornwall. He was director of a multinational bank with a branch in New York. I think he may have been doing something funny, illegal really, with some of the funds that trace to that Cornish branch. The head branch is in London, and the money seems to originate from New York, route through Cornwall, and then carry on to London, Dublin and Geneva."

"Go on."

"Well, this is what I don't understand. Two things, really: one, why go through Cornwall first? Why not just send the money to whatever ultimate branch it needs to end up in? And secondly, why does the sum of money going into Cornwall not match with the sum of money leaving Cornwall?"

"Maybe it was transferred somewhere else and you don't have all the information?"

She shook her head. "I doubt it. My files are quite extensive."

"Then, perhaps some of it has been skimmed?"

"It appears that way, just over twenty per cent is missing."

"The money coming in from New York, is it from one source?" he asked.

"A lot of it tracks to an individual with the name Flegenheimst, although there are also smaller sums from a variety of other accounts; all going to the same account in Cornwall."

Daniel knew the name, vaguely. He had heard it, this much he knew, but he couldn't place where.

"It reeks of organized crime, doesn't it? I regret calling on you but I wanted to navigate this without ending up dead in the Thames, if you get my drift."

The thought made him shudder. "I would have to do some digging."

"I have an appointment with the bank manager in the London branch tomorrow. Of course he hasn't a clue why I am really meeting with him. I cloaked the meeting request in a fabricated newspaper story I said I was writing."

"I'll come with you. You may need some protection."

"From a bank manager?" She laughed.

"Look, you don't know what you are up against. Not yet anyway."

"No," she conceded. "You are quite right. The young man who was supposed to give me the information I needed was shot a few days ago on a Cornish beach. It was horrific. Which is why I decided to get in touch with you. I figured you might have some understanding of the lay of the land. Not here, necessarily, but in New York."

She was referring to his past and it pleased him to say what he did next. "I've been out for some time."

She smiled at him, this time properly. A slow, creeping smile that reached her eyes and caused the edges of them to softly crinkle. For a moment he caught a glimpse of her in twenty years, at fifty, and thought she would be just as stunning as she was now.

"I'm very happy to hear that. Well…" She took a final sip of her drink, draining it to the ice cubes. He admittedly found this wildly attractive. "I don't believe you can help me then." She looked so pleased with him that he felt a surge of pride. He had been a lost cause his entire life. A criminal. A gangster, a marauder, an outlaw. And now he was cleansed of it all. He had told her before he left England last year that he was going to make a new start and he had.

"But that doesn't mean I don't still know who the players are. I am sure there are new faces but the structure will have remained the same."

She had wound her silk scarf around her neck as if preparing to leave, and he wondered where Harry was? Should he offer to take her to the cinema himself? It was a ridiculous notion, he thought, as he enviously stared at the scarf. He fought the urge to touch her. Instead he leaned forward, inhaling her scent. Violet. That was it. He clasped his hands together to stop them from shaking.

"So," he started. "Tell me about the movie you are seeing this evening."

18

LILLIE

B y three thirty the next afternoon she found herself on Threadneedle Street staring up at the limestone facade of Ainsworth Capital. She was early. Half an hour early, to be exact, and she cursed herself for not planning better. The street was busy, its bankers and stockbrokers spilling out of their offices for a cup of tea, or more likely a pint, before returning back to their desks to toil over the numbers for a few more hours. They strolled in groups, threes or fours, or sometimes half a dozen of them—the brims of their hats touching as they leaned in to discuss something they didn't want overheard.

She could hardly expect the manager to welcome her early arrival, so she took to the outdoor patio of a small and cramped cafe across the street and ordered an espresso, glancing around at the clientele. The glittering and bob-haired customers of last night were absent in these parts—having been entirely replaced by moustached, side-burned, and bespectacled men in fine wool suits and impeccably polished shoes. Having not even been there ten minutes, she spotted her accomplice circling their planned meeting spot, stopping eventually to languorously smoke a cigarette on the stone steps in front of the bank.

She watched him carefully for a few minutes before eventually giving him a wave and standing up to pay the bill. She couldn't help but feel an unwelcome sense of trepidation as she picked her way across the road to join him. He had startled her last night at the restaurant, and she hadn't really understood how he had managed to find her. He was man of hidden and dangerous depths and she would be wise to remember that.

He carefully stubbed out his cigarette before she reached him.

"Hello." He smiled at her, but it was tentative, as though he wasn't sure how to greet her in the daylight.

For a man she hardly knew, and one with such a horrifying past, he was remarkably disarming when he wanted to be.

"Ready?" she asked him.

"Of course. Today I am one immensely capable reporter's assistant." He paused, clearly aware of the absurdity. "Which is something I can honestly attest I have never been. Lead on."

She looked at him. He was the furthest thing from an assistant that she had ever seen. He had chosen his clothes with care. A light tweed coat the colour of sand, a pressed white shirt with a nondescript tie, beige trousers that blended remarkably well with his otherwise overtly expensive shoes. Had he been the man befitting today's clothes, she could imagine him being a fine conversationalist, a menace on the tennis court, and an impeccable partner for a foxtrot. As it was, he may have been these things, but he was also something much, much darker. His presence, however, was necessary given the topic of conversation she was embarking on with the branch manager: how large was the extent of criminal influence in the world of cross-border banking?

It was a cover, of course, a lead into her real motive which was much more specific: why would money be missing from

Mr. Flegenheimst's account? And why would he have it diverted through the Cornwall branch in the first place?

They made their way through thick glass doors, each pivoting smoothly on great brass pins, and approached the information kiosk.

"Lillie Mead to see Mr Rosenthal, please. We have an appointment." The receptionist nodded and touched a button on her switchboard.

The bank was a tribute to American classicism: its order and symmetry reflected in the pared-down Federal-style of its columns and balanced geometric spaces. To their right was a line of teller booths, dwarfed significantly by a soaring, coffered ceiling and enormous suspended globe lighting. To the left was a reception area, its marble floors bare and hosting clusters of barely worn, mahogany and leather club chairs. Beyond, and down a long corridor, were where the offices of the bank's more senior staff were housed.

"Mr Rosenthal will see you now. Down the corridor and second door on your left."

Lillie thanked her and, wordlessly, the two of them followed her directions.

Rosenthal was an archetypical banker. His diminutive stature told of long days at a desk with little in the way of outdoor pursuits. Balding, his face mostly obscured by large, round spectacles that reflected the light and caused an irritating mirroring, Lillie pegged his age at approximately fifty—although she could have been off by a decade either way.

"Thank you very much for seeing us today, Mr Rosenthal. May I introduce my associate Mr..." She hesitated, realizing she hadn't thought of a name for him. "Mr Daniel Hawke." At least if she used the correct first name she wouldn't forget it in a pinch.

"Pleasure to meet you both. Please, please, have a seat. Can I offer you anything to drink?"

"No, thank you."

"So, tell me, I understand you are doing a story for an international paper on global influences on the banking system, or something or other?" He waved his slender hand in an offhand way, giving the impression he was being dismissive.

"Not exactly. I believe you may not have been given the correct reason for my visit today. I apologize if it wasn't made clear to you." She glanced at the man next to her and he urged her on with an almost imperceptible smile. "What our paper is interested in is the extent traditional banks are used with regards to housing funds for what some governments might label 'criminal organizations'."

Rosenthal did nothing to conceal neither his surprise nor his disdain. "Oh! Miss Mead, surely you don't think Ainsworth Capital, or any other esteemed English bank, would ever engage with criminality in any form. No, no, no...it's preposterous." His hand was waving now, as though he were swatting flies. "Which newspaper are you with again, was it *The Washington Tribune*?"

"The *Oxford Daily Press*." It didn't sound nearly as significant, and she winced inwardly.

"I see. I haven't heard of it," he said pointedly.

She felt Daniel shift next to her and she willed him to keep quiet. In these situations, it was usually better to ignore the disparagement and carry on. Rosenthal was a snob, pure and simple, and Lillie had had much experience with the type.

"I'm surprised. We tend to cast our net quite widely throughout England and Europe, and even the United States from time to time, however it can be a little far for us to cover regularly." She gave him what she hoped amounted to a disarming smile.

"There is nothing whatsoever that I can help you with with regards to *that* story," Rosenthal continued. "Our checks and balances ensure that we only engage in business relations with legitimate entities. You have wasted not only your time, but mine as well, coming here today."

"Mr Rosenthal," Lillie tried again. "I have no doubt from my five minutes sitting here with you that your branch only operates with the utmost integrity, this is glowingly obvious." She watched as Rosenthal visibly relaxed into his more familiar, self-satisfied stance. Pleased, she continued, "Is there a chance some of the smaller county, or indeed the foreign branches might, oh, how shall I put it, have less professionalism than the London branch?" Appealing to his conceit, she hoped, would get her further than criticism would.

"I would hope not, Miss Mead, but as I'm sure you can well attest to—being an American overseas—things are hardly done in other countries as we do them in England." He sniffed. "There have been deficiencies in the past and although we try to stamp these things out quickly, there are restraints placed on our reach. As you know, the Americans are particularly reluctant to adapt, and the French are absolutely hopeless." He let his insult weigh on the air between them.

Until now Daniel had remained very quiet. He was scribbling on a notepad he had produced from somewhere and, had Lillie not known differently, he appeared the exemplary assistant. Resting his pen on the notepad, he looked up. "If I may interject, Miss Mead, could I just ask a question of Mr Rosenthal?"

Lillie nodded at him, surprised.

"Is it possible that the London regulations at Ainsworth Capital might cause an American citizen wanting to bank overseas to, perhaps, bank through international branches instead? Say, Ireland, or perhaps even a small county branch, Cornwall conceivably, in an attempt to evade the excellent restrictions you have in place here in London?"

"It is possible, I suppose," Rosenthal admitted hesitantly. "Although they would absolutely be caught out eventually. Our system is extremely adept at spotting anything that may be untoward."

"Of course, of course..." Daniel was scribbling again and when Lillie looked sideways at his pad she noticed a jumbled mix of letters and the odd doodle. She stifled a smile.

Lillie attempted to continue the train of thought. "And tell me, when money is received into, say, the Cornwall branch, and then transferred on—would there be a record of every other branch it goes to, whether it be in England or elsewhere?"

"Of course. Each branch would be clearly listed with a routing number."

"Have you ever had a situation where the amount of funds coming in doesn't match the amount outgoing?"

"If that were the case, presumably some of it would have been withdrawn by the client along the way, and this would be clearly identified on the financial statement."

"But if it weren't withdrawn by the client, as you say—what would be the reason for the numbers not matching exactly?"

"Well, there are banking fees, obviously, so some would go there."

"And what percentage is taken in fees?"

"It depends on the account but it is usually a set sum, and this would be clearly marked."

"Around twenty per cent?"

"Oh goodness, no! Certainly nothing like that. No one would bank with us if we took that kind of compensation. No, no no."

"Have you ever heard of a client by the name of Flegenheimst?" She was in hostile territory now, and she knew it.

The bank manager stared at them, his mouth agape. He snapped his lips shut with some force. "I cannot possibly discuss clients with you."

"So you confirm he is a client?"

"I do nothing of the sort." The manager was pulling at his

tie now, as though it were threatening to strangle him.

Lillie pulled some account papers out of her bag. She calmly continued. "These account statements show that Mr Flegenheimst, an American with investments in Ainsworth Capital, appears to be missing a great sum of money. Twenty-two per cent, by my calculations."

"How did you get those?" Rosenthal asked furiously. He aggressively leaned across the desk towards her as if to snatch them out of her hands and Daniel instinctively moved his body nearer hers. She felt him tense. "Those are private documents!"

"Let's say Mr Flegenheimst gave them to me. Are you prepared to answer my questions?" Backing down wasn't really her style, and she was emboldened by Daniel's presence in the face of this imposter. He knew exactly what she was talking about and for the first time she wondered if he wasn't in on it.

"Certainly not." The banker retreated back into his chair, keeping a wary eye on Daniel who had softened his position but hadn't moved. He smelled of tobacco and vanilla soap, she noticed, and while he had relaxed somewhat, his left hand was gripping the arm of her chair—his knuckles white with the effort.

"I see," she said, standing up to signal their meeting was over. She wasn't going to have any more success with the man. "I suppose I shall just have to print what I can from this meeting."

"If you print a thing, I will have you sued."

Rosenthal wasn't a man to be coerced, it seemed, which was disappointing but not insurmountable. Lillie picked up her bag and she and Daniel moved towards the door. They hadn't gained much from their visit but she knew this: wherever the money had gone, the head branch in London was acutely aware of it.

She looked back at Rosenthal and gave him a winning smile. "I will take my chances."

He had already picked up the phone on his desk and was dialling.

~

IT DIDN'T TAKE LONG.

By the time they had left the bank and emerged back into the sunshine on Threadneedle Street, they were being followed. At first it wasn't obvious, at least not to her, but Daniel had already chosen their route back to Mayfair in the least direct, most haphazard fashion. Instead of talking about what had happened inside their meeting he shot her a strong look that told her not to say a word. She obliged, not really understanding why, until she glanced behind them and saw a very determined, thick and heavy-set man who looked nothing like the other bankers on the street. He was half a block behind them, and appeared to have them in his sights, for he was steadily gaining on them.

This didn't really worry her, at least not initially. It was, after all, bright daylight and what could he possibly do to them on a street chock-full of people? It wouldn't be dark for hours and by then they could certainly shake him.

"Rosenthal could call the police, you know, which would be a great deal more dangerous to you than this joker behind us." She snuck a hurried look at Daniel. Was he taller than she remembered? His hair perhaps just the slightest more silver at the temples? It reflected the sunlight and when he glanced at her, she noticed he had flecks of amber sprinkled throughout his grey eyes. His skin was tanned from the summer and it made him look even more athletic than when she had last seen him. The clothes he had chosen to play the assistant made him look an entirely different man. Legitimate, came to mind. There wasn't any doubt women would find him handsome. Today he looked as though a woman could get past the forbidding landscape he usually cloaked himself in. His chiselled chin and strong cheekbones were mellowed by his attire, and it was easy to forget his terrifying past in his present role: her accomplice, dare she even say, her friend. She chided herself for momentarily being distracted from who he really was.

"He won't call the police," came the reply. "He's buried in it too deep. But don't discount the man following us. He is a professional—although not a legitimate one."

"How can you tell?"

"Lots of giveaways. The one I like the least is the bulge under his left arm. Classic Pinkerton goon squad attire."

"Who is Pinkerton?"

"Security firm. Hires out for businesses, governments... although their work is, at times, hardly legal. They are a nasty bunch we would do well to avoid." He steered her again into another wrong turn.

"Where are you going? This is the very opposite direction of where we need to go."

"Just want to be certain, and now I am. Drink?" He stepped quickly into a small doorway, abruptly pulling her in behind him. The bell over the door tinkled as they stepped across the threshold and Daniel moved them quickly away from the window. She caught a glimpse of the goon carrying on past.

She shivered and Daniel glanced down at her. He had the most disconcerting way of looking at her. Intensely direct, as though he couldn't decide if he should kill her or ravish her, his grey eyes so deep that they seemed to have no bottom.

They hadn't gleaned much from their afternoon at the bank, but her suspicions had been confirmed. Cornwall would likely operate with a few less checks and balances than London or New York. It was conceivable that criminal money would be less conspicuous if it flowed through there, which was presumably why Flegenheimst had chosen it. Prohibition profits, she reasoned, or gambling, or a bit of both.

They took their seats at a small table to the right of the bar in a section without windows. Daniel took the chair with a view to the door and she sat down across from him. Neither of them said a word until their drinks had been delivered, a French 75 for her and an Irish whiskey for him, along with a delicious plate of hot, fried potatoes. They picked up their glasses in silence and each took a long drink.

She wasn't sure if it was appropriate to ask the question but she did it anyway. "Are you carrying a gun?" she whispered.

He shook his head, swallowing. "I should be, though."

She nodded her agreement.

"I've put some inquiries out since our meeting last night." he continued. "Based on the initial reactions to my questions, I would wager this Flegenheimst is mob related. Not a small player either. He won't be pleased his money has vanished into thin air."

"I can imagine. But will he really be able to do anything about it? He is an ocean away and as we witnessed today, the walls of Ainsworth Capital are thick and slimy."

"Agreed. Although he will have people here too, you can be sure of that."

"Do you think the duke and Rosenthal were in it together? It would be embezzlement, pure and simple, if they were. Something easily achieved by two bank officials entrusted with large amounts of illegal cash."

"Possibly."

"If they killed the duke then I am sure they will be gunning for Rosenthal."

"Which would explain the muscle at the tip of his dialling finger." Daniel took another long drink, draining his glass. He glanced at hers and then ordered two more.

"I shouldn't," she said, as the waitress put them on the table. She didn't want to become intoxicated and loosen her guard. Against him or the thug on the street.

"Just keep me company," he replied gently. "You needn't drink it if you don't want to."

Lillie picked at the plate of the potatoes, realizing after the first few bites that she was ravenous. The clock on the wall read six thirty and she wondered where the time had gone? He picked up his fork and did the same. They munched in silence and she noted that eating from the same plate was a very intimate gesture, and yet it was one she didn't mind doing with him. She glanced around the pub. It was slowly filling up with the after-work crowd, and the noise levels had increased. She realized she was now half-way through her second drink and he had finished his and switched to water.

"Should we find a taxi?" she asked eventually. "It's too far to walk to Mayfair."

He nodded his agreement and waved for the bill. "Safer, too."

He paid up and they gathered their things and made their way back onto the street. His demeanour changed instantly now they were back outside. He was no longer relaxed, instead his eyes moved constantly to surveil their surrounding. Taxis seemed to be in short supply, and they waited for fifteen minutes to no avail.

"I think I would rather be moving than be a sitting target. Are you fine to walk a little?"

"Of course," she replied, and they headed west towards Mayfair.

The sky had darkened somewhat as the clear day had begun to give way to an overcast evening. The air was cooler now and Lillie walked briskly in an attempt to warm up. St Paul's Cathedral loomed to their right, its pale and unassailable dome surprising her, as she had lost track of where they were now, but it provided a beacon of comfort in its familiarity. A New Yorker in London always felt a little out of sorts.

Daniel's strange trajectory had taken them south towards

the Thames and now they were walking along the river with only the water and a few vessels to their left. They passed Blackfriars Bridge and carried on at a good clip. She wondered how they would find a taxi here, but didn't question his choice of route. She scarcely knew the city herself and was in no position to question his navigational skills.

He reached behind and found her hand; a gesture she found terrifyingly close and inappropriate, and then he stopped and pulled her towards him in a tight embrace. He buried his face into her hair and for one startling moment she thought he might force himself on her. Instead, he whispered urgently into her ear.

"He is here, behind us. Listen to me." He was pressed into her and she could feel his heart beating and noticed hers had begun to match it. She could smell the whiskey on his skin. "When I say run, do it. Fast. And don't stop, do you understand? No matter what, do not stop." He breathed, and she nodded her assent, feeling her legs buckle a little. He released her as suddenly as he had embraced her, and she swayed a little.

He set off again, a step ahead and they rounded a bend where the river curved and the pavement gave way to a path less travelled. Should they try to hide somewhere? A long line of abandoned warehouses took up where the road ended and she wondered if they shouldn't cut back into the heart of the city. Out here, the day dwindling and the light fading, she was beginning to feel exposed. The river bank became sand as Daniel cut around the warehouses and kept to the water's edge. She hadn't been in this part of the city before and had lost all sense of where they were.

For the first time she risked a glance back and saw the man was gaining on them, almost jogging in an attempt to keep up. He was hardly inconspicuous—although shorter than Daniel, he was a great deal heavier, with a black thatch of receding hair and a prominent forehead. He was as ugly as he was determined, and she fought the urge to break into a run. Seeming to read her thoughts she felt a quick squeeze on her forearm, urging her not to.

Out of what appeared to be nowhere they were blindsided by a second man—one she stupidly hadn't seen. Nor had Daniel apparently, as he was tackled with such force that he was ferociously flung to the dirt, his body colliding with hers mid-fall. She stumbled back, miraculously staying on her feet, and just narrowly missed being thrown to the ground with them.

The man who had been following them was upon them now, and he made a lunge for her while the other man struggled with Daniel. She quickly darted out of his way and toyed with running, but ruled it out. If he didn't catch her he would certainly shoot her in the back and she decided not giving him a bull's eye target would certainly suit her purposes better.

"Somebody...please!" she screamed, "Help us..."

Her words came out choked and the grunts of the man who had tackled Daniel were oddly but instantly silenced. She looked back to see Daniel brandishing a short, wide blade covered in blood. She frantically eyed him for injury before realizing it was the man on the ground who wasn't moving. Daniel, by contrast, was incensed. The look on his face as he turned his unleashed fury towards their tail would have stopped a German army tank. A ripple of terror ran through her. He stalked towards the man following them, and the man began to back up and reach for his left-side holster. Before he could get to his gun, Daniel was upon him and the two of them struggled for the firearm. Daniel slashed the man's forearm in the process and Lillie winced at the howl of pain he made.

The gun was halfway out of the holster when it went off, its sharp crack reverberating off the empty warehouses and splashing across the dusk. Something hot seared across Lillie's arm and for a moment she had the sensation that she had been set on fire. Daniel had the gun in his possession now and kicked the man hard in the back of the knees causing him to crumple to the ground. Daniel kneeled, pushing his knee into the man's throat and pointing the gun directly at the man's forehead. The tip of it made a deep, red mark on his skin.

"Who sent you?" he asked him.

But the man just shook his head.

Lillie watched in fear, knowing full well what Daniel was apt to do to him. The edges of her vision were beginning to blur and the searing pain across her arm had given way to a deep throbbing. The two men before her suddenly felt as though they were miles away.

"Private security?" Daniel asked again, his voice sounded as though it were underwater.

The man nodded this time, in the hope of having his life spared, then added. "Kill me and they will just send another."

Daniel nodded his understanding. "I'm not feeling too lenient towards you right now."

"I won't give you any trouble," the man answered. "I can be reassigned." He knew he had been defeated. "But you two, you are going to have to watch your back. They know your hotels, your movements. All of it."

Lillie tried to concentrate on them but there were white splotches across her vision. She leaned over, trying to get the blood to rush back to her head, then felt her legs crumple.

"You with him?" she heard Daniel say from a far corner of the universe, to which the man grunted his affirmative reply, and then the world went dark.

～

SHE COULDN'T HAVE BEEN unconscious for more than a few minutes and when she came to she realized she was bleeding from a graze across her upper arm. A slow ribbon of red winding its way down over her elbow and disappearing into the fabric of her blouse, oozing a swath across her cuff and smearing itself slowly past each button, staining their pearled surfaces.

She felt Daniel kneel beside her and place a hand across her wound, felt the tear of silk as he ripped the fabric to get to it. She reached up and touched the back of his hand, and he jumped, obviously not realizing she was conscious.

He said nothing while he held steadfast—pushing his weight into her skin to stem the bleeding. She let her hand rest on his wrist for a moment then trailed it back to the ground. Were those his hands that were trembling? Or was her body in shock?

She closed her eyes and felt his hands gently run over her body, his touch clinical as he searched for any other injuries. Apparently satisfied he resumed his pressure across her arm.

"I'm alright..." It was only a whisper, but she heard him exhale and felt the pressure lessen.

He removed his bloodied palm and inspected what little he could see of her wound in the fading light. It was nearly dark now and the scent off the river had changed with the twilight—a heady dose of damp moss and reed. She struggled to sit up.

"If you do that you are likely to start bleeding again," he warned gruffly.

She noticed the second man was still lying unnaturally still, face down, his body half submerged at the river's blackened shore.

"I'm alright," she repeated.

"For someone who is alright you seem to be remarkably bloody."

She put a hand up to her head while he followed it with his eyes. "I think it's my head more than my arm, to tell you the truth...I must have hit it on the way down."

"Mm. I'm not surprised. Stay still. I'll be right back."

"No...we have to get out of here," she said, weakly defiant, and attempted to glance around. Who knew if there would be others?

"Just for a moment..."

He took long, measured strides to the water's edge and she watched it lap at his beautiful shoes as he searched the dead man's pockets. They would be ruined, she thought bizarrely, given what had just happened. Finding what looked to be a wallet, a letter of some sort, and a handful of keys, he pocketed the items and quietly rolled the man's body into the water. He waded out, the water creeping up his trouser legs and darkening the fabric as he gave the body a final shove, watching as it began its journey down the river into the darkness. Reaching into his pocket he retrieved a handkerchief and dipped it in the water.

Turning, he saw her staring him. He sighed and started back up the bank towards her. She said nothing as he reached her side and carefully began to dab at her wound. She winced and he gently grasped her shoulder to keep her still.

"I'm glad he's dead," she said with finality, staring out to the horizon. "He would have killed both of us if you hadn't..."

"Yes."

Her blouse was ruined: where it hadn't been torn it was covered in blood. She looked down at it and attempted to pull her sweater over the whole mess.

"Can I just..." His hand dangled the wet and bloody cloth.

"It's good," she finished for him, pulling the sweater tighter.

"Let's get out of here. If they come for him..."

"I know." She nodded. "And the other one?"

"I let him go. He's no longer a threat." He pulled her to her feet, letting his hand linger too long. "I'll get you home," he said, by way of excuse.

19

DANIEL

er hotel was far enough away that by the time they reached it his pants had almost dried in the warm night air. He stood in front while she searched for a key she had obviously lost.

"Get another from the front desk," he said, rather more brusquely than he had intended. He was frustrated with himself. With the whole evening. With killing a man in front of her very eyes—for now would she ever be able to see him for who he could be?

She nodded, apparently unaffected by his tone, and they entered the nearly empty lobby. He waited while she retrieved a new key, surveying their surroundings. They knew she was staying here. The thought made him feel ill. Tomorrow she would need to find a new hotel. He walked her to the elevators and decided he would see her upstairs and check her room before he left her. And even then he wouldn't be going far.

"I've asked them to send up something to drink. I thought we could use it," she told him over her shoulder as they made their way down the hallway.

This surprised him. Nodding, he watched as she opened the door. It was a suite, which relieved some of the awkwardness he might have felt had it only been a bedroom and he took a seat on a large, comfortable sofa while she went into the other room, presumably to change.

A doorman arrived with a large decanter of whiskey, two glasses and an assortment of finger sandwiches. Daniel fumbled in his pocket for a tip, feeling the dead man's keys as he did.

When she finally re-emerged she was wearing a long, loose, linen blouse of the palest blue over a slim dark skirt, looking every bit the American she was. The gash across her arm had evidently stopped bleeding but he wondered if they shouldn't have it stitched.

She walked to the sideboard and poured them both large drinks.

He stood and met her there feeling the brush of her hand as she handed him his. She took a long sip and breathed out deeply; the tantalizing scent of peat, mixed with anise and caramel filled the air between them and he inhaled it, then did the same with his. She held his gaze and he realized he was becoming comfortable with the intensity she stirred in him. Was he somehow becoming addicted to the ridiculous range of emotions he felt in her presence?

"So?" She raised a delicate dark eyebrow. "I guess we hit a nerve somewhere."

He admired her ability to adjust and be matter of fact in the face of what she had just witnessed.

"Looks like it." He swallowed, feeling a burn down the back of his throat.

"What do you know about the Fenian Brotherhood in New York?"

"You think that is who we are up against?"

"It's a theory, although admittedly the Flegenheimst name

hardly fits." She had a faraway look on her face and he glanced again at her arm. She had been grazed with a bullet an hour ago and she was standing there as though nothing had happened. It was unnerving.

She continued. "It was just something the duchess said to Harry—that the duke wouldn't travel to Ireland...ever." She poured herself another drink and topped his up. "Never mind. Sit?"

"I think you should see the hotel doctor." He gave her what he hoped was an intimidating stare but admittedly, when it came to her, he was as useless as a cart without a horse. She ignored him.

He took a seat on the end of the sofa while she sat a comfortable distance away, placing the whiskey bottle on the sofa table, and curling her legs underneath her. Her feet were bare. He could feel the alcohol begin to warm his face and fingers and the room had taken on a fuzzy haze. Where was her fiancé, he wondered? Was he likely to show up?

"Why do you think it's them, the Fenians?" he asked as he began to empty his pockets onto the table. The dead man's keys clanged the glass.

"I don't know. It may not be. The money originates from organized crime of some sort, I'm sure of it, and you've confirmed Flegenheimst is of that world. The way it trickles in, the various originating names, one American beneficiary hiding his cash offshore. The jumpy bank manager. And the dead director and dead bank clerk, of course. Maybe that's the trail. Maybe the duke was moving it for them to Ireland and that is the missing twenty-two per cent. Maybe he wasn't lining his pockets at all." She reached forward and retrieved the wallet, placing its contents on the table before them. A couple of soaked photos, a woman smiling back at them, another of a fairground booth and a couple of dirty-faced kids standing in front of it. Her face was suddenly sad and she pushed them away.

She sat back against the sofa. "But then why kill him? Unless..."

He thought her tongue sounded as thick as his felt.

"Unless one has nothing to do with the other," he finished for her, realizing he was having difficulty pronouncing his vowels.

She sat up and retrieved the whiskey bottle from the table, pouring more drinks into their glasses. If she wasn't careful she would very likely get him dangerously drunk.

"I wish you could have asked that man...your attacker, what he knew."

"I was a little busy trying to not get killed," he answered. "And anyway, he was just the hired thug. He wouldn't have known anything of value."

He wanted to be dangerously drunk, he decided after a moment, and took a gulp of his drink eyeing her while she did the same.

He pointed to her arm. "I think you need stitches."

"So you've said," she retorted, and he realized how much he loved a strong-minded woman, regardless of how infuriating they could be. "I'll deal with that tomorrow."

He glared at her. "The sooner the better, or so they say."

"It's disinfected and bandaged. And just who is 'they' anyway?"

He laughed. Something he rarely did. He was feeling wildly carefree despite the evening they had just had. He thought fleetingly about the dead man floating down the river and it sobered him somewhat. She was sitting close enough that if he reached out he would be able to touch her. It tantalized him, and he longed to sit on his hands to stop them betraying him.

"So, who would want a duke dead?" she asked. "And a clerk, for that matter." She was leaning over the table fingering the keys and looking at the rest of the wallet's contents again. He could smell her: flowers and whiskey, and dried blood.

"Let me look at your arm..." He leaned forward, fully expecting her to roll up her sleeve for him, sad that her beautiful skin would forever have a scar there. The top of his head brushed her chin and he realized he was too close, the whiskey affecting his judgement.

"Sorry..." he apologized, pulling back and raising his eyes to hers. "Actually, I can't...say..."—everything was becoming muddled, the room spun, he touched her shoulder and pressed her gently away from him—"...that I'm sorry because I'm not really..." He wasn't making the slightest bit of sense and he knew that if she was too close to him it would spell disaster.

He struggled to get control of himself.

Was she as drunk as he was? Was he insane? Did women throw caution to the wind like men did?

Of course not.

The air between them electrified him. He imagined what it would feel like to lean in and kiss her, then slowly devour her with his whole being.

He realized she was looking at him. Afraid, perhaps? Angry?

He cleared his throat uncomfortably. He was a fool. Dropping his eyes he felt instantly sick at his mistake. He took another sip of his drink and tried to compose himself.

"So," he started, attempting to change course, there wasn't any point addressing his ridiculous behaviour. He pointed to the ring on her finger. "Engaged then?" He felt the moment begin to slip away from him, thankful he was back on solid footing, his thoughts, gratefully, still somewhat private.

She nodded and with great reluctance he put his drink down. He had had enough liquor.

They sat in silence for a long time—side by side, their bodies only inches from one another, each of them lost in their own thoughts, the candles the housekeeping staff had lit flickering their animated shadows off the papered walls.

When she finally spoke it was with a clarity that surprised him. "I just don't know if I can marry him."

He exhaled. "Because?"

"He left me once and I haven't forgiven him."

Daniel sighed, reaching for his glass. "Stupid man, leaving you."

She seemed to mull this over then said quietly, "I think perhaps drinking whiskey together, you and I, isn't a good idea."

He laughed for the second time that night.

~

THE NEXT MORNING Daniel arrived back at the hotel with a thick head and low-grade nausea. He found her in the breakfast room sipping a cup of coffee and toying with a plate of toast and eggs. He watched as she pushed them around, nibbling on the edge of her bread reluctantly before abandoning it entirely and pushing the plate away.

"You feel like I do, apparently," he said, taking a seat opposite her.

She looked up at him with a smile that he longed to see every morning.

"It looks like that has been attended to?" He pointed to the bulk on her arm under her blouse.

"Hotel doctor, thankfully. A few stitches."

"Good." He motioned to a waiter for a cup of coffee.

There was a silence between them as he struggled to find something to say about his error in judgement the night before.

"Listen, I'm sor—"

"Don't say a thing," she interrupted. "It wasn't all you. I kept pouring the drinks. I'm as much to blame. I wrote to you—

sought you out—and you've been...well, you saved my life last night. Things got a little...never mind, it's over now."

He sorely wished it wasn't but he nodded his agreement all the same. He wanted to ask about her fiancé, but it was none of his business so he kept quiet and sipped the coffee the waiter had brought.

"First order of business is to get you out of here," he said matter-of-factly, changing the subject.

"Yes, I agree. Best to keep moving. I've made a reservation at Brown's. Harry has already left for Oxford so I won't get any resistance on that account. He despises staying anywhere else." She glanced around, taking in the pleasant surroundings.

"I've asked around, the Fenian Brotherhood does have a group in New York. Quite a large one actually. They were pushed out of Buffalo in the 1860s after which they dispersed somewhat, but their biggest pocket of support appears to be in the New York area."

"Perhaps American sympathizers are still funding the anti-treaty IRA. The violence in Belfast shows no sign of abating. Presumably there would be a constant need for firearms and military equipment. They are fighting the British Army, after all, it can't be easy. I read somewhere that seventy to eighty per cent of the IRA is against the treaty. Liam Forde, Ernie O'Malley, Rory O'Connor—they have quite a following."

Daniel nodded, even in America, Ireland made front-page news.

Lillie continued, "I suppose it's possible that a portion may have been transferred elsewhere to buy military supplies, perhaps, or political favours—I just don't have all the information."

"Mm, possibly. Ireland as a seat of discontent..." he mused. "With a rebel army in need of assistance."

"They are at war, after all, regardless of the treaty that was signed. And, someone has been skimming—either for themselves, or for a splintered Irish resistance. It's not a bad theory." Lillie stated it matter-of-factly. "Of course it's just one theory amongst many. Oddly though, the duke spent much more time at the branch in Cornwall than a director of the bank usually would. He seemed to be quite hands-on, in fact. His death, along with that of the other clerk, certainly points to something untoward. And, of course, Stefanie is still missing. As far as I can tell, she was the only other clerk who executed the duke's orders."

"Sounds like Stefanie is the one you need to track down."

"Felix Petters is working on it, but as he is still in Cornwall —which is likely exactly where Stefanie *isn't*—there hasn't been much success on that point."

"Do you think you might consider abandoning this whole thing and heading back to Oxford?"

Lillie frowned. "I thought we just discussed moving hotels? I haven't yet put this all together...and shouldn't we report this man's death to the police? It was self defence after all."

"Absolutely not. And be tied up in an investigation? We did nothing wrong, and whoever he was isn't worth your investigation being stalled and police resources wasted. He was an assassin, plain and simple. End of story." He was acutely aware of the irony. He continued, "I can keep on monitoring things here and will communicate anything I find out. In the meantime, you can and should operate on the very likely assumption that this is IRA money and they are probably gunning for Stefanie. She is their only loose end."

They sat in silence. Of course, he, if anyone, understood what a *loose end* meant.

"Or it's simpler than that. It's American mob money and the Duke and his crony stole it. I just think that to come all this way and then leave without any definitive conclusions is a waste. And something else bothers me; the duchess. She was sort of... well, cagey with me—I can't really put my finger on it."

"It's not a waste. We know we have caused some very dangerous people a great deal of angst."

She gave him a hard look and he reached for his coffee, taking a long sip before he spoke again.

"Go pack your things. I'll wait here and accompany you to Brown's."

She gave him another frown. "I don't think I hired you to make my travel arrangements."

He ignored her. He wasn't fooling himself into thinking he had any influence over her. She would do exactly as she liked but the look on her face told him she knew she needed to get moving.

"Fine." She sighed with annoyance, placing her cup down and rising. "I'll be right back."

He nodded. "One more thing," he added cautiously. "About another matter. Forgive my forwardness but here it goes..." He winced inwardly. "Perhaps you shouldn't marry him."

She didn't seem surprised at his words and instead looked at him, long and hard, her eyes a swirl of sadness, regret, defiance. He felt as though she had struck a match and set him on fire.

"I'll think about that," she said quietly, putting her napkin on the table. "I guess I'll have to."

At once he regretted and yet selfishly celebrated the complication he had likely brought her with his words. Or was he fooling himself into thinking she actually cared about his opinion?

"Well, anyway," he continued, getting up from his chair, "it's none of my business, of course." He was bumbling around now and he willed himself to have some restraint. "Get your things," he added, bringing the conversation to a close.

Although he felt panic that he wouldn't see her again after what he had just risked saying, he was reassured knowing where her cottage in Oxford was—at the end of a lane, past the shops and the village green, a cobblestone path that led to an arched front door painted robin's-egg blue...

He watched as she retreated from the restaurant and made her way across the hotel lobby—taking the ashen pieces of his broken heart with her.

20

LILLIE

There was a familiarity about the man standing with his back to her in the lobby of the hotel, although it only registered in passing. She noticed him, albeit subconsciously, as she breezed across the etched, marble floor towards the stairs—that recognizable stance, the grooves in the back of his neck, the coffee-coloured hair. Perhaps the realization eluded her, for she hadn't the time to linger, and noticing bystanders as she hurried through the reception area en route to her room to pack wasn't something she was inclined to do that particular morning; unless, of course, they were burley, private security hires with guns hidden underneath their left arms. Which this one wasn't.

Yet, the way he moved, the colour of his herringbone suit—blackened navy with the finest charcoal threading—she had seen it all before. She caught her breath as she passed, then, startled, she stopped and turned back swiftly. He was still turned away from her, leaning in across the polished counter and asking something of the hotel clerk, a plumpish, but attractive woman who appeared to be flirting with him—or he with her? It was difficult to tell. Her empty-headed laughter tinkled across the room.

The fog lifted and Lillie's heart leapt into her throat as she had the sudden rushing realization that she had left a wanted man back at her breakfast table. The familiar back turned from the desk and she found herself staring into a pair of sharp blue eyes that she knew very well.

She blinked a few times, attempting to focus, and wondered if she was seeing things. It couldn't possibly be...

"Jack?"

The paleness of his skin surprised her, especially given the summer they were having. But that wasn't all. Here he was, back in London, and he had obviously come for her. It irritated her, she realized, and in addition to being pleased to see him she also had the unwelcome impression that she was being tracked.

He smiled and walked towards her, leaving the hotel receptionist gazing after him. He was thinner than when he had left Oxford over a month ago. She hadn't spoken to him since and she realized she had yet to open the letter Harry had given her. She had been so distracted with her story, and so flooded with the inevitable doubts that come when one is absent for such a long time, that she had tucked it away in her coat pocket thinking she would read it when she had a moment to herself. That moment hadn't come.

"Hello, Lillie." He moved towards her. "Surprised to see me?"

"Well...yes actually...I am. What are you doing here?"

"Didn't Harry tell you I was coming?" His eyebrows were raised, perplexed and surprised all at once, in addition to being mildly suspicious. Lillie realized that while they were in the lobby, they had a full line of vision to the restaurant. Had he already seen her? And for that matter, had he seen who she was breakfasting with? Would he remember him?

"No, unless he left a message, and I didn't get it. To tell you the truth I haven't seen him this morning." She eyed the polished wood reception desk behind him, along with the annoyingly attentive receptionist who was happily manning it, and wondered why she hadn't thought to check in with them? She supposed being attacked and nearly killed the previous evening had thrown her off her game.

She nervously fiddled with a loose thread on her blouse.

Jack was staring at her. His eyes roved from her face to her arm, which was bulkily bandaged underneath her blouse, and back up again. It wasn't an easy thing to hide, unfortunately. "I finished working on...well, what I was doing, and checked in with Rumple who said you and Harry were in London. I thought, well why not? I hardly want to be in Oxford if you aren't there. Incidentally, what is this?" He reached over and gently touched her arm.

"Nothing—it's, well, later..." She glared at the desk attendant who was blatantly eavesdropping and the woman reluctantly slunk away. Lillie understood that much of Jack's work was classified but it did irritate her that he had been gone a month and offered no explanation of what he had been doing. She glanced behind her to the restaurant. The table she had been eating at had been cleared and re-set. There was no sign of Daniel—he must have seen them. She felt herself exhale in relief.

"Is everything alright?" Jack followed her gaze towards the breakfast room. "Lillie?"

She brought her eyes back in an effort to deter him. "Yes, yes, of course, it's just I was heading up to my room to pack some things. I was planning on switching hotels today."

"Oh?"

"Just for a little change of scene," she added, hastily.

Something to the right of where they were standing caught her eye and she realized with a glance that Daniel had moved from the restaurant and was standing beside the exit door in the lobby. A bold move, considering. He had a puzzled look on his face and she could feel his eyes boring a hole through Jack's back and settling on her. Lillie prayed Jack wouldn't turn around. It had been some time since that day in the Oxford chapel when Daniel had slipped Superintendent Petters' net, but Jack was sharp enough to not forget a face.

"Well, I'll accompany you, shall I, and you can tell me what you are working on." He motioned towards the stairwell.

She nodded and risked a final glance towards the door.

The place where Daniel had stood was now empty, and he was nowhere to be seen. A momentary flood of relief washed over her.

By the time they reached her room and unlocked the door, Lillie's nerves were shot. Jack took a seat on the sofa and pulled her down beside him.

"I've missed you," he murmured, brushing his lips across her forehead and leaning in to kiss her. She willed herself to relax. The kiss lingered, as did the claustrophobic guilt that came with keeping secrets. She wondered how Jack managed to do it on a daily basis?

When they parted, she had a pit in her stomach the size of Scotland.

"Are you going to tell me about your arm?" he inquired again.

"Oh, this? It's nothing. I slipped getting out the bath and scraped it along the side of the sill. There must have been a sharp piece of cast iron and it tore the skin."

"Would you like me to have a look at it for you?" He trailed his hand up and down her arm gently.

"No, it's fine, really. The hotel doctor fixed it up." She wanted to change the subject. "Are you going to tell me where you have been all this time?"

He smiled at her. "You know the routine. It's classified—but

I can tell you the food was dreadful. Anyway, I hope to have a couple of weeks in the London office before they send me anywhere again."

Lillie nodded, hiding her irritation.

"And what is the story you are working on, my dear? Rumple relayed that you were in Cornwall for a time."

Why did he expect her to tell him all the goings-on in her life while he stayed mute on his? She didn't feel like telling him a thing, but, realizing she was being childish, attempted a change in tactic.

"It's an international banking story, really," she began. "A director of a bank in Cornwall was murdered and one of the clerks at the bank is now missing. Presumably she is involved in some way, I'm just not sure how. I came to London to try to find her as I believe she may have been in touch with an old boyfriend of hers who lives here—Alek something-or-other. I am trying to track him down in the hopes he leads me to her— but it's a long shot. Anyway...why don't I fill you in later. I should be getting my things together to check out."

"I find it odd you want to go to Brown's when you always stay here. You could stay with me in the flat you know, there is a spare room—forgo the whole hotel experience?"

Jack had a flat not far from Claridge's, although he had spent little time there since Lillie had bought her cottage in Oxford. When he was working he would use it as a city base, but every weekend and holiday he spent with her. In her current state of mind the very last thing she wanted to do was stay with Jack.

"I have to work, its just easier to do that without distractions."

"So, I'm a distraction?" His face fell, and she instantly regretted her words.

"No, of course not. But you know, writing takes concentration. I can hardly do it when I am in my own home somedays, much less someone else's. There's always something else that commands my attention—plants in need of water, a kitchen in need of a tidy, weeds in need of a pull."

Jack looked doubtful.

"I'll pack my things and then we can walk together," Lillie said, putting on a false smile. She wondered where Daniel had gone and if she would see him again. She suspected that even if she didn't see him, he would certainly be seeing her. The thought made her oddly comfortable and that, in turn, made her uncomfortable. There was no winning.

She made her way to the bedroom to pack her suitcase.

21

LILLIE

"It's good to be back, I can tell you that with certainty. Cornwall feels somewhat...*remote*. Out-of-touch, perhaps. Certainly foreign. It's hard to believe it's part of England, really. The locals seem so extraordinarily—*relaxed*. Not that that's a bad thing. Quite the contrary, in fact. I only wish I could be a little more laissez-faire in my own life. And yet when one is immersed in it, it's as though nothing else exists outside of it. Does that make any sense?"

"A great deal of sense. When I think of Manhattan, it's like I never really lived there at all. Isn't it funny how time passes in a new place and without pomp or ceremony it just becomes... well, *normal* I suppose."

They were walking through St James's Park and the gravel path crunched under their feet sending up small clouds of dust and soiling the tips of their shoes. They were having a very warm summer and the city was beginning to parch. The grass had the bleached look of a hay field and even the summer flies had fled. Lillie had never seen it so dry.

Petters had arrived in London just over a week after Lillie had. Jeremiah and his aunt had returned from their trip and

Petters planned to take him back to Oxford with him. So much had happened in the short time that Lillie had been in London without him. And while she yearned to tell him about it, she knew very well she couldn't reveal everything.

"Spoken like a true ex-pat," Petters joked. "Although you really haven't enlightened me on where you are at in the investigation. Do you still think this whole thing might be Sinn Fein related?" He narrowly avoided brushing shoulders with the oncoming hordes of summer tourists. Petters didn't like touching strangers, and Lillie smirked as he brushed imaginary germs off his ivory dress shirt. It was far too warm for a jacket and he had his slung, perfectly folded and pressed, over his forearm.

"I'm still not sure." Lillie replied, carefully sidestepping the question on how she knew what she knew. "I didn't get that feeling from the bank manager, and certainly the names are hardly Irish, but it was just that statement that the duchess made—that the duke wouldn't travel to Ireland, ever."

Petters gave her a hard look. "So a wasted visit to the bank then? All those waves made and nothing concrete?"

Lillie thought about this for a few minutes. They came upon a green-and-white kiosk selling iced teas and passed it by. She changed the direction of the conversation. "Tell me what you have learned in Cornwall."

Petters cleared his throat and lowered his voice, even though there was no one within earshot. "Still no sign of the girl..."

"Hmm. So still a missing person but nothing to suggest she is dead?"

"No, not yet, anyway. But still, no sign of Stefanie and the fact that she's had no communication with her aunt is vexing. Angus's death is still unsolved. The police don't have many leads either. Apparently there were two men who checked into a small hotel on the coast outside Newquay two days before

Angus died. They used aliases unfortunately, so nothing to track them by, but the hotel clerk swears up and down that their accents were Scottish."

"And the hotelier was English?"

"Canadian actually. Has lived in Cornwall since the end of the war though, so I would think he would be able to pinpoint an accent."

"You'd be surprised. I still have difficulty. Could they have been Irish and he was mistaken?"

"It's a possibility. The police are trying to find anyone else who may have conversed with them or sold them something, served them in a restaurant or a pub—what have you—but we are going to have to wait on that one. I did, however, telegram the Swedish police and have them correspond with that friend of Stefanie's."

"And?"

"She says she hasn't heard from her—so I seriously doubt she has made it back to Sweden."

"And you think she is telling the truth?"

"Well, that is always the big question, isn't it? Although, in this case, yes I do because she was very forthcoming on another matter."

"Oh?" Lillie stopped walking and faced Petters. The late afternoon sun was low in the sky and sliced through the atmosphere like glass. She held up an arm to shield her eyes.

"She gave them the full name and address of Stefanie's former boyfriend, Alek. The one who she was madly in love with and who left her to marry an English woman. Broke her heart, apparently."

"And you think that for some reason Stefanie might have gotten in touch with Alek?"

"Possibly."

"Her aunt said they didn't keep in touch."

"True, but her aunt may not have had all the facts."

"It's a long shot, Felix. If he married and moved on, he would hardly still be her confidante—although I do rather agree with you, it's as good a place as any to start looking."

"Mm. She is a young woman alone and terrified and it is possible she will reach for the only lifeline she can grab."

"So we track down Alek."

"Ideally, yes. And I am way ahead of you. I have his addresses here in London. Both home and business."

Lillie smiled at her friend. She liked the way his mind worked—quick, efficient and always looking for the next act. He was methodical, it was true, even stubbornly dogmatic at times, but he had the one thing that made a good detective into an excellent one: intuition.

"Are you sure you aren't making a mistake leaving the police force? You seem to be very good at this," she teased.

Petters didn't answer, instead turning on his heel and continuing his walk down the dusty path into an early mauve twilight.

22

LILLIE

"Hello? Harry, is that you? I can barely hear you..."

Lillie was settling in at Brown's hotel that evening and was about to draw a bath when the front desk put the call through. There was a rush of something that sounded like wind and Lillie pressed the earpiece of the hotel telephone against her ear.

"Lill...it's the...oh, damn it...Rumple...fix..."

"Shall I hang up and try you back then?" she asked.

There was nothing but static now and she waited impatiently, tapping her foot and glancing at her watch. It was nearly eleven o'clock, no wonder she was so exhausted. She longed to flop down onto the bed and sleep for days. She stared at its inviting blue-and-white quilt and feather pillows.

"Lillie! Can you hear me now? There, I think that's fixed it. Thank you, Rumple."

"Yes, yes. Much better. I can hear you now."

"Good. Listen, I've had a call from the duchess this afternoon. It seems there have been some odd goings on with regards to her personal household bank account. There has been a steady trickle of money going out, and she hasn't withdrawn it. It became rather more substantial over the past few days."

"Is the account with Ainsworth Capital? I assume it is."

"No, actually it isn't. This is a personal account she uses for running her house—staff payroll, gardeners, that sort of thing. It's with a local Oxford bank."

"Perhaps there is another signatory on the account—her butler, or a housekeeper? It wouldn't be the first time a lady was fleeced by someone in a position of trust."

"No, I quite agree, but she insists none of the household staff has any authority on this particular account. In addition, she has noticed some things missing from her home. A bit of silver, some jewellery, odds and bobs."

"Sounds like petty household theft from a staff member, Harry."

"She insists she has had the same staff for years and things like this have never happened before."

"I'm not sure what you think this has to do with the case?"

"Perhaps nothing, but I thought you should be aware. Oh, and I almost forgot. The Secretary of State's office wrote about a passport renewal."

"Is the duchess planning a trip?"

"No. It wasn't her passport they were referring to, it was the duke's."

"He must have applied for a renewal before he died. Was there any date reference on the letter they sent?"

"I asked that but she didn't seem to know."

"Harry, I certainly appreciate the update but I'm not sure any of these things actually mean anything important to the duke's murder."

"Well, that's the thing. The duke's passport renewal was rushed. He was planning a trip to the West Indies, it seems, and needed it promptly."

"I see. Did he and the duchess often travel there?"

"She has never been, and he never mentioned it to her."

"So you think he was planning on making a run for it?"

"Possibly. And perhaps he was taking Stefanie with him—or wanted to before he...well, expired."

Lillie thought about this. Had Stefanie left the country? she wondered. If so, then Petters would have been wrong about her reaching out to Alek. Wrong, also, about her being in London. She had never known Petters to be wrong about anything.

"Are you still there?" Harry was saying, then as an aside, "*Rumple! I think it's broken again...I swear, if I employed a wet dishrag...*"

Lillie cut him off, "I'm here, Harry. Sorry, I was just thinking."

"Say, why have you changed hotels? Tell me the truth." He didn't wait for her to answer. "Incidentally, have you seen Jack? I hear he is fresh off the trail of hunting communist sympathizers. It all seems a little paranoid, if you ask me—but then no one ever does, oddly."

He was gently baiting.

"I'm working, Harry, and it's easier to do that without distractions."

"I see, well, I do suppose some of those London hotels are so terribly lovely that it's hard to imagine yourself anywhere else."

"Something like that," she answered.

"I see. Well, tell you what, I could use another trip to London. Rumple has been on at me about taking him to the city. Wants to buy some ridiculously expensive ties from a fashion house, Patou, Pate, some name I can't actually remember. I do wonder if I am paying him too much. Why don't I head there tomorrow? I'll even venture over to the dark side and join you at Brown's, shall I? Although it does pain me terribly to see someone else in my suite at Claridge's. I don't suppose I will need to reserve a room—I can't possibly imagine that *particular* hotel would be full—is the clientele terribly uncouth?"

Lillie could hear Harry arguing with someone in the background. Rumple had obviously reentered the room.

"Yes, yes, I know that! I meant 'we'...well, that's what I..."

She waited.

*"Oh, for goodness sake, of course, Rumple. Although I have seen the ties he designs and they rather belong in Sloane's collection than on a neck...*Lillie? Lillie, are you there?"

"I'm still here, Harry."

"Anyway, *we* will head to London tomorrow and I will give you a hand while Rumple flounces around the city as though he were attending a Parisian parade."

That thought cheered her. "I'd like that, Harry. I really would."

"Good, that's settled. Oh, and I forgot to mention, Rumple says your roses are doing remarkably well this summer. He has been at the cottage every second day. He says he is using coffee grounds for fertilizer. Have you ever heard of anything so absurd?"

"Whatever Mr Green Fingers thinks appropriate I am grateful for. Please thank him."

A tap on her door startled her.

"Harry, I've got to go. There's someone at the door. See you tomorrow."

Hanging up she pulled open the door to reveal Jack leaning languidly against the doorframe.

"Hello."

"Jack, this is a surprise."

"Are you in the middle of something?"

"I just hung up with Harry."

"May I come in."

Lillie opened the door wide to let him pass. He smelled of cedar and rose, laced gently with Scotch. The smell reminded her of the night with Daniel and she immediately shoved the thought out of mind.

Jack turned to look at her, reading her face as expertly as always, "Something isn't right with you and me, and I figured we might as well hash it out."

Lillie closed the door and invited him to take a seat on the sofa. She sighed, sitting down next to him. It seemed she would never get to that bath. In an instant she realized she had gone beyond tired to wide awake and on guard. Did they have to do this now? It was nearly midnight.

"I hardly think we need to 'hash' anything out, Jack. You have been gone for some time and I have been busy with the newspaper. That's all."

"Ah yes, but you haven't been busy planning our wedding, have you?"

If nothing else, he was certainly perceptive. She thought about a retort; giving him a good lashing back. Why should she be planning a wedding while he whittled around the world doing God knows what in the name of intelligence? It wasn't as though her work was unimportant. But he was right, she wasn't even thinking about planning a wedding.

"And," he continued a little unsteadily, "you seem different. As though you have changed your mind, perhaps? Or something has happened since I left?" He reached over and brushed his finger over her bandaged arm, sending a shiver through her body. He leaned in and kissed her neck.

"I'm not...different..." She thought back and realized she hadn't really told him all that much about her investigation, and nor did she want to. There was just too much that needed to be kept hidden. From everyone.

"You are, a little," he said, pulling back and looking at her. "You aren't the same Lillie I left a month ago. Do you still love me?"

"Of course I do."

He stood up and pulled off his jacket, then slumped back against the sofa, stifling a yawn.

"Good. Then let's hurry up and get married shall we?" He closed his eyes.

She studied him carefully. He was slightly intoxicated, but not enough to seriously impair his judgement. If she hadn't smelled it on him, she wouldn't even know he'd been drinking. He was terribly handsome, and he loved her. He was a man in complete control of his life, and responsible for many lives around him. He was good, and kind—albeit sometimes his decisions with regards to her were made in error. She would be lying if she said he didn't make her heart flutter. Of course he did. But something—and she couldn't really put her finger on it —made her resistant to getting married. Perhaps it was because of his long absences, required for work, of course. Or the fact that he had lied and disappeared during the war. Or that he continued to put his career ahead of their happiness. But didn't she also do that? Was she not asking for heartache?

She let out a resigned sigh and realized she had forgotten what they were talking about; although looking at him it seemed it hardly mattered.

He was fast asleep on her sofa. She, unfortunately, was wide awake.

23

STEFANIE

She was nearly out of money.

Stefanie pulled her worn bag onto the unmade bed and hastily recounted what was left, feeling the bills and cold coins slip against her fingers. She hoped she had somehow made a mistake.

She hadn't.

Slipping the meagre funds back into their hidden pouch in her shoulder bag, she finished packing her small duffel and looked around the room. Although she was still staying at the same hotel she had shared with Alek, there was no way she could pay for it now. He hadn't returned since that dismal morning she had woken to find his wife angrily banging on her door. It had been days since the confrontation and Stefanie had held on, hoping he would come back, and fearful every time she left the hotel that she would be locked out on her return. A bill for the room had been slipped under the door. And another, and another. One each morning, their presence akin to a poisonous snake slithering through the gap under the door. She knew Alek had paid cash for the first few nights but that was all he had done. She was amazed they hadn't already asked her to leave.

Where had he gone? Was he afraid to return? Afraid his wife would divorce him? Was he injured? Dead? What the hell was going on?

She began to feel the anger rise and she pushed its creeping tentacles away. There was no use giving in to it. She needed to give him the benefit of the doubt.

But no note? No correspondence?

How could he do this to her? Just leave her. Not keep his promises.

She shoved the last of her things into her shoulder bag. She could stay no longer.

It was time to get lost.

24

LILLIE

"I haven't seen her."

The man sitting across the desk from Lillie late that morning was a terrible liar and she scrutinized him critically. He wore a very smart navy-blue suit. His exceptionally light blonde hair brushed the collar of his jacket and his clothes were cut slim enough that his athletic build could be seen through the thin wool. She could certainly see what Stefanie saw in him.

"Really? I would have thought, based on your history, that she may have been in touch with you." Lillie wondered how much she should reveal about the case and decided very little.

There was noise outside his office: voices in the hallway, some too loud for the surroundings, reverberating off the polished marble floors that were in desperate need of rugs to muffle the general din. Alek got up from his desk, walked around her chair and closed the door. She caught a whiff of expensive cologne.

"I am a married man, Miss Mead. I hardly think my wife would appreciate me spending time with an old girlfriend."

He was wading into his own mess quite easily, Lillie

marvelled. She wondered how his wife would feel seeing their names in print?

"Who said anything about spending time with her? I just wondered if she had written to you."

"I just meant..."

Lillie cut him off. "I know what you meant."

Irritated, she glanced outside and noted the sky had clouded over—deep, dark, and heavy, with the promise of rain. She silently counted to ten; losing one's temper was hardly a fine way to start the day.

He was sitting unnaturally still when she refocused her attention on him, and she wished fleetingly that she had brought Petters with her. They had considered it, but concluded that having two of them there would seem as though they were ganging up on Alek. Lillie had opted to go it alone. It seems they had miscalculated.

"Stefanie could be in a great deal of trouble." She decided she would change tack. With any luck she could appeal to him another way. "She may have been privy to something at the bank—something illegal—or asked to do something illegal, perhaps something she didn't even realize *was* illegal. Whoever has killed the director of the bank, and his associate, is likely also gunning for Stefanie."

He sat quietly. Expressionless.

"Alek," she sighed audibly. "You loved Stefanie once, very much I imagine. I can't think that now you would just wantonly throw her to the wolves."

"Miss Mead, if there were anything I could tell you, I would do it without hesitation."

Lillie knit her brows together thoughtfully. Was he trying to tell her something? Could he not talk here? She glanced around. They were in a private office with the door shut, surely he could speak freely?

Studying him carefully, she stood up and slipped her business card across the desk towards him. "I'm at Brown's for the time being, if you think of anything."

Alek nodded, then pulled at his tie, loosening it. He got up to shake her hand. "You are right about one thing, Miss Mead. I do love Stefanie very much."

He was doing it again. Letting her know there was more than he was saying. He had purposely used the present tense. *I do love her*. Not *did*.

She should have brought Petters with her.

~

LUNCH WAS SERVED to Lillie's hotel room shortly after one o'clock by an exceedingly tall, and impossibly slender waiter. She had just returned from her meeting with Alek and, as she eyed the silver tray being carried through the room, found she was surprisingly ravenous. Discord feeds the appetite, she thought ruefully. The waiter carefully lifted a polished and gleaming cover to reveal the finger sandwiches she had ordered, all neatly arranged on a crystal plate. He motioned to the berries and clotted cream for dessert and offered to pour her tea.

"No, thank you, I can manage."

"As you wish. And a letter came for you, madam. It is just here." He retrieved a small, pale blue envelope from the edge of the tray with a long and slim gloved hand and placed it on the table in front of her.

"Thank you." Lillie reached into her purse and brought out some coins for his tip.

When he had retreated from the room and shut the door, Lillie opened the window adjacent to the luncheon table and watched as the skies opened up to the most magnificent summer rain. She inhaled deeply, watching it wash the summer filth off the now glistening pavements, the excess water dancing down the street.

The letter did not have a return address, but her name was written with impeccable penmanship across the front. She knew who it was from immediately. She sliced it open, poured some tea and began to read:

Dear Lillie,

I trust you had an uneventful journey to your new hotel. This city feels somewhat forlorn now that I am no longer with you. I have endeavoured to ascertain further the origin and intent of the man with the accounts we have investigated.

Although I had started with some preconceived notions of who he might be; American, of course, and involved in a business that is, shall we say 'unregulated'—there really don't appear to be any connections to Ireland. At least not yet. Of course, I needn't explain to what I am referring, as you gave the theory to me, however any signals to that effect are not forthcoming.

As for the hire who followed us, I am not entirely sure he was in the employ of the bank manager. It may have been coincidental that the timing coincided with us leaving the bank, or, he may have been tailing you for some time. Or I may be completely mistaken—for if not hired by the bank, then who? And why? I fear we are being led on a wild goose chase.

All this is to say that we are nowhere further, completely befuddled, and I fear still in possible danger—or shall I say, likely danger, for that is truly what I believe. Not knowing your enemy makes you a target, my dear girl, and I urge you to take precautions.

I will, of course, continue to follow what few leads I have, and hope that the coming hours and days will reveal some bit of information that might help. I will continue to send anything I discover to Brown's Hotel, however please use this return address to let me know

when you move on, so I can ensure you receive any future corre-
spondence.

HERE HE HAD GIVEN what looked to be the address to a private residence in Knightsbridge. Perhaps he had a friend in London? Why had he not told her this? Should he have? She chided herself for being so petty. Why would he have told her?

I WOULD ALSO, after much thought, like to apologize for my forth-
right remarks on your impending nuptials. I have no business giving
an unsolicited opinion on your happiness, except to wish you as
much of it as you so obviously deserve. If the world were a different
place, and I a man who had chosen a different path, perhaps things
would be different.

But wherever life may take you, or with whom, please remember
that if you ever need me, for any reason, I will always be here.

Yours always,

D

LILLIE PUT THE LETTER DOWN, perplexed. Daniel was being careful with his words—not signing his name, saying nothing that could be fully understood by an outsider. It was no wonder he hadn't ever been caught for anything. The man was smart, careful and calculated. He was so many things. She thought back to the night by the river: his intensity with her, his searing gaze, his ability to be so gentle and caring while simultaneously killing their attacker. She shuddered.

She would have to fill Petters in on everything, which was a thought that made her immensely uncomfortable. If he knew that Daniel had helped her in London, would he not immediately have him arrested? Assuming he could find him, of course. He had left well enough alone after Daniel had left Oxford, searching for a time and then giving up after having no leads. But he didn't know where he had gone and if Lillie were to tell him, it was conceivable—even likely—Petters would find him.

And Jack, what would he say? It was unforgivable, her turning to an assassin for help. She had a retired police investigator and a spy at her disposal, yet would turn to a criminal to aid her investigation? It was ludicrous, and they would see it as downright dangerous. Which is why she had purposely not said a word about it to anyone.

She carefully folded the letter and got up to tuck it into the lining of her suitcase. Until she decided what to do with the information, the letter certainly wasn't something she wanted anyone getting their hands on.

Harry would be arriving in the city shortly. He would be the only person she could tell about it all without facing reprisals. She was glad he was coming for she needed a friend, and with Primrose still up North with her parents, she felt alone and terribly homesick—for her cottage in Oxford certainly, but also for a life she seemed to be deviating from.

She retrieved a piece of hotel stationary from the desk drawer and carried it back to the luncheon table. After she had had a few of the sandwiches and another cup of tea, she settled down to write:

DEAR D,

Thank you for your letter and the update on your inquiries; the lack of conclusions are troublesome indeed.

I have undertaken my search for the woman we discussed, and while I have some idea that she may be here in London, I have yet to find anything concrete. With the exception of my intuition (which *tells me she is here) I seem to be running up against a variety of closed doors.*

But I shall persevere.

The other night seems very far away now and I didn't get the chance to say goodbye to you properly. That next morning in the hotel lobby certainly complicated things and I was as surprised as you looked to find my visitor standing in the reception after our breakfast. I suppose we had decided I should leave anyway, but everything happened in such a whirlwind that...Well, never mind, I hardly need to explain to you, do I?

Anyway, I thank you for your candor and help, more than I can ever say. I go forth with this new information that you have so generously provided. Please be careful there, as I will here; whomever we are dealing with will very likely have a lot to lose.

I think you should consider going back to America now, there is only a downside here in England for you.

Warmest regards,

Lillie

PUTTING down her pen and finishing the last of her tea, she sealed the letter and quickly scribbled the address on the front. She was tempted to deliver it to Knightsbridge herself, but no, she would have the hotel clerk courier it on her way out. She needed to walk, clear her head, get her thoughts organized for her column that week. Jeremy wouldn't be impressed if she didn't at least get something down on paper for this week's issue.

She ran her finger over the address on the envelope, imagining its destination. A white stone townhouse perhaps, with a black door and a brass handle. Would there be a woman there? A male friend? Someone who was in the same business he had been? Someone with criminal connections? In Knightsbridge? It hardly seemed so. It was more likely a woman. Someone he was involved with? Why did this thought plague her so? She imagined him, lounging on a long, velvet, art deco sofa, his long legs stretched out before him, whoever he was with curled up next to him, the room cloaked in fog from her cigarette. Daniel. A man who sent a shiver of fear up her spine and yet intrigued her with his alarming magnetism.

What was wrong with her?

She put the letter in her bag and pulled on her raincoat. She would fetch an umbrella from the doorman on her way out.

25

STEFANIE

The red-brick townhouse, with all its gingerbread swirls and polished black hydrangea-filled window boxes, was for sale. Even in the rain, which had petered out somewhat, its facade was grand. It steamed now, as the heat of the day evaporated the water from its face.

The estate agent tasked with its sale was a slick-haired, overtly extraverted man in his late forties with a rapidly slackening jawline. The same could be said of his waist, Stefanie noted, as she walked up the newly painted steps and approached him. She shifted the borrowed notebook and pen into her left hand so she could shake with her right, adjusted her unfamiliar glasses, and gave him what she hoped passed for a professional smile.

She had stashed her worn bag in a row of hornbeam hedging down the street, stolen a more becoming dress from a grossly unmonitored shop on Piccadilly, and made her way here, to Chelsea, to see the duke's townhouse for herself.

Or, more precisely, to see what was inside.

"Hello." The ballooning agent came forward to shake

Stefanie's hand, peering around her with a look of confusion on his face as he did so.

"Good morning, Pricilla Bond, I'm a buyer's agent for..." She wracked her brain for a company name, and, remembering a sign she had seen a few times since her arrival in London said "...Hamptons."

The agent looked at her quizzically.

"Are you on your own? It's a very unusual practice to send a woman."

Stefanie cut him off. "My employer is currently at another showing, I'm afraid. I offered."

"I see." He didn't looked particularly convinced. "I didn't realize Hamptons was in the residential housing market. I knew they did art and silver, and the odd nautical vessel, but this is a surprise."

She silently scolded herself for her lack of preparedness. "Yes, it's new for us, and we don't often get many requests—many people don't think of us as such—but this particular client is a very good one and when he's in town, he likes to keep the majority of his business in-house."

"And will he be arriving shortly?" The agent looked around as though he expected him to materialize out of the surrounding air.

"I am afraid not. He resides abroad, in the Loire Valley, actually." She was making it up as she went along and hoped she was convincing. "I am here to review the property for him and his wife."

"I see, another foreigner buying up our prime stock." He sighed, audibly, and turned to unlock the door.

Stefanie glared at his back as he led the way into the townhouse; he was a caricature of classic English pomposity. Why shouldn't a foreigner buy stock if a Londoner wasn't going to? Even a make-believe one.

"An extravagant foyer, as you can see," he was prattling on

already. "Early Georgian, and so obviously reflecting an aesthetic preceding the American vernacular influences that have so ruined classic architecture."

If there had been any doubt the agent was a snob, it was confirmed immediately.

"Of course, it has been updated, but in keeping with the original Palladian purity—you can see the nod to Rococo here in the Boucher." He motioned to a rather large nude that dominated the staircase. "Of course, this painting will reside with the current owner and isn't part of the overall package."

Stefanie nodded, taking in the rooms with the analytical intensity of an accountant. She couldn't care less about style and architecture.

They had moved into a large drawing room with windows that overlooked a small but impeccably maintained garden. The sun streamed in, reflecting the room's polished surfaces. There wasn't any dust to be seen.

"Some of the furnishings can be purchased separately—the current owner hasn't room for everything in her country home, you see..."

It was a perfect opening and Stefanie jumped at it. "And why are the current owners selling?"

"Just owner, singular, I'm afraid. The duchess's husband passed away quite suddenly and she doesn't plan to spend much time in the city." He leaned in and whispered as though they might be overheard. "I hear there are some financial troubles, so if your client wanted to make an offer I should encourage it."

The foreign-buyer bias was completely forgotten when it came to a quick commission, it seemed.

"I'll pass that along."

"Please do." The agent was moving now into a small library off the drawing room. "This room was used extensively as a study when the duke and duchess were in town. I can't say I am particularly fond of the heavy panelling, but it could easily be refinished to a shade more befitting the rest of the house. Of course, as it is quarter-sawn oak one should be encouraged to keep it."

The library lacked the large windows of the main rooms, and it was cold, even with the warmth of a summer's day. There was a large, white marble fireplace in one corner which Stefanie imagined would need to be lit at all times in order for the room to feel cosy. A long, Louis XVI desk held a commanding presence in the centre of the room, its deep green chair pushed back as though the duke had recently gone for a cup of tea. She felt a pang of longing for him, and imagined him here with his family, in this place so far from Cornwall and their hidden life. She didn't know what she expected to find here and she couldn't very well go rummaging through his desk drawers with the estate agent glued to her every move. What she needed was some understanding of why the duke was murdered. It could have been related to the bank, certainly. And if so, wouldn't there be some trace—something by which to understand why someone would want him dead?

She held her hand to her head. "You know, I'm not feeling all that well." Reaching out unsteadily she put her hand on the desk. "Could I possibly have a glass of water—I'm sure it's just the heat, I'm so sorry to trouble you."

"Of course! I'll just dash to the kitchen and see if I can't find a glass...please, take a seat." He pulled out the green desk chair and Stefanie sunk into it.

Would it be enough time?

"...and perhaps a biscuit or something? I just realized I forgot to eat breakfast and it's possibly making me a little light-headed," she called to his retreating back.

That would keep him a little longer.

As soon as he left the room, she got busy on the drawers. The top ones housed nothing more than pens and various clips, a few business cards, and four assorted glass paper-weights. She didn't waste any time on them. The lower drawers had the duke's files, and she impatiently flicked through them, looking for anything she might recognize from the bank.

There were the usual things one would expect in household files. Staff payroll ledgers, a receipt for kitchen repairs, inventories for wine and silver, assorted letters from friends abroad.

She began on the next drawer with frustration. Here she found files related to the bank and she flicked through them at a slower rate, not wanting to miss anything. Notice of directors' meetings and their corresponding minutes, expense reports for dinners and hotels, curriculum vitae for potential new managerial positions. She had no idea the duke had been so involved in the day-to-day business of Ainsworth Capital. Most of the correspondence had nothing to do with the Cornwall branch but was stamped London, New York, Paris, and Dublin. Their central branches.

What was he doing in Cornwall then? Was it just that he was in love with her and was using it as an excuse to visit more often? Or perhaps...A file caught her eye. It was buried far at the back of the drawer and she wouldn't have seen it had she not pulled everything forward and noticed the dark red leather it was encased in. She pulled it out and looked at it, glancing up from her seat for the estate agent. It was marked *Private and Confidential* in sharp gold lettering across the front and bound with a leather string.

She could hear the footfalls of the estate agent coming back with her water and she quickly pushed the thin file up her dress so it wrapped around her ribcage.

"Here we are." He was carrying a glass of water and a plate of biscuits.

"Oh, that is so very kind of you." She could feel the leather of the file sticking to her skin as she reached forward for the glass.

"And I found these in the kitchen, a bit stale but not too bad," he placed the biscuits in front of her and Stefanie quickly gobbled one down with her water. "Feeling any better?"

"Yes, much, thank you. It must be this heat." She carefully got up from the chair keeping a hand across her middle so the file wouldn't fall out. "Well, I think I have seen enough of the house to recommend it to my client." She smiled.

"But don't you want to see the upstairs bedrooms? There are four of them, and a new powder room, along with a charming balcony off the master bedroom which overlooks the garden." The agent swiftly finished off the rest of the biscuits, leaving a trail of crumbs on the front of his shirt.

Stefanie wavered. She didn't want to look unprofessional and rouse his suspicions, but at the same time she could hardly walk around with an unsecured file under her dress.

"It isn't necessary, I know my client will want to see the house so perhaps I could arrange for a second visit once I have spoken to him. He is due to arrive in London next week."

"I see, I see. Certainly, but tell him not to delay. This particular listing will be snapped up."

26

LILLIE

Harry's train arrived early that evening. A pleasant anomaly in a country where post-war trains tended to be tardy at the best of times.

Lillie had spent the afternoon wandering the streets of Knightsbridge looking for the address Daniel was staying at. She had planned to send a courier but finding herself with the time, she had changed her mind at the last minute and gone herself. She eventually found it—an imposing block-front house on a street lined with the very same type of houses running both east and west as far as the eye could see. This particular house looked no different from any of the others except that the greenery in front looked as though it hadn't been watered in some time. The day's rain was giving it a good soak, but judging by the extent of the wilt, it would be too little, too late.

Her knock on the door could be heard reverberating off what sounded like a barren interior. She peered into a window to the right of the door and although it had a sheer pulled across the glass, she could make out enough of the room to see that it was nearly empty. She knocked again, loudly, but eventually gave up after a few minutes and instead slipped the letter through the mail slit in the door. She had wondered if she shouldn't hang around a little, in case he came back, but decided against it. She had work to do and what did she really hope to gain by seeing him again? The sooner he left England, the better.

The rain had ceased by the time she reached the station, giving way to a bright but low-in-the-sky sunshine. Rumple had promptly made his way from Paddington to the West End to behold his illustrious designer, leaving a waft of cheap cologne in his wake, but not before loudly ordering Harry to shoulder his cases onto the pavement.

"I ask you," Harry huffed as he hauled one of Rumple's three suitcases into an awaiting cab. "Who exactly is the beast of burden in this situation?"

Lillie held the second case out to him while Harry made room for it in the boot of the car. Or tried to.

"We are going to need a larger car," he stated bluntly, standing up straight and wiping a whisper of perspiration from his forehead. "Where is our driver, anyway? I can hardly be expected to swelter out here in this heat while he does God knows what in the station. Either he arrives here forthwith, or he shall return to a lost fare. Is it any wonder I don't live in this horrendous cesspool of a city?"

"You love coming to London, Harry, you always say so. I think perhaps you might be in need of something to eat and a drink—"

"I would like nothing better, my dear. Oh look, here he comes now...about time, too," he grumbled under his breath. "Oh, good of you to join us, old chap. Delightful to have a driver, perhaps you might be able to give me a hand with these?"

Even an insult sounded polite when an Englishman delivered it, Lillie couldn't help but notice. Their driver opened his passenger side door and handily lifted the two remaining cases into the front passenger seat, along with Harry's small leather bag, and opened the rear doors for them.

Lillie smirked at Harry as she got in. "Doesn't seem all that hard, now, does it?"

"Oh, shush," he reprimanded.

Their car made its way through the now steaming streets, a delicious lack of traffic shortening their journey to a mere fifteen minutes. By the time they arrived at the hotel the sun was just starting its descent beyond the horizon, its departure giving rise to the most majestic sunset.

"Hotel bar?" Harry asked as their driver handed off the bags to a waiting porter.

"Count me in."

"And are we expecting Jack this evening?"

"I really haven't heard."

"Well, perhaps it's better that way. I have a feeling you and I are in need of a little chat." He gave her a wink and waved at the reception desk on his way by.

'Good evening, Miss Mead, sir..., welcome back to Brown's,' came the murmured reply.

They annexed a small table near the bar and Harry brought their drinks over himself. A rather large, dry sherry for Lillie and Scotch for himself.

"I ordered us some soup as well: celeriac and pea is today's blend, two flavours that couldn't possibly go well together, so I was curious more than anything. So"— his glass made a clink as he set it down on the table—"tell me..."

"Tell you what?" It was no good trying to conceal anything from Harry.

"What's happened since I've been away, of course."

Lillie toyed with the cutlery on the table. "I made some inquiries, interviewed one of the bank managers. Managed to discover I was being followed, so someone is on to us, of that I have no doubt."

"Is that how you received that?" He pointed to her arm. She had re-bandaged her wound that morning and although she had used thinner gauze, it still showed through her blouse.

"Mm. Yes, but please don't mention it to Jack. I haven't told him what really happened. I gave him some story about the bathtub, I just didn't want to have an argument about it."

The sherry tickled her throat.

"But you managed to get away?"

She nodded, swallowing.

"Alone? You fought off your attacker alone, did you?"

"What are you getting at Harry?"

"My dear, I am trying, with obvious futility, to ascertain just what has happened to you since I left London." He cut her off as she was about to reply. "And don't tell me for a minute that you were on your own when that happened." He nodded to her arm.

She looked up at him and sighed.

"Out with it," he commanded.

"There really isn't much to tell..." she began.

"Balderdash!" He took a large sip of his drink, and then repeated, a little more gently this time. "Out with it. And incidentally, I have all night."

Lillie looked at him with resignation.

"It doesn't leave this table, Harry."

27

LILLIE

They were following him.

It had been Harry's idea; cooked up the evening before over the remains of the celeriac soup, a curry remoulade, and an excess of port. But it was a good idea nonetheless, and one that Lillie had been keen to go along with. If Alek was hiding Stefanie's location, then it would be the only way to smoke her out.

Felix Petters had returned to Cornwall earlier that morning in order to interview the Canadian hotel keeper who, with a sliver of probability, may have met Angus's killer. It was a long way to go for a small task, but at the very least he might be able to get an update on any leads the Newquay police might have. Jeremiah's aunt had taken the boy back to Oxford and had offered to remain there with him until Petters could return home. The two of them were becoming quite a good parenting team, Lillie had mused, and wondered how long it would be before Petters was married.

Lillie had risen early and met him for a cup of tea before his train departed.

"Be careful here, Lillie," he had cautioned, stirring an

unusually large amount of sugar into his cup of Darjeeling. "Even if Stefanie is in London, and even if she holds most of the answers as to who would kill the duke and Angus, it isn't worth getting yourself killed for. Ultimately, you are a reporter, not a detective."

"Stop fussing and drink your tea," she'd retorted.

"I saw your column this morning; very well written," he complimented. "Although I'm not sure splashing Stefanie's name and picture on the page is helpful to our case." He glanced at his watch keeping an eye on the time.

"No? I disagree. We need her, Felix, and the sooner the better. Otherwise we're just running around chasing our tails and I may as well get back to tending the flowers in my garden."

"Oxford does sound a great deal more appealing than this hot and dirty city right now." He glanced out of the hotel restaurant window with a look of mild disgust. "And with that, I must go or I shall miss my train." He rose and picked up a tidy leather bag that looked as though it had been recently oiled. He really was the most fastidious man she had ever met.

Lillie stood too, wondering if she should shake his hand or give him a brief hug. She decided they knew each other well enough now for it to be the latter.

"Good luck." She smiled, feeling a pang of guilt that she hadn't told him more about her time in London. At the moment, it didn't affect Petters' investigation, but there may come a time when it would and she dreaded having to explain it to him.

"It's about method and determination, my girl, and not a thing about luck." He gave her a wink, pushed his chair in, and departed, leaving a sense of confidence and the smell of lavender soap in his place.

~

THE SOUND of Harry's footfalls beside her brought her attention back to the present. Alek had left his townhouse at a quarter to nine that same morning and was now heading west along the pavement at a brisk pace. Lillie and Harry were following a few hundred yards behind.

She had chosen an out-of-fashion wide-brimmed hat to wear that morning, navy blue and finely woven with the briefest of veils which fell over enough of her face that only the tip of her chin was exposed. The dark colour, she hoped, would obscure her identity enough that Alek wouldn't recognize her if they got too close. She had purposely chosen clothes she hadn't been wearing when she had seen him in his office, even going so far as to ensure she was wearing different colours. Her navy blue dress was tubular in shape, with a wide, dropped waistband which was gathered at the left side with two silk alabaster roses. The pleated skirt stopped mid-calf and her low, wellworn Mary-Jane pumps assured her that her feet would be comfortable, however far she needed to go.

He turned at the end of his street and headed past a smattering of cafes and bakeries, up to the next corner, and then disappeared from their view.

"Hurry," Harry scolded, and she increased her pace to a jog to catch up. "I would dislike losing him now—it would make my missing breakfast for this escapade seem all the more inconvenient."

"I told you to set a wake-up call. Had I known you were lounging around in bed I would have woken you myself. I've been up since the crack of dawn. Really, Harry, you would make a terrible detective—you must know what they say about the early bird..." She instantly lowered voice as they rounded the corner and had Alek in their sights once again. His pace had slowed.

"Lillie, do I look like someone who would request a worm

with my tea?" He stopped quickly, holding out his arm to keep her from walking.

Alek had gone into a small coffee shop about one hundred feet ahead of where they stood.

"You are going to have to go in after him, Harry. I can't do it, he will recognize me."

"If I do then I won't very well be able to follow him later on, will I? I trust you realize I am a memorable person."

Harry flicked his flaxen hair back and Lillie had to reluctantly admit, for all his arrogance, he was right.

"I'll wait here while you do a walk by of the shop window. It's big enough that you might be able to see if he is meeting anyone."

"He could just be having a quick cup of something en route to his office."

"Except he isn't anywhere near his office. It's entirely in the other direction. He is carrying a briefcase but I can assure you, he isn't going to work. Now hurry so we don't miss anything."

Harry started off, looking every bit as though he were a gentleman out for a morning stroll, pausing briefly at each store window along the way as though he were shopping for something. When he reached the coffee shop he hesitated in front, pretending to search his pockets for something, a cigarette perhaps, or a handkerchief, and then he continued slowly past.

Lillie crossed the road so she wouldn't be seen, and walked briskly past the cafe to where Harry now stood at the end of the street.

"So?"

"He is meeting someone all right." Harry lit the cigarette he had apparently been searching his pockets for.

"And?"

"And you won't believe who it is." He inhaled and blew smoke into delicate rings above her head.

"Who?" Lillie demanded, getting frustrated with the delay.

"I mean, it's possible, I suppose, that he knows him somehow..." He picked a piece of tobacco off his lip.

"Harry! Who was Alek meeting with?"

"Well, that's the strange thing...you really aren't going to believe this. I'm not sure I even do."

"Harry!"

"My dear, it was Jack."

28

LILLIE

"You can hardly go storming into that unsuspecting coffee shop as though you have been shot out of a cannon, now, can you?" Harry was presently attempting to form a variety of shapes, other than the standard rings, with his cigarette smoke. He frowned as they came out as little clouds resembling nothing much at all.

Lillie snatched the cigarette out of his hand and threw it down onto the pavement, grinding it out with the toe of her shoe.

"I'm astonished, Harry. And furious! Why wouldn't he mention it to me—something, at least! Here I am, running all over the city, and all the while he is in touch with the only man who probably knows where Stefanie is, and he says *nothing*? *Nothing?*"

Harry gave her a guilty look. "I may have told him a little bit more about the case than perhaps you did."

"Meaning what exactly?"

"Well...names, specifically. I thought possibly that he might be able to help find Stefanie so I gave him Alek's name on the off chance that he might be able to get some additional information. He certainly has more access to resources than we do—I was just trying to help."

"Well that just infuriates me, Harry! I don't expect to help Jack in his line of work and I *certainly* don't want his help in mine! How *dare* he not tell me!" She stopped her tirade to think about this for a moment. "Do you think there is more to this than just Jack finding Alek for us? I mean, if he was doing it to help us, why didn't he mention it to me? There must be something more going on here—which is typical Jack, isn't it? Always playing his cards close to his chest." She suddenly felt depressed. Would she ever really know him?

Harry gave her what he probably hoped was a diffusing shrug. "I don't have to tell you, Jack's business is always secretive. Whatever is going on, it will be classified, you know this. He can't tell you. I'm sure he would like to, but he won't be able to. There's no point getting angry."

"Aren't you sick of Jack's *business*? Because I am. Sick of the secretiveness, sick of the lies, sick of not knowing where he is. Sick of it all!"

She was pacing back and forth now and could feel a creeping rage threatening to suffocate her. An elderly couple out for a morning walk rounded the corner and, getting a look at Lillie's face, quickly crossed to the street to avoid them.

Harry was leaning against the wall of a large building that looked like a bank of some sort with windows the size of giraffes. The shadow it gave off was enough to shield him from the sun and she walked over to join him there. She took a deep breath and exhaled slowly, willing herself to calm down.

"Let's just wait here, shall we?" Harry said softly. "See what shakes out." He patted the wall and she leaned her back against it, lifting the veil of her hat as she did so. It was bloody hot already and she could feel her face beginning to perspire.

"I suppose they have to come out eventually, but then what? Confront them?"

"Not necessarily. In fact, I believe things are always better executed when we don't come at them head on."

"Meaning?"

"Being a little more...nuanced, if you will. As it stands, what do we know right now?"

Lillie sighed. "Stefanie is still at large. Alek likely knows where she is. Alek, oddly, appears to know Jack, which means he may somehow be involved in intelligence, or is an accessory in some regard. Either to Stefanie's disappearance or the duke's murder, or both."

"Yes, and?"

"Well, the obvious, the duke and Angus are dead. And we have some idea that their murders involve Stefanie."

"Correct."

"And we think there is some connection with the bank, because Stefanie was working on some of the duke's files when she disappeared—and of course, there is also their affair."

"And then there is the aside case of the man who gave you that nasty little gunshot graze on your arm. Hired either by a couple of rascals at the bank, or worse, the American mob. And not to complicate things, but they could have also been hired by the Sinn Fein."

Lillie thought about this for a moment. "Yes. You remember the duchess mentioning Ireland in her conversation with you when she said the duke would never travel there."

"Mm. Curious."

"Harry, is it me or is there something very odd about this case?"

"Meaning?"

"I don't know. It feels as though there is a puppeteer some-where, pulling everyone's strings and watching as they dance around and around but don't ever really get anywhere."

"Mm. Which begs the question ..." He paused and Lillie waited for him to finish. "Just *who* is the puppeteer?"

He fished out another cigarette and flicked his lighter, inhaling deeply. This time his shapes were perfect.

29

STEFANIE

S he had to queue for the telephone kiosk in King's Cross Station. The stench of the flooring, devoid of a good cleaning and accompanied by the heat it gave off, made her feel nauseous. She wondered, not for the first time, if she could be pregnant. The people in front of her consisted of the current occupant of the booth—an elderly man who was waving his hands around in anger in an attempt to intimidate the person on the other end, as if they could actually see him. A young, smartly dressed woman holding the hand of a small child, and a middle-aged man wearing a bowler hat, who was picking at his teeth with the corner of a business card and tapping his well-polished foot impatiently.

Stefanie clutched the newspaper she had bought that morning in one hand, and her worn bag which housed the duke's file in the other. She was still wearing the glasses she had used at the townhouse, and had her hair pulled back and tucked at the base of her neck so the small, cloche hat she wore fit. She glanced at the picture in the newspaper, relieved the girl in black-and-white print looked nothing like the bespectacled woman now waiting in line for the telephone. It wasn't difficult to alter an appearance, especially in a large city where everyone was bustling about and not paying attention anyway.

The angry, elderly man had moved on, and the woman with the child was now in the booth speaking in a hurried tone. At least the cost of making a telephone call ensured no one lingered for long. The child was opening and closing the door to the booth, enraptured with the click of the door and peering at the closing mechanism as though attempting to solve one of the world's great mysteries. The man with the bowler hat was anxiously checking his watch. It wasn't long before the child had slammed his finger in the latching mechanism, letting out an enormous wail; the bowler-hatted man moved on in a blur of exasperation, and it was Stefanie's turn.

"Oxford 4653, please," she asked the exchange, then listened for the ringing.

"*Oxford Daily Press*," a pinched, female voice answered.

"Yes, hello. May I please speak with one of your reporters, Lillie Mead?"

"I am sorry, Miss Mead is not in the office this week."

"Oh...I see." Her disappointment was palpable. "Is there somewhere I can get in touch with her? It's in reference to a story she is working on."

"I see. Miss Mead is in London at the moment, but I can put you through to her editor."

The last thing she wanted to do was give her whereabouts to someone else. There were already too many people who knew enough to find her.

"No, thank you, I just really needed to speak to Miss Mead. Isn't there any way you might be able to tell me where I can find her in London? It's very important, and I think she will want to see me."

"Well, it isn't really our policy, and I can't say for sure, but"—she lowered her voice—"usually Miss Mead stays at Claridge's when she visits the city, however I just received some correspondence from her and the return address was Brown's Hotel." She cleared her throat. "Although I can't confirm that you will find her there this trip."

"Thank you. I appreciate that." Stefanie hung up and shifted her bag.

It looked as though she would be staying in London a little longer after all.

30

LILLIE

T he hotel lobby was quiet that evening as Lillie crossed its etched marble floor to check her messages with the clerk.

"Just one, madam, from a gentleman in Oxford. A Mr Jeremy Winston." He handed her a folded slip of paper and Lillie thanked him, making her way to a cluster of wool-backed armchairs and sinking into one of them.

The note was brief. Jeremy was requesting her third instalment on the murdered Duke story and he wanted a progress report. She glanced at her watch, and decided she would call him tomorrow. It was too late now and the newsroom would be closed; and with her article not yet finished she wasn't in any rush to speak with him.

It was nearly time for dinner and she expected Harry to be down any minute. She watched the reception desk, which was quiet at this time, its attendants lingering, chatting mutedly amongst each other, one yawning from sheer boredom. The lobby lighting dimmed with the onset of evening, and she could see candles being lit in the dining room, the flickering light reflecting back in the crystal lining the bar. There was a jingle of ice as a waiter filled a silver bowl.

Reluctantly, she got up and decided to find them a table. She hadn't spoken to Jack since he had been spotted with Alek that morning, and the disappointment and frustration she had felt with him hadn't yet had time to wane. Even more debilitating was the confusion she felt surrounding it all. He hadn't lied to her exactly, but he had kept the truth hidden and regardless of his job, his security clearance and all that nonsense, shouldn't he have tipped her off that he knew at least one of the actors in her saga?

Entering the dining room, she was given her choice of tables and she picked one far from the door with a snippet of a view of the lobby so she could watch for Harry. She sat down and ordered a Dubonnet with a twist of lemon and extra ice. Lazily sipping it, she pulled out a notebook and began arranging points for her article—it would make writing it that evening a little easier. As was always the case with her, she was never quite sure how much she should reveal. Her column had taken on the flavour of an exposé involving cross-national banking and the role of politically or criminally motivated individuals, but now with a great deal of money missing and an elusive connection to Ireland that was seeming more nebulous than concrete—she wondered if she wasn't completely misguided in her methodology. But, she could hardly change it now. She took a long sip of her drink and watched as the dining room began to slowly fill.

And then, without any warning, he was there. Jack. In the darkened doorway of the restaurant. She watched him as he moved with the precision of an exotic cat. She couldn't tear her eyes away from his lithe body, which was draped in an exquisite wool suit, his skin recently bronzed by the English sun. He must have been outside the past few days, perhaps working on another case that didn't require him to toil behind his desk. He had sidled into a seat at the bar, and the leather seat sank perfectly under his weight, his back to her. He hadn't seen her, and it was enough just to watch him, as yet unnoticed. Perhaps she would gain an advantage, she thought, or the upper hand. Unlikely. She would never achieve that with him; but did it matter? Weren't they in love? Weren't they about to be partners in life?

Her thoughts were too loud, she realized with regret, for in that instant he turned and saw her. His smile, she reflected, would melt a glacier. He was in front of her in an instant, and motioned to the empty chair. She nodded and a fresh wave of frustration, fuelled by drink and curiously mixed with desire, threatened to knock her clean off her axis.

"Did you have a good day?" She was taunting him, although he had yet to notice.

"Quite good. And you?"

"Not particularly."

"Oh?" He looked genuinely interested, a perfectly benign expression on a clearly open face. A sociopath could not have been more convincing, she thought irrationally.

"Jack. Don't give me that," she snapped at him.

"Lillie, I really haven't a clue to what you are referring but I can certainly tell you are angry with me about something. Care to elaborate?"

"And give away all my secrets? Hardly. You certainly aren't giving away any of yours."

He frowned at her but didn't rise to the provocation. He was smart enough to know that throwing fuel on an open flame would only set the table on fire.

"Whatever you think you know," he finally said with some reluctance. "I can assure you, you don't."

"No, I quite agree, I'm sure I don't! And isn't that the point? I don't know a thing and your...your *loyalties* aren't to me at all, are they? Not when they lie with the state, or the establishment, or the service, or whatever you want to call it!" Her voice rose and the couple at the table next to them glanced over nervously. Jack shot them a charming smile and they went back to their endive salads, embarrassed.

"Perhaps we should take this up in private." He redirected his eyes towards her.

"Jack," Lillie sighed. "Unless you are going to tell me just exactly what you are doing having coffee with a subject in my investigation, then I am about ready to call it a night."

"Ah," he breathed. "I see. Well...I won't insult your intelligence by denying it, Lillie, but you know I can't..."

They were interrupted by a hotel clerk who stood at the head of their table. "Madam? I am terribly sorry to interrupt, but there is a young lady in reception asking to speak with you."

"Thank you, I will be right there." Lillie nodded, pushing back her chair and getting up.

"Shall I wait here until you come back?" Jack asked hopefully.

"I don't see why. Unless you have something you are willing to tell me, Jack Abbott, there isn't anything else to say tonight," she snapped irritably.

"Lillie, that isn't fair...just come back here to the table and let's talk about it..."

She wasn't looking at him, but she nodded anyway, anxious for their conversation to end so she could see who was in the lobby. There appeared to be a flurry of activity around the front doors and she hurried away from the table to get a better look, distractedly giving Jack a little wave of her hand as she left. She could hear him push his chair away from the table and sensed that he, too, was curious about the commotion.

By the time she reached the lobby a split second later, the porters, who had previously been languishing at their stations, were scurrying around like agitated squirrels. The lobby clerk was coming out from behind the desk and shouting at something going on in the middle of the room. Harry had just stepped off the elevator and stood, motionless, watching the scene unfold before them.

In the centre of the room were two men and a woman, who appeared to be the source of all the activity. One of the men had the young woman by the arm and was nearly dragging her across the floor while the other pushed bystanders out of his way—much to the astonishment of the hotel staff who were, with futility, trying to stop him. The woman was putting up a good fight, leaning away from the man, dragging her feet, and hitting at his arm, but his sheer size ensured he had the advantage. One particularly brave desk clerk had thrown himself into the fray and was flung aside as neatly as one would discard an apple core. By this time, the man doing the dragging had reached the front doors and Lillie could see there was a long, low car idling in front of the hotel with a driver, whose face she couldn't make out, at the wheel. The driver jumped out of the car when he saw that the man and the protesting woman were near, and swiftly opened the back door. The woman was shoved in, her bare legs briefly visible before the thug tucked in after her.

The woman's blonde hair was in complete disarray from the struggle and it was the shock of it—a long, bleached ribbon of white against the unlit night and viewed through the back window of the car—that gave Lillie a sickening realization. Could the woman who had just been violently torn from the lobby of Brown's Hotel be Stefanie?

31

LILLIE

"Who was that?" Lillie hollered, as she broke into a run towards the pavement in pursuit.

"The woman who was here for you, madam." The hotel clerk was running after her, huffing, and trying to read a piece of paper he had clutched in his palm. "Stefanie something or other, I can't make it out...but these ruffians, they just took her!" He was waving to man at the front desk. "Call the police immediately!"

"Get me a car, as quick as you can!" Lillie yelled to the doorman, but before the words were even out of her mouth, one had materialized—its driver, thankfully, someone reassuringly familiar. Lillie pushed through the front doors, catching the sleeve of her blouse on one of the handles and tearing the cuff.

"Thank God, Rumple!" She jumped in the back seat, followed closely by Harry. She could hear Jack loudly protesting from the side of the road, and through the passenger window she watched as he furiously waved his arms at the car.

"Lillie! Rumple! Don't you dare follow!" She could hear him say as he threw his hands up in frustration.

Rumple squealed away from the curb, ushering the car into the darkness and leaving Jack behind.

"I'm terribly sorry, miss, but it was now or never. Another minute and we would have lost them."

"Never mind, Rumple. There! Isn't that them ahead, do you see?" She squinted through the windscreen and pointed at the row of cars a few blocks ahead. One was weaving this way and that, desperately attempting to overtake a team of two horses and their carriage, as though looking for a gap through which it could disappear. Not finding one, it veered sharply to the left and disappeared down a side street. "Step on it, Rumple! I don't want to lose them."

Harry's manservant did as he was told, swerving out into the oncoming lane of traffic in order to overtake an old lumbering car in front of them as it wheezed its way up the street. He made the same left turn as the other car had done moments before, and they caught sight of it just as it made another sharp left. She sincerely hoped they had the right car, but its erratic driving made her confident they did.

The two cars sped handily through the streets, dodging traffic and pedestrians, rounding corners at considerable speed and once in a while, Lillie actually felt they were gaining on them—only to be disappointed when the distance would stretch out once again. The evening had brought with it the smog of a thousand coal-burning factories and the air lay heavy with a hazy pollution.

"I say, old sport," Harry quipped, leaning in to the corner they were taking. "The next time we rent a car let's go for something a little jauntier, shall we? This bloody fog isn't helping matters—it's no wonder I prefer the countryside."

Rumple didn't reply, his focus on the road ahead.

Harry continued, "Your sense of timing is impeccable as always, Rumple. How did you know?"

"I was just arriving back to the hotel, sir, and I saw Miss

Mead following those two thugs out of the lobby. It was just a matter of changing course, really...Look! There, they've ducked into that roundabout, probably thinking I would lose sight of them."

Thanks to Rumple's sharp eye, they were gaining on them once again and this time they got close enough that Lillie could make out a flash of blonde hair in the rear window as they entered the roundabout. At least now she was sure it was the correct car. The two cars exited the roundabout and sped down a darkened road towards Camden Town where the streets were thick with vendors still doing an admirable dinner business with the labour crowd—pickled whelks, pea soup, and fried fish were offered up alongside the hearty and usual fare of pies, sandwiches, and baked chestnuts. The smell of fish entered and then swiftly, and thankfully, exited the car as they whizzed through the hurried streets.

"Where are they going with her?" Lillie said, more to herself than anyone.

"It's brazen, certainly," Harry answered. "Imagine kidnapping someone right out of an hotel lobby in front of God knows how many witnesses. I would expect they were planning to hide her somewhere tonight and not let her get to you. She obviously has some information she wanted to pass on and someone caught wind of it."

"She is a dead woman, isn't she?"

"Not necessarily. She may be useful in some way and as such, stay her execution—in a manner of speaking," Harry added.

Rumple called to them from the front seat as he rounded a particularly sharp corner. "Hold on!"

The resulting crash took Lillie by complete surprise, and she was flung, shoulder first, into the back of Rumple's seat. Harry was also thrown forward and sailed right into the front passenger seat, losing one of his shoes mid-air. Rumple managed to stay upright and behind the wheel, but his head hit the side window with such force that the glass shattered, causing the shards to rain in around them.

For a brief moment, the universe was completely silent. Only the ringing in Lillie's ears let her know she was even alive. They seemed to stay, suspended in that state, for an eternity.

"Miss?" Came a voice, small, diminutive, and seemingly childlike through the broken driver's-side window. It sounded a million miles away, drowned out by the chasm of silence beyond her ears. She groaned as she tried to extricate herself from the back of Rumple's seat. A searing pain ripped through her shoulder. "Miss?" The voice repeated. "Are you going to be alright?"

There was a sliver of light coming in where the window used to be and the person doing the talking was blocking most of it with their small head. Or so she thought.

"I'm sorry, miss." There was a loud sniff. "It's my fault. I was in the road and I shouldn't have been, I was chasing my cat when out of nowhere I saw the car. And now...now I've gone and killed someone."

The voice began to cry—long, choked sobs that sounded more like a clogged drain than a boy—and the sound of it, along with the groaning from the front seat, gave Lillie the strength to get upright, if only to silence it all.

"Harry?" She managed to squeak out, the pain from her shoulder shot across her chest as she moved.

He groaned in return. "I'm alright...but Rumple, he doesn't look too good..." Harry reached over and brushed glass off Rumple's head which was slumped against the steering wheel. "He's breathing." Harry gave him a little shake and Rumple moaned in return.

"I think your friend needs a doctor," the little voice commanded, the sobbing apparently finished now he realized everyone was alive. "And soon. Should I go and get an adult?"

Well, that would be helpful, Lillie thought miserably, since the three of them in the car didn't seem to be able to help themselves. With relief she heard a faint bell, its drring sound, its muffled echo against the fog, a beacon of light sluicing through the darkness. Lillie sincerely hoped it was an ambulance heading their way.

"Wait!" said the voice. "I think that's for us. Yes, yes it is!"

Lillie could hear him hopping up and down on the pavement as the ringing got louder and louder. "Over here! Over here!"

She decided to attempt to get out of the car and help him with what little energy she had left. The ambulance was nearly on top of them by the time she managed to get the door open. It was bent on its hinge and she had to resort to kicking it ajar. Even then she only just managed to get it wide enough to slither out. Rumple had started to move one of his arms. It was barely noticeable at first, but was swiftly followed by him turning his shoulders and pushing himself off the steering well. A spray of glass fell onto the dashboard. Leaning against the crumpled car for assistance, she leaned into the driver's-side window to examine him more carefully, which was difficult given the dim light. His face was covered in tiny cuts and he would have a nasty goose egg on his head. But he was, thankfully, alive.

They had lost Stefanie, but they were all alive.

32

LILLIE

"Not a particularly enchanting evening, was it?" Harry said, rubbing his forehead where it had hit the dashboard a few hours earlier. A large, angry-looking bump was beginning to rear its head. He reached into his whiskey glass and fished out some ice, wrapped them in a napkin, and pressed the whole mess to his head.

He continued petulantly, "No dinner, a kidnapped girl, and a hefty automobile repair bill. To say nothing of the hospital stay poor Rumple has to endure this evening. Quite a lot of stitches, I can imagine. He won't be happy about that—old chap is terribly vain. No doubt he will be looking like a patchwork quilt in a hurricane by tomorrow. I shan't be surprised if he wants to borrow some of your powder for the remainder of our stay."

Lillie looked up from their table in the hotel bar towards the lobby. Alek, who presumably had been called by Jack after Stefanie had been kidnapped, was pacing back and forth along one edge of a large rug in the centre of the room. His blonde hair was dishevelled from constantly running his hands through it, and was now standing up in tiny tufts. The sight of the two of them together irritated her.

"I'm sorry, Harry. I shouldn't have involved either you or Rumple in this. None of this would have happened had it not been for my interference. Perhaps I should take Jack's unsolicited advice and find another occupation. The last case I was on drove him nearly to madness. There might be something in it, come to think of it..."

"Ouch," Harry winced as the hotel nurse inspected a nasty cut he had on his forearm. "Don't be silly, my girl. Besides, who would hire you? If it weren't for Jeremy Winston hoping to get into your knickers, you would be frightfully unemployable. And anyway, nothing good ever comes without a bit of a struggle."

Lillie scowled her disapproval.

"It'll need to be cleaned," the nurse reprimanded, clucking with dissatisfaction, as though he could have helped it. "It's a bit unorthodox to be treating you here." She pursed her lips and took in the hotel bar surroundings. "I would prefer we move to the medical room."

Harry looked up at her sharply. "Do you serve whiskey there?"

"Of course not!" she huffed.

"Then I shan't be going. Any medical establishment that doesn't serve at least something alcoholic to console its patients is hardly deserving of my funding. Just do your best. I say," Harry called to a passing waiter. "Is there any chance of getting a bite to eat? And while we are at it"—he held up his empty glass—"how about another drink?"

"Of course, sir, I will bring you a menu and will bring your whiskey to you in a tick."

Harry directed his attention back to Lillie. "Jack didn't seem very pleased with us, did he? Madder than a wet hen would be more accurate."

Lillie glanced in the direction of the lobby. Jack had been engaged with the local police when they had returned via a taxi from the hospital. "Not pleased," as Harry put it, was an understatement. He had been absolutely furious. In fact, he had not said two words to her since their return, preferring instead to glower in her general direction while he conversed with the attending officers and waved the nurse over to them.

Lillie did have to reluctantly admit he seemed to be at his best when in a position of authority. Having said that, he could be terribly severe when he wanted to be, but she had already made up her mind not to be influenced by his increasingly obvious disapproval. He and Alek had their heads bowed together now as though they were planning on stealing the crown jewels. After about ten minutes, Alek got up from the chair he had been inhabiting and made for the front door.

She glanced at the clock on the wall. It was after midnight and she felt exhaustion creeping in like a king tide.

"No, he certainly wasn't. Harry, would you mind terribly if I went up to bed? I have an awful headache and I want to be up early. There is a tremendous amount to be done if we are to find Stefanie."

"Not at all, my dear. I will hold fort here until things in the lobby die down somewhat. Sleep well."

Lillie got up and nodded to the nurse who was now dousing Harry's wound with an antiseptic, much to his protest, and went into the lobby to speak to Jack.

He was sitting with a plain-clothes officer in the corner of the room, his long legs stretched out in front of him, looking as though he were conducting an interview of some sort. She would have thought it would be the other way around. Having half a thought to slip away unnoticed, she decided in the end to say goodnight, even though she was still angry with him for his secrecy, and he with her recklessness. Would they ever agree on anything?

He looked up as she walked over and, getting out of his seat, he moved forward as though to take her hand. Perhaps he had softened his position somewhat.

"Calling it a night, are you?" he asked, looking a little gentler than he had an hour ago.

"Yes, I just wanted to come and say goodnight." She turned her attention to the detective who was scribbling something on a notepad. He hadn't bothered to get up. "Any idea where they might have taken Stefanie yet?"

"No leads, ma'am, but I have a team of officers combing the streets. In all likelihood they will have holed up for the night and plan to move again in the morning. If that's the case, it's unlikely we will have much luck tonight. While I have you here, why do you think she finally decided to come out of the wood-work and seek you out?"

"That's a very good question, and one I don't know the answer to. Perhaps she has some information she hadn't had previously. Or maybe she just realized staying underground indefinitely was more difficult than she thought."

"In what way?" The detective asked, peering up at her through his thin glasses.

Lillie thought this an obtuse question. "Well, detective," she began slowly, attempting to hide her annoyance. "A lack of funds for one thing; she isn't a wealthy girl. Being likely alone and not knowing anyone in the city, with the exception of an old boyfriend"—Lillie glared at Jack as she said this—"and being on the run from someone who obviously wishes her harm can't be easy—case in point, her being violently dragged out of this very lobby a few hours ago."

Jack raised his eyes as though there were something fasci-nating on the ceiling and rocked on his heels, his hands tucked behind his back. His anger seemed to have given way to amuse-ment, and she studied his upturned face briefly, before settling her stare back on the detective.

He hurriedly scribbled a few more notes down and then rose from his chair. "Thank you, Miss Mead." He gave her a curt nod. "Mr Abbott, we shall be in touch." He gathered up his suit jacket and walked across the lobby.

She gave Jack a hard look as he reluctantly tore his eyes away from the ceiling.

"What's on your mind?" he asked carefully, not wanting to irritate her further.

"Is that the best we can do? Really? *That* detective who insists on asking idiotic questions and doing very little of his own thinking?"

"You know as well as I do that there are all sorts of nuances the police use in their questioning. Often what they are asking is not what they seek an answer for, they are getting to it in another, more crafty way."

"Well," she said, "Felix Petters is a great deal more competent than that neophyte—it's a shame he isn't here helping find Stefanie. He probably wouldn't have lost her in the first place. What a complete shambles."

"Please sit. Just for a few minutes. I want to discuss something with you."

She did as she was asked and sank down into the chair the detective had been occupying.

"Fire away," she said, yawning. "I don't suppose this has anything to do with your meeting with Alek today?"

"It does actually, although I don't think you are going to like what I have to say." This piqued her interest. Was he *actually* going to talk about it with her?

"Jack," she smiled. "It wouldn't be the first time."

He took a deep breath and she caught a delicious smell of his cologne. "I need you to drop this story. Right away."

Well, she thought, it was hardly unexpected. When *hadn't* Jack asked her to drop a case?

"Are you going to tell me why?" she asked, narrowing her eyes.

Jack leaned in closer and lowered his voice. "As you know, Alek is involved in shipping."

Lillie nodded.

He continued, "Well, he works with a company headed by his wife's father. Alek isn't there in any real decision-making capacity. Since he married and joined the company, his father-in-law has kept him at arm's length; and while he has an enviable salary and good title, he doesn't have any real authority."

"Go on," Lillie urged, pleased she was finally getting some information on the young Swede. It was certainly more that she had been able to glean from him.

"It seems he has discovered some...anomalies in the shipping manifests."

"What sort of anomalies?"

"Well, this is where it gets interesting. Over the past year and a half he has found multiple incidences of their container ships not carrying what was listed and declared on their manifests."

"I'm not following you, Jack. Were the ships empty when they should have been full?"

"Not empty, no. They were carrying other, illegal items, instead."

"Drugs?"

"Guns. Hand guns, for the most part—.45s and 9mm mainly —and a significant amount of ammunition. Also other weaponry, some rifles, gelignite explosives, grenades..."

"Where were these shipments originating?"

"New York, mostly. Sometimes Boston. There was one ship last year out of Halifax carrying a considerable number of Ross rifles, but that was a one-off."

"I would think those rifles would be going for a song after

all their glitches and troubles during the war. Really, who would want them? But, let me guess where they were going."

Jack nodded, gravely. "I think you know."

"And I don't suppose they were being used by the British Army stationed in Ireland."

"There is no record of us receiving these shipments, no. And I have checked, extensively."

"Do you think this has something to do with the duke's murder? Is there a connection?"

"Fulbright Shipping does its banking with Ainsworth Capital, but so do many companies, so that on its own isn't remarkable."

"No. And there aren't many banks who offer branches in New York, London, and Dublin, so from what I can tell, Ainsworth has the lion's share of industry business. Even Lloyd George's party banks with them, so we can hardly say the majority of their business is sinister."

Jack nodded. "It does make it rather difficult to track down criminal behaviour."

"I don't understand, did Alek get in touch with you about this?"

"Not me as such, but one of our departments." Jack shifted in his seat. "I admit, I searched his name, and Stefanie's, when I got back from my last assignment. Harry gave me the specifics." He looked at her face and she made a miserable attempt to hide what she was thinking. "Don't be angry with him. He knows I have access to things you don't and thought it would help. And then this came up, which was either odd or oddly coincidental —I'm not sure which, yet."

"So Alek is an informant. He is informing on his own company. It isn't necessarily connected to whatever Stefanie is caught up in—in fact, it probably isn't connected at all."

"But Harry suspects your case has a connection with Ireland—he told me as much."

"Only because the duchess, a woman who is the least transparent person you will ever meet, had suggested it. But Jack, I hardly think we can take her at face value."

Jack leaned back in his chair. "I see. Well, I suppose I figured if anything shook out, maybe I could help you, or at the very least warn you off." He gave her a pointed look. "Of course, I should realize by now that warning you off anything just makes you sink your teeth in further."

"When did he reach out to the department exactly?"

"Some time ago. I believe it was October of last year. Why?"

"Hmm, so not so recently, and certainly previous to all this mess. Just a thought, and this is a reach, but do you think Stefanie might have been hired by the bank *because* of her connection with Alek? But how would anyone know about it —" She trailed off, grasping for the association—was the bank laundering money for the company?

"It makes more sense than chalking it up to a coincidence, certainly, but still, it seems a tenuous connection. I doubt the bank nor the shipping company realizes Alek is an informant. If they did, he would likely be dead like the other two."

"You think the bank or the company might have murdered the duke and Angus? It seems a little nefarious for a corporate entity, doesn't it? Anyway, if they did, perhaps they suspect Alek but want to be sure. In the meantime, what are you doing to protect him? If Stefanie can be made to disappear, shouldn't we assume the same for Alek?"

"Yes, I have a man on him—well, two actually. One in the house masquerading as the butler and another he isn't aware of on the outside. Of course, I don't have to tell you that none of this leaves this room. I really shouldn't be telling you any of this."

"I know." Lillie leaned in to give him a kiss. "I *am* happy we are finally both working from the same playbook, though."

"Go to bed," he replied. "You look as though you have been hit by a lorry."

"Something like that," she retorted ruefully.

33

STEFANIE

She was in a room. It looked to be a back office of some sort, its usual occupant an untidy but efficient person it seemed, for the desk was extraordinarily organized in a haphazard way but the shelves behind the desk were in need of some attention. A riot of ledger books, novels and loose paper spilled from a large bookcase that looked as though it were listing to the right, causing it to take on an appearance of a community library, dangerously adrift and devoid of its skipper.

Where she sat now, on a stuffed and threadbare divan that prickled her bare legs, was across from the only door into the room. The door wasn't large, but it was solidly built of oak and had a heavy, worn iron handle. The door was located at the end of a long corridor, which two men with palms of sandpaper had forcibly dragged her down on the way in. The only other way out of the room was through a small window made of wire mesh encased glass, beyond which she could only see darkness. She had already tried the door handle, and it was, as expected, locked. She had half a mind to go through the window, or at least try, but she doubted she was in the building alone—the two thugs who had happened upon her in the hotel lobby wouldn't have gone far.

But they hadn't, had they? *Happened* upon her, that is. Obviously, she had, unbeknownst to her, been followed, and she wondered for how long? She had stopped fighting them after she had been strong-armed into the car at Brown's. Stuck between two men who smelled of sweat and iron, it was the prudent choice to sit still and try to navigate her rapidly changing surroundings. If she were to get away, then at least she might be able to find her way back. Or so she thought, but not knowing London at all she had rapidly lost track of their location as the scenery changed and the miles sped past. Shouldn't they have blindfolded her? She supposed they didn't think she would escape. Perhaps they were right. Perhaps not.

They had searched her, roughly and with intent, as though what they wanted could be shaken out of her. Her bag, which one of them must have grabbed from the lobby of the hotel because she certainly wasn't still hanging onto it after she was *happened* upon, was also searched—its lining sliced as though whatever information she might have could have been crushed into its tiny space.

There were voices outside the door of the room now, and she strained to hear what they were saying. She crept from the sofa and moved toward the door. The voices carried, coming nearer to her and then further away, as though they were walking up and down the corridor. She didn't recognize any of them. All men, and nearly all of them with American accents. She supposed the man who she had followed back to the warehouse by the river had been tired of waiting for information on the missing funds and had decided kidnapping her might be more expeditious.

She wondered if the diminutive hotel porter, the one with the thick glasses and crooked haircut, still had her file? She hoped by now it might have been delivered.

34

DANIEL

His stay in England was probably a terrible idea. It was rash, dangerous, and illogical—and it really wasn't like him at all, Daniel thought miserably while standing on the edge of the platform at Waterloo Station. The pavement smelled of fried chips overlain with some sort of rotten fruit. Peach, perhaps, or apricot. A large swath of something orange and dried, likely the source of the smell, was narrowly avoided as he reached down and picked up his briefcase.

He was ostensibly in London to see a school for disadvantaged youth, at least that was what he had told the immigration officer when his ship had docked over a week ago. It was quite a successful school, actually, and even though he was only using it as a cover, its headmistress was still expecting him for brunch. If he didn't hurry he would miss it. He felt his stomach growl its discontent.

His life was beginning to feel complicated and for the first time in a long time, the paths laid out before him weren't clear. *Lillie.* He was drawn to her like a fly to honey, and he wouldn't be at all surprised if he were swatted for it. He had a hard time remembering the last time he had been so careless. But he had his suspicions and a man could hardly be faulted for seeing them through. He *wanted* to discover that it had been Lillie's fiancé who had had the thugs follow them—at least then he might be able to convince her not to marry him. He didn't know her well but he knew that she wouldn't tolerate that type of interference. He also knew he had to be careful with his intentions—for certainly just because one wishes for something it doesn't necessarily make it so.

He ruminated that perhaps his only saving grace was the expanse of time that had passed between when he had committed two murders on English soil, and his return now. If he was fortunate his photographs would have slowly and steadily faded from the public consciousness over the past year. If he was *unfortunate* he would run smack into the police officer who had been tracking him at the time, just as he was hailing a cab. Hoping he was the former, he made his way through the Victory Arch and exited the train station with all the false confidence that he was exceptional at portraying.

He glanced at his identification card while he extracted a bill out of his wallet, now sweaty with the heat and stickiness of a London summer. It wasn't the best forgery, he would be the first to admit. But, having been out of criminal circles for some time, he had had to rely on a second-rate supplier who could produce it quickly. These things were never very good when they were rushed, and he was careful not to handle it too much for fear the fresh ink would smudge.

He reached one long arm up and hailed a taxi and the car weaved itself into an almost impossible parking spot beside him. "Haverstock Hill," he told the cab driver through the open window. He opened the door and got in. "Alexandra Orphanage, please."

The driver nodded his assent.

Daniel pulled his hat lower over his eyes and stared out the window as the car cruised swiftly through enemy territory.

35

FELIX PETTERS

He was standing amongst the ruins of the small hillside cottage that had once been the home of Stefanie and her aunt. It had never been a pretty cottage: its sagging roof a testament to its age and lack of a patron; its haphazard windows either too small or too few for it to be considered a handsome building. Yet it had had a sort of Cornish charm to it, especially where a well-established creeping Virginia had obscured its architectural flaws. Oddly, the vine was one of the few things left after the fire had swept through. That, and a remnant of the wall it had once covered. Now the wall's smouldering foundation was all but gone, causing it to lean horribly inward.

Petters rubbed at his chin and extracted a handkerchief from his pocket. Even in the fresh air of the morning, the smoke lingered and burned at his throat as he waded through the ash. There was an investigative team there too, two detectives with their evidence bags and magnifiers set up. The local police had requested them, and they had arrived from London early that morning on the overnight train—gliding in with a respectable and confident quiet. Their thin black overcoats were removed now, folded carefully over the hood of a black police car which was acquiring dust as rapidly as a junior detective could brush it off. The heat of the day began to creep over the black cliffs and toward the beaches and with it came the smell of seaweed and salted fish.

Stefanie's aunt, Clara, had been taken by the ambulance attendants a few hours ago—she had some burns to her arms and face, and some minor smoke inhalation but was alive. The doctor expected her to be released shortly. And while it appeared, at least initially, that this had been an unfortunate accident, the presence of the arson team told him differently.

Petters stared out at the water. A flock of cormorants, their blackened feathers glistening in the morning sun, danced through the air and occasionally disappeared into the water in their endless search for breakfast. He envied their oblivious-ness to the human world surrounding them all.

"Apparently they can dive up to a hundred feet, those birds. Better fishermen than we are really, and they don't need nets."

The voice behind him startled Petters, and he turned to see its source. One of the arson investigators was mopping at his forehead with a dirty shirtsleeve. His face was smeared with soot and where his eyes had watered there were long streaks of white cascading down his cheeks.

The man continued, "I understand from Detective"—he glanced down at the soiled clipboard he was carrying—"Mar-ley, you are to be read in on our findings?"

"Yes, thank you. What have you got?" Birds forgotten, Petters turned to face the man.

"Looks like it was an incendiary fire for certain—deliber-ately set. There is accelerant residue around the back door and then again here." The man pointed to where the front of the house had once been. "Probably kerosene, maybe turpentine, too early to tell, but the signs are there." He motioned with his arm to an area left of the creeping Virginia. "We have some localized burning, which tells me whoever set it released the majority of the fuel here."

Petters couldn't see much but he didn't doubt the findings. "Not the most sophisticated arsonist, surely."

"No. Relatively easy to detect for anyone who knows what to look for."

"But surely the woman should have been able to get out?"

"You would think so, but I wouldn't be surprised if she was incapacitated in some way first. Drugs, blow to the head, whatever. Doctor at the hospital should be able to tell you more."

Petters nodded.

"Anyway, those details aren't part of our investigation. I'll write up my findings before I leave for the evening train and have the report delivered to Detective Marley by tomorrow."

"Right, I'll let him know. Thank you both for coming."

Petters shook the man's hand, regretting it immediately as he watched the ash transfer onto his own.

He waited until the man's back was turned then surreptitiously wiped it on the parched grass beside him.

36

LILLIE

Surprisingly, Harry was already in the breakfast room when Lillie came downstairs. The morning sun was streaming through the leaded glass windows and highlighting not only his golden hair, but also the thin layer of dust that had accumulated overnight on the bar turned coffee station. A waiter was doing a poor job of wiping it down, leaving more streaks than when he had started.

Even more surprising was the man sitting across from Harry.

"Rumple!" She rushed forward to give him an uncharacteristic kiss on the cheek. Normally she wouldn't have, but she was so relieved to see him after their accident that she wantonly disregarded his usual English reserve.

"Miss Mead." He shifted uncomfortably and attempted to get to his feet. She thought she detected a little colour in his cheeks but it was difficult to confirm through the myriad of cuts and bruises.

"Please, don't get up," she added hurriedly, seeing a thin line of stitches laced across his upper forehead peeking out from under their bandage. "You look good," she lied, trying to keep her eyes from betraying her dismay at his appearance. The waiter, apparently now finished with his inept housekeeping, rushed over to pull out Lillie's chair and she took a seat. He gave Rumple a doubtful look as he departed. What did they look like, the three of them?

Harry's bruises had also begun to show, although his were minor in comparison to Rumple's. A faint but broad discolouration extended across his brow and curved upward towards his hairline. She, luckily, with the exception of one above her right eye, had most of her contusions hidden; although her hip bone looked as though it had been pulverized, as did her shoulder. She noticed she was quite sore if she moved the wrong way, and she had had an interrupted sleep because of it. She wondered how Stefanie was this morning, or even if she were still alive?

"Coffee? Tea?" Harry motioned to a waiter.

"A coffee would be divine, thank you," she told him.

When her cup was full and the waiter had departed, Lillie gave them her news. "I've had a call from Felix Petters this morning and something terrible has happened in Cornwall. Stefanie's aunt's cottage burned to the ground yesterday."

"How coincidental," Harry mused, raising his eyebrows.

"Yes," Lillie agreed. "But even more disturbing is that her aunt was in the house at the time. She is at the local hospital, but he expects her to be released today. She was lucky—she escaped with just a few minor burns."

Rumple shook his head slowly. "How terribly sad."

"Just what in the hell is going on?" Harry was uncharacteristically exasperated. "Was it an accident, or intentional?"

"An arson team from London has been investigating, their report should be in the Newquay police's hands now. But they told Petters they believe it was deliberately set."

"Unbelievable." Harry looked grim.

"It is very nasty, indeed. Petters is going to wrap up there and then I am afraid he is heading back to Oxford."

"He won't come here? To London? We could use him if we are going to track down the girl."

Lillie was heartened to hear that Harry wouldn't also be abandoning her. Petters' unexpected announcement that he was leaving had left her forlorn.

"He's had a call from the duchess and apparently she doesn't want to continue employing him as a private detective any longer."

"That's absurd! Her husband was murdered and Petters hasn't yet finished his investigation." Harry slammed down his cup of tea and all three of them looked surprised when it didn't shatter into a thousand pieces.

"She says it's all too emotional for her and she doesn't want to carry on. I wonder how much of that is true. Perhaps it's financial—now that the duke is gone, her budgetary outlook may be much bleaker than it already was and she did mention to Petters that the London townhouse is up for sale." Lillie sipped at her coffee and wondered. Something about the woman had never quite sat right with her. "Anyway, Petters can't afford to be on a wild goose chase and not get paid for it, so he has decided to go home and dust off his shingle. He needs to be available for whatever other work comes his way."

"It must infuriate him, though, all the same."

"I'm sure. You know him, a perfectionist if ever there was one. To leave something so obviously undone is sure to drive him around the bend. Still, I'm here, and while I might not be a classically trained detective, there does seem to be some manpower on this case now with Stefanie's disappearance." She thought fleetingly of Jack. The possible Alek connection would ensure assistance from his department, or so she hoped, although it wasn't really something she was permitted to mention.

"And what of the Canadian hotelier?" Harry asked. "Was Petters able to ascertain the nationality of the men who checked into the Cornish hotel around the time Angus was murdered? Perhaps the same men are responsible for the fire."

"A dead end, apparently; no pun intended. Petters tried to get him to identify a Scottish and Irish accent and the poor man was wrong every time. I told you, being from North America, our kind isn't immersed enough to know one British Isles' accent from another. At least not consistently."

The three of them sat in silence for a few moments, each lost in their own thoughts. Lillie didn't notice one of the hotel staff had quietly glided up to their table. She startled when he spoke.

"Miss Mead?"

"Yes." she glanced up sharply at the sound of his voice.

"I'm terribly sorry I didn't get this to you last night. With all the commotion...and that poor girl being kidnapped from the lobby..."

He handed her a dark red file.

"Who is this from?" she asked, turning it over. It was bound with a leather string and marked *Private and Confidential* in embossed gold lettering.

The young man peered at her from behind his thick glasses, they gave his eyes an overly large and undeniably comic appearance. "Oh, yes of course, I should have said—the girl who was kidnapped, she wanted you to have it."

All three of them stared at him, uncomprehending.

"But that's impossible, I don't understand..." Lillie searched his face for clarification.

"She handed it to me, the moment those horrible men came through the doors after her. She had her back turned to them but still, I thought surely they would have seen it, but they didn't. It was all terribly upsetting. She didn't get a chance to say anything to me, other than your name, and I pushed it under the nearest chair so her wishes would be granted. In all the chaos, I forgot it was there until this morning and I just fished it back out." He dropped his eyes. "I am so deeply sorry for the delay."

"Goodness, don't be sorry, old sport—thank heavens for mediocre housekeeping services. How marvellous that you remembered it," Harry chimed in.

"Yes, very good work," Lillie added encouragingly. "Thank you."

They watched the young man depart and Lillie unwound the keeper string on the back of the file. Inside were a number of pages and she carefully extracted them, laying each one on the table before them. They consisted mostly of bank statements and balance sheets. Amongst the deposit and withdrawal slips there were also a series of newspaper clippings, a couple of photographs, and some handwritten letters. She pushed the bank statements towards Harry and he started to sort through them while she concentrated on the newspaper clippings.

Rumple had placed two of the photographs in front of him and he put them side by side. He was staring down at them quietly, with a puzzled look etched on his face.

"Do you suppose she got this file directly from the duke's house?" Harry asked. Lillie tore her eyes away from Rumple's injured face in order to concentrate on what Harry was saying.

He continued once he had her attention. "These are their bank statements, or at least some of them are. The others appear to be numbered accounts and it is going to take some detective work to find out who the account beneficiaries are."

Lillie frowned. "You think Stefanie might have stolen this file?"

"How else would she come by it? Unless the duke gave it to her before he died. But why would he? This all seems to be quite personal financial information. I certainly wouldn't be handing it around like sweets at a country fair."

Rumple was still staring at the pictures in front of him and was now rotating them, back and forth.

"Look at this." Lillie handed Harry one of the newspaper clippings. "Seems strange they would keep newspaper articles on grifters and common criminals."

There were at least a dozen of them, all from different newspapers, and all the individuals had evaded the capture of the authorities. In most cases, their photos were splashed across the page asking for public assistance in locating them. She pushed the rest of the clippings across the table to him.

"Mmm, yes." Harry sorted through them, pausing to study each, then carrying on to the next. "And why keep them in a file with banking information? They are hardly complementary items."

"Maybe they just threw everything together in haste, some people are terrible at file-keeping. Perhaps they are looking for someone? An old relative, or friend. Someone who has gone over to the dark side."

"Yes, possibly," Harry mused, putting the clippings down. He glanced at Rumple and addressed him pointedly. "I say, you seem quite taken with those two photographs, care to share your thoughts?"

Rumple slowly raised his eyes to them. He turned the photographs around so Lillie and Harry could see them better.

"Ah yes." Harry leaned in to study them. "The duke wasn't a terribly handsome man, was he? Not that one should speak ill of the dead, but it does beg the question: what *did* that lovely young lady see in him?" He picked up the photos and looked at them more closely. "See here, this one must have been taken a few years after the other." Harry pointed to the duke's forehead. "Looks like he had quite the recession in his hairline over the period of a few years. Terrible thing for a man, losing one's hair. Makes one seem dreadfully old in a rather short amount of time." He handed the photos to Lillie.

There was something off about them. Not at first glance, maybe, but if you looked at them long enough there was a discrepancy to them. She pulled out the newspaper clippings and lined them up above the photos.

She looked up at Rumple. He stared back, as though willing her to come to the same conclusion he had. "You don't think..." she began carefully.

Harry interrupted her, oblivious to what she was seeing. "Certainly I do. Age may not be directly linked to hair loss but it does muddy the water. Of course there are always pieces that can be purchased. I had a frightful uncle when I was little, the old chap wore his false hair like a badge of honour. Used to remind one of a dead ferret nestled on top his head..."

"Harry!" Lillie silenced him. "Look at these again, take a closer look," she shoved them towards him, turning each photo and clipping around so he could see them properly. He dutifully studied them in silence while neither she nor Rumple spoke.

After what seemed like an eternity, Harry looked up at them both. "You know, I don't think these two pictures are of the same man at all, are they? There is an uncanny resemblance, certainly, but there is something about them together...and then also in relation to these..." He turned the newspaper clippings back towards her.

"I quite agree," Rumple murmured.

"The cheekbones are similar in the photos," Lillie continued. "And the forehead. But the shape of the eyes is slightly different, this one is more hooded than that one," she pointed out her findings. "And the right droops more than the left in this picture, which I assume is the duke based on the clothing he is wearing. This other man looks to be dressed in something nearer rags and notice his eyes: brighter somewhat, more lid showing."

"And even more telling, that particular photo bears an

uncanny resemblance to this man." Harry pointed to one of the newspaper clippings.

"A grifter," Lillie said, flicking once more through the other newspaper articles.

"Mm, yes, although I am not familiar with the term. But this grifter, vagrant, whatever—looks remarkably like our dead duke." Finding what he was looking for he extracted one and held it up so Lillie and Rumple could see it. The photograph was of the same man with the brighter eyes. "In fact, all these grifters look the same actually, don't they? If you can see past the different hair styles, and beards, and moustaches—they are the same bloody man! Just different aliases."

"*Charlie Linton.*" Lillie read, picking up one. "*Missing, presumed to be en route to Devon in an attempt to evade the Metropolitan Police. Wanted in London for assault and theft. Anyone seeing this man is urged to contact their local police station to report.*" She looked up at them both. "Devon."

"Not far from Cornwall," Rumple continued.

"What are you saying?" Harry asked. "That this man and the duke, were somehow accidentally mixed up? Or their bodies were?"

"Or one was purposely put in the place of the other," Lillie stated flatly with a creeping trepidation.

"And you think it was this Linton fellow? That he was killed and made to look as though it were the duke?"

"Or that he was killed because someone mistook him for the duke. Either way, if that is the case, it would lead to one very disturbing conclusion—"

Harry finished her sentence with gravity. "That the duke is very possibly still alive."

Lillie nodded. "Yes, and for some reason or another, he doesn't wish to be found."

37

DANIEL

He awoke early and reflected on the woman who ran the orphanage he had visited yesterday. Under normal circumstances, had a woman been so flamboyantly flirtatious with him, he would have woken up in a bed not his own with a thick head and regrets as deep as the Grand Canyon.

As it was, he was alone and relieved.

It was refreshing to be on a new path, a changed man. He thought it as he dressed and made his way outside his small hotel—it put an added spring in his step. As the flat in Knightsbridge was just a place to receive correspondence, he wouldn't dream of taking the risk of staying there. Instead he had taken a room at a former coaching inn turned public house in Hammersmith. Even though he completely trusted Lillie, he wouldn't put it past her friend, the detective, to have her followed. As he walked, he reflected that a London morning wasn't so very different from a New York morning. The bustle had yet to start but the early risers were clucking around the pavements, walking dogs, putting out newspapers, baking bread.

He inhaled deeply, taking it all in; the dewy ground in the park, fresh laundry on the line, the slow roast of coffee as it permeated the air.

It would be difficult not to go to Brown's this morning. It existed like the North to a compass wand, a pull so great it was impossible to ignore, and nearly unimaginable to deviate from. There was no rational reason for his feelings toward Lillie Mead. She was a reporter, for God's sake, a woman used to covering crime, writing from the side of morality, espousing the values of acceptable social behaviour—something he had never adhered to himself. The only thing they had in common was their country of birth, after that, they were chalk and cheese, oil and water, wine and...

The honk of a horn disturbed his thoughts.

He had tried to cross a street and made the mistake of looking the wrong way into the traffic. A classic North American mistake that almost caused him to be pancaked onto the cobblestones. He gave his head a shake, trying to dislodge his daydreaming and focus on the task before him.

He needed to figure out who exactly had hired the thugs who had followed them, because if their assumptions that it had been the bank manager were wrong, then there existed another, entirely different threat out there. If there was one thing he was certain of: until they knew who killed that Duke in Cornwall, Lillie was putting herself directly into the line of fire. And this was something that he was feeling increasingly uncomfortable with.

38

STEFANIE

S he woke with a crick in her neck and a metallic taste on her tongue. She had been captive now for two long days.

Stefanie sat up and rubbed at her neck, attempting to smooth out the cramp in her joints, feeling her skin itch from the horrible fabric on the ancient sofa. It smelled as an old man might: unwashed and rotting. Her face was rubbed raw from where it had rested on the horsehair cushions. After the night she had had she was surprised she had even slept.

She had been questioned by a small but menacing man who had been brought into the room just as she had been falling asleep. He had repeatedly asked the same questions, over and over again into the wee hours of the morning. They regarded the bank's policies and directions she might have been given. None of which she was able to recall. She had transferred thousands of pounds for hundreds of people. Nothing was special or poignant. It was just numbers: account numbers, balance numbers. She had had very few answers for him, and his manner had become increasingly icy the longer the questions went on, the realization sinking in that she knew little or nothing of where whatever money they were looking for had gone. By the time he had finished questioning her, she had been convinced he was going to lean across and slice her throat but he had just calmly got up and left the room.

The building was now quiet, imbued with an eerie vacancy that caused her to wonder if her captors had gone, and left her there—locked in that haphazard office with its overflowing bookcases and unfinished ledger books.

She pushed back her hair, wound it into a small knot on top of her head, then stood up and stretched. She was still wearing her shoes and her feet were cold under their frigid leather. Despite the summer heat, the room felt positively glacial. Someone had put an old, threadbare blanket in the room overnight, and she threw it over her shoulders while she walked to the small mesh window and stood on her tiptoes so she could see out. There was a scent of something on the blanket, something familiar, although even as she gathered it around her, she couldn't quite place it.

It appeared she was in an industrial area of some sort. There were a few dilapidated warehouses across a wide dirt road which was scattered with rusting machine parts and the odd broken-down cart. There wasn't another living soul around, which was probably why they had picked this place.

It was early, she reflected, judging by the haze on the horizon. The sun had yet to fully come up and the blue overhead still had the remnant hue of an evening, the fading moon giving its last salute at half-mast. Perhaps these warehouses would come alive in a few hours and she might find someone willing to help her, although even as she thought it, her eyes gazed miserably over the scene before her. Abandonment greeted her.

She padded back to the sofa and curled up into a ball, kicking off her shoes and attempting to warm her toes by tucking them up beneath her. She adjusted the weight of the blanket over her shoulders and pulled it around her.

She would wait, she decided. Just a little while longer. And if she really was alone in this cavernous old building, then she would kick out that window—or die trying.

39

LILLIE

It had been a day of dead ends, false leads and unanswered requests for assistance. Lillie flopped down in an extraordinarily comfortable armchair in the hotel lounge and ordered a sherry.

"A large one, and Andalusian if you have it." She smiled at the bartender, who was polishing glasses in anticipation of the pre-dinner crowd.

He brought it out from behind the bar and then disappeared behind his mountain of glassware once more.

She took a long sip and reflected on her call with Felix Petters.

"I need you here, it's terribly self-centred of you to just disappear," she had told him in no uncertain terms.

"And I wish I could be there, truly. But Jeremiah is just back from his aunt's and I really must be a father first and a detective second. Especially since the duchess has fired me."

"Which is odd, don't you think?"

"A little. Or maybe not, I really don't know. But listen to me, Lillie—whoever set that fire to Stefanie's aunt's cottage either thought something was in there or was sending a very strong message—they very nearly killed the woman."

"Presumably if whoever set the fire had something to do with Stefanie, they would know she wasn't there."

Lillie thought of the red file the hotel porter had given her. It was hidden under a mound of clothes in her hotel dresser but she really must find somewhere safer for it. She didn't dare tell Petters on the telephone that she may possibly already have something that could blow this whole case apart. The more people who knew, the greater target they all became.

They had rung off and Lillie had headed to the police station to discover what was being done to find Stefanie. At least on that score she was satisfied. The detective who had so annoyed her the evening Stefanie was taken was thankfully off duty and the officer heading up the manhunt seemed a great deal more competent. He had the city broken into quadrants and then further divided depending on density and population. Eight small groups of officers had been assigned to various areas, depending on their local expertise. Moreover, contact had been made with any county within a fifty-mile radius of London in case the threesome had slipped the net and were on the run. Road checks had been set up, farmers had been notified, shopkeepers had been given pictures of Stefanie to display in their windows.

Lillie had spent the better part of the afternoon in his smoky office, watching as the detective inhaled cigarette after cigarette, washing the tobacco down with copious amounts of coffee, not really caring if it were hot or cold so long as there was plenty of it. He was a tall man—middle-aged, greying at the temples, with ruddy skin that prematurely aged him. He wasn't a stickler for protocol, seeming instead to shoot from the hip and ask questions later. In any other police procedure she would have been ushered out of the building as quickly as one could say "jack rabbit", but either this particular detective didn't respect police etiquette, or he simply paid it no regard at all. Instead, he appeared to barely notice his surroundings or who was occupying them at any given time.

He was hyper-focused, Lillie observed, and his particular point of focus that afternoon was a large, burlap board that took up the entire west wall of his office. It sported an extensively detailed map of London, on which he had pinned tacks of various colours—each denoting some sort of coded plan or a location of officers. To Lillie, it appeared so haphazardly random that only a codebreaker might crack it; yet the detective seemed able to fully grasp its meaning and when he wasn't otherwise engaged on the telephone or bellowing across the station, he hurriedly moved the pins this way or that.

By three o'clock the detective seemed to be having some success and the pins began to converge. He sat down in his desk chair, pushing up his glasses and rubbing at his eyes. He had appeared rather surprised to find Lillie still there, quietly sitting across from him, scribbling notes for her article.

She had reached into a basket at her feet, which had been provided by the hotel kitchen that morning, and pulled out a sandwich which she'd pushed across the desk towards him in an act of appeasement. "I thought you might want something other than coffee."

He nodded his thanks, still looking slightly baffled at her presence as he unwrapped the waxed paper and bit into it.

"I should have thought you would be long gone by now," he said with a mouthful of bread. He swallowed, then continued. "I can telephone the hotel if we find her, you needn't stay."

Lillie questioned her own judgement on keeping the muddle of the Duke's death quiet, but she didn't know anything for sure and the last thing they needed was to send the police barking up the wrong tree and delay finding Stephanie.

"It looks as though you might be getting close to something?" She motioned to the tight group of red pins centred around a cluster of streets in the garment district.

"Not sure, probably nothing, but worth investigating anyway." He continued to munch and stared up at the board, calculating. "A few eye witnesses to some sort of shenanigans around there last night—may be related, or may not." He swallowed loudly. "Go home," he said eventually, but not unkindly, as he crumpled up the sandwich paper and tossed deftly into a bin on the other side of the room. "There may be nothing to report from here for hours, or worse, days. Either way, I'll let you know."

Lillie sighed, "But you think she is a alive?"

He raised his eyebrows, resulting in a sharply creased forehead that gave her confidence. "Probably," he said carefully. "At least that would have been the intention when they nabbed her. Otherwise, they would have eliminated her on the spot."

"I see. Well, please do let me know whatever you find out."

The detective nodded, his glasses once again on the bridge of his nose, his eyes flickering over the map of the city. It seemed she had already left his thoughts even though she was standing not five feet away.

He said in an offhand way, "Thanks for the lunch."

His eyes had never left the map as she'd let herself out.

Now, back at the hotel, she glanced up at the clock on the lounge wall. Half past six. She sighed, leaning further into the comfortable chair she had commandeered in the hotel bar, while she sipped her sherry. She supposed she should really go upstairs and change for dinner with Harry, but she feared if she went upstairs she might not make it back down.

She shifted, feeling her bruised hip, and an overwhelming tiredness wash over her. It felt good to just sit still. Jack had left a message with the front desk saying he was working and wouldn't be able to join them. She supposed she had better get used to that and wondered if she ever would.

The pre-dinner crowd had just begun to trickle in and Lillie noted with amusement the hurried faces of men who wanted their cocktails before their wives joined them. She watched as they anxiously tossed their drinks back before heading to the dining room.

"Hello..." said a voice behind her, and before she had a chance to turn the voice hurriedly spoke again. "Please don't turn around, it's better if you pretend you aren't talking to me. In case..."

She recognized the voice instantly and felt her pulse quicken. Surely he wouldn't be so brazen as to be here still, in London.

She carefully took another sip of her drink and forced herself to choke it down. The bartender had moved on to cleaning the silverware now, his cloth flicking this way and that, but he was too far away to be eavesdropping. There was an elderly couple at a table fifteen feet away but owing to their age and distance, she didn't think they could hear a thing. As usual, Daniel had been very calculating and careful in his approach. The only danger to them now was Harry arriving early, or Rumple sauntering in.

"You certainly aren't who I expected to see here," she whispered. "Taking quite a risk, aren't you?" She felt her skin tingle.

"I like to live dangerously. What fun would it be otherwise?"

"Not much fun spending one's time in a jail cell," she reprimanded. "I hear the meals are dreadfully dull."

"Is that so?" he said, and she imagined his mouth turning down in a little grimace. "I really have no intention of finding out." She heard him adjust his position in the chair, the leather softly protesting. "I thought I would let you know I remained in town in case you need anything."

She frowned, wishing the pounding in her chest would subside. "You sound as though you have gone for a drive in the country and are offering to pick up some milk."

He gave a little chuckle. "That doesn't sound much like me. I decided to see an orphanage while I was here, actually. And thought I would swing by and see how you are making out."

She could hear him stirring in the chair behind her and she caught a whiff of his soap. She longed to turn around, and swivelled ever so slightly so that she might catch a glimpse of his profile.

"An orphanage?" She asked with incredulity. "You certainly are somewhat of an oxymoron, aren't you?" She glanced around the room furtively, looking for Harry and for once being grateful at his habitual tardiness. "Well, since you are here and so wantonly disregarding your freedom, I may as well fill you in. Stefanie was kidnapped two days ago, from this very hotel as she tried to slip me some information. The police are searching for her but they haven't a thing to go on. At least not that I know of." She paused, feeling his eyes on her. "And I think the duke might be alive. Possibly—as ridiculous as that sounds."

He was quiet for a moment. He did that sometimes—that saying nothing—and she realized she was getting to know his mannerisms. He *processed*; always calculating and recalculating. He wasn't a man to rush.

She waited patiently until he finally spoke. "It would be an elaborate ruse, convincing the police and a coroner that someone is dead when in fact he isn't."

"Mm, quite so. Which is why I need to be careful on that assumption; it does seem rather far-fetched."

"Have you told the police?"

"Not yet."

"It could have everything to do with the disappearance of the girl. But I'm sure you already realize that."

"Possibly. But I figured it wouldn't change their modus operandi so there really wasn't any point saying anything until I could prove it. Can I turn around now? It seems rather odd to be talking to the air."

"I didn't think you liked to take risks." He said it quietly, in a voice that could have come from a pillow as easily as the chair behind her. She felt her hands get warm.

What *was* it that he did to her? Was it fear? Trepidation? It would be easy to say he scared her. And logical. Except saying it wouldn't make it so. For some inexplicable and utterly irrational reason, she felt safe with him. A man who had killed people. It was absurd.

Giving in to her yearning, she turned to face him, realizing as she did so that he had already swivelled his chair around and was watching her. His grey eyes had a peculiar look to them—a fleeting amusement coupled with a strong intensity she was beginning to know well. She felt a shiver run down her spine.

"I found out who hired the man who followed us after our meeting at the bank" he said carefully, his eyes giving the room a quick, measured glance then settling back on her.

"And?" she urged. "Don't keep me in suspense."

"I think you might be surprised." His eyes bored into hers.

"It wouldn't be the first time," she retorted, holding his gaze, realizing with frustration that her nerves were a mess.

"It was a government hire. Security services, it seems."

This, admittedly, stunned her. Through all of it she had been certain—no, *more* than certain—that whoever was sent to follow her was part of the criminal underworld—either hired by that despicable bank manager, or the man who held the accounts they were looking into. It only made sense.

But *this*? This was Jack's department. SIS. Secret Intelligence Service. Plain and simple—and she felt her world spinning.

"I don't understand..." she stammered. Her mind swirled: Jack in the lobby of the hotel the morning after their attack by the river. Coincidence? The timing was too perfect. How long had he really been in London before he came to her hotel?

"Nor do I. My source in London is very reliable but he can only get so far without arousing suspicion, so it isn't really possible to find out who hired them, or why. But suffice it to say that you, my dear, are in all likelihood still being watched." He fiddled with his glass and she watched as his long fingers wrapped themselves around the crystal and brought it to his lips.

She opened her mouth to say something but stopped suddenly, seeing a familiar figure coming towards them.

"Lillie!" An exasperated voice boomed from the doorway, loud enough for neighbouring tables to turn and look. "I thought we said we would meet in the dining room, I have been searching everywhere for you." Harry ushered himself into the lounge in a waft of expensive cologne and perfectly tailored clothes, waving to the bartender on his way past. "I've got a table waiting, hurry up now. Is that what you are wearing to dinner?" He stopped in front of her table and looked her up and down, frowning when he got to her shoes. Despite her distracted mindset, she looked down at her day clothes; a dropped v-neck knitted vest over the top of a thin, shell-coloured blouse paired with a bold, navy geometric-patterned skirt. Admittedly, it was hardly dinner attire, especially since her companion was standing before her in a terribly expensive fedora, a silk ascot scarf that must have cost as much as her monthly salary, and a perfectly pressed lilac dress shirt.

"I know Brown's is quite modern, but really, my dear, shall we not try to at least make a bit of an effort?"

Lillie's head snapped up in his direction, hoping he wouldn't notice the man sitting behind her. She shifted her body to hide him, feeling a brief brush along her shoulder, and as she stood up she risked a glance behind her. There was nothing but an empty chair and a half-finished drink, the smudge of a fingerprint on the glass being the only remnant left of him.

"Good evening, Harry," she said reluctantly, brushing imaginary lint off her skirt as she got up, buying time to regain her composure. "I didn't expect you until a little later." She gave him what she hoped was a dazzling smile, tossed back the remainder of her sherry, and left the empty glass on the table. "Forgive my appearance but if it's all the same to you, I suggest we don't stand on ceremony tonight. Shall I lead the way?"

She turned away before he could read the disappointment on her face.

40

STEFANIE

There was blood dripping down her calf. Where it met her shoe it had darkened the leather from tan to almost black, making it look dirty, as if she had paid precious little attention to her attire, allowing it to become soiled beyond repair.

The scrapes up and down her legs were deep; the wire mesh from the kicked-out window had torn her flesh and it was now turning from red to a tinged purplish green. Looking down at them, she hardly believed they were hers for she felt nothing at all. They would crust over eventually, she thought, but enough time hadn't yet passed. It had only been an hour since she had crawled through the jagged hole she'd made in the window's mesh with her incessant and frantic kicking, the glass shards plucking at her skin as she'd wriggled through a space barely large enough for her to push her shoulders and hips through.

She had waited until dusk to make her exit. She was keeping a steady pace, any fatigue she might have felt was banished by the sheer adrenaline that coursed through her veins. She was out. Free. Away from her captors, and if it were up to her, they would have great difficulty tracking her. The room she had escaped from was now forgotten as she hurried through the London back streets—alleys, sunken doorways, the darkness, all her allies.

They would have realized by now she was gone. Her captors checked on her every few hours, their great hulking silence an unnerving constant in a desolate, captive existence. And they would, in all likelihood, look for her in the same place they had found her before. Brown's Hotel. So, this time, she would need to be much more careful. She thought of going directly to the police, where perhaps she would find the help she needed in order to stay safe. But it wasn't her preferred route out of this mess. She didn't want to have to explain her disappearance, her role in the bank and the things the duke had asked her to do.

No, she would stick with her original plan and find Lillie Mead, she decided, feeling a twinge of pain from the shards of glass that were embedded in her lower leg. And when she did, she would find the answers she needed to stay alive.

41

LILLIE

She was hot and mildly intoxicated. Dinner with Harry had been painstakingly long, endured only with copious amounts of wine which the waiter continually poured to make up for the spectacularly slow service from the hotel kitchen. Her salmon hadn't materialized until nearly an hour after she had ordered it and Harry never did get his filet mignon, instead settling for a breast of chicken that was surely meant to be someone else's dinner. All the apologies in the world had done little to make up for what seemed to be an unusual but vast incompetence.

"I don't understand—this blundering around would never have happened at Claridge's," Harry had vented. "They had our orders, and they were the ones to make the menus tonight. Had we known they had to spear your salmon from the Thames themselves, I shouldn't think you would have ordered it!"

"I hope that isn't where they got it from, Harry..." Lillie picked at her dinner, losing her appetite and thinking instead of what Daniel had told her before Harry had arrived.

A government hire. Sent to surveil them? Was the attack a mistake or intentional? If they had done nothing perhaps that man wouldn't have ended up dead. It was chilling. And it made not the least bit of sense. Of course the big question remained, did Jack know about it? She wondered whether she should tell Harry this new development but decided not to for the time being. She didn't want to explain where the information had come from.

They had parted in the lobby after dinner, and Lillie had checked her messages with the front desk, hoping to have something from the detective on his search for Stefanie. She had also hoped to have something from Daniel after having him slink away at the sight of Harry, but she was disappointed on both accounts. There was nothing at all for her.

Now back in her room, she flung open her windows to let in the evening air, the tinkle of laughter and a steady roar of car engines trailed upwards and into her third floor room. She glanced at the clock beside the bed which read eleven and marvelled at how awake London still was. Had she been in Oxford, the only sign of life outside at this late hour would be a fox scuttling along a fence in search of its next stolen meal.

She peeled off her skirt, blouse and stockings and stood in her slip as she wet a wash cloth with cold water and pressed it into her face. She wasn't the least bit tired. Wired, more like it. Pulling on a sleeveless nightgown and a silk wrap with three-quarter-length sleeves, she sat down at the desk under the window and began to make a diagrammatic chart. She circled names and linked those circles with other circles when she was sure of the connections and squared them off when she wasn't. The duke was at the top, circled with Angus and Stefanie, then another fork from Stefanie to Alek and Alek with an arrow pointing to SIS and then Jack. *Jack.* What did he know? There was also the duchess, squared as an unknown quantity, her children—probably uninvolved and therefore pushed to the side—and then the connection between the shipping company, Ainsworth Capital, and Ireland. Or not Ireland, she mused, as she scribbled in the margin. For the man on the river that Daniel had killed she drew a dark, indelible arrow from his circle back to SIS. And who had started the fire that injured Stefanie's aunt?

A knock on her door startled her and she wound her wrap tighter around her body as she made her way towards it. It was almost midnight.

"Who is it?" She hardly wanted to open it at this late hour and meet the same fate Stefanie had. There was every likelihood she was also a target.

"Jack," came the reply.

She pulled the door open and stood back to allow him in. Then she swiftly shut the door again.

"Good evening." He smiled down at her.

"It's a little late, Jack." She frowned at him.

"I just finished up at work and thought I would check in on you. May I?" He motioned to the sofa and she nodded. "I won't stay long," he assured her.

"Shall I order you up a tray? Tea? Dinner?"

"I'm fine," he replied, taking a seat and stretching out his legs. "I had something at my desk a few hours ago."

"I am glad you came, actually, I have something important to ask you." She walked back to the desk and with her back turned to him flipped over the piece of paper she had been sketching on.

"Ask away," Jack prompted.

"Well, first, a confession. I lied to you," she started. "But then I guess you already knew that, didn't you?"

He watched her carefully, saying nothing. He was assessing what she knew, of this she was sure, and he carefully hid his surprise.

"What about?" He continued the charade.

"The injury to my arm. I didn't slip in the bathtub. I was accidentally shot by one of the thugs you had tailing me." She glared furiously at him, nearly unable to control her rage. He hadn't moved an inch and seemed to be calculating a response.

Instead of responding to her statements, he calmly asked, "Do you want to tell me who the man on the river that night was? The one you were with after your meeting at the bank?" At least they were getting right to it. No beating about the bush.

Lillie barely contained her anger. "Are you quite serious?" she spat back. "You have me followed, and then lie about when you got back from wherever the hell you were—obviously you must have been here in London for quite some time if you were up to speed enough to hire a private security firm to spy on me."

"It was a mistake, I freely admit that. They weren't supposed to get that close and they certainly weren't supposed to have firearms. I suppose it was your companion who killed one of them?"

Lillie wasn't going to admit to anything. "And why, exactly, were you having me followed?"

"I think you know I have always been very concerned about your occupation. What you choose to do for a story, the people you choose to get involved with—they are extremely dangerous individuals. You can hardly fault me for wanting to make sure you are safe."

"Of course they are dangerous! I am a crime reporter. I'm hardly interviewing for the gardening section."

"And the man you had with you? Is he someone you are involved with? Is that why you have been dragging your feet on setting a date with me?"

"It's nothing like that!" she snapped, ferociously.

"Oh?"

"Certainly not. I hired him myself. For protection. He is just security, that's all." She was lucky Jack hadn't got a visual of Daniel, for he would have surely remembered him from a year ago.

"I think," Jack started softly, "that you have been nearly as secretive as I have. Why don't you come over here and let's put this all behind us." He motioned to the space beside him.

As she mulled this over, there was a tap on her door. She glanced at the clock on the side table. Ten minutes past midnight was far too late for a visitor; even Harry would have had the good sense to call first. Oh God, she thought with panic, what if it was Daniel? She would have some difficulty explaining that one.

Jack tensed. He rose slowly and collected his coat from the back of the chair. He reached inside the pocket and produced a small pistol, which glinted in the dim light of the room. He moved towards her and she involuntarily shivered.

"Who is it?" she asked through the closed door.

"It's Stefanie." The voice came hurried and panicked. "Please, Miss Mead, could you let me..."

Lillie flung the door back with such force that it hit Jack's shoe and then bounced back to where she caught it. The girl came through it quickly and hurriedly shut it behind her. She stood in the doorway, her tall strength a foil to Lillie's much smaller frame, and glanced around, settling her nervous blue eyes on Jack, who was still wielding the gun. He slipped it back into his coat pocket.

"Stefanie, my God, are you alright? Your legs, they are bleeding—quite a lot..." Lillie snatched up a cloth from a pile of clean linens the maid had stacked in a French Empire hutch of exquisite craftsmanship, and crouched down to have a better look at the mess of the poor girl's legs. "Please, come and sit down. Jack, can you have a look—"

They guided the girl to the sofa and Lillie ran to the bathroom for some water. When she got back carrying a rather large glass, Jack was kneeling on the floor inspecting them. He dabbed the cloth he was holding in the water and attempted to clean away some of the blood with it.

"I think they need to be stitched. Lillie, can you call down to the front desk, ask them for a needle, some thread, a bottle of their strongest scotch, and a bucket of ice."

Lillie picked up the telephone receiver on the desk and dialled. She waited as it rang, keeping an eye on Stefanie's face. She must have been in a great deal of pain but her face barely showed a thing. If Lillie expected a weak and terrified young woman, she was to be disappointed. This girl was a tour de force.

"No answer," she said to Jack.

"Hang up and try again," he commanded.

"How did you get away? Where have they been holding you?" Jack asked Stefanie while Lillie redialed.

"Where, I don't know. Some warehouse district. As for getting out, that was with great difficulty. I kicked out a window but getting here was even harder. I hardly know London at all and I feel as though I have been going in circles for ages. Finally I found a few landmarks and I asked a street person for directions and while he was hardly coherent, he did manage to get me pointed in the right direction."

"We need to call the police immediately," Lillie said, still listening to the ringing while she imagined the night attendant asleep at the desk. "They have search parties all over the city."

"No." Stefanie put a hand out. "Not yet. It can wait until the morning. I can't bear to be questioned by the police tonight and, to be honest, I don't know who I can trust." Lillie thought about this. The waste of public policing resources overnight bothered her, but she didn't want to spook the girl and have her run off. She also realized that the girl might be right. Who could they trust? The police, obviously, but what if the reach of her kidnappers extended that far and her location was leaked by someone in the force?

"Still no answer! Never mind, I'll go down to reception myself." Lillie slipped on a pair of shoes, wrapped her silk robe a little tighter and headed out the door. At least the time of night assured her she wouldn't be seen by many people—she didn't want to take the time to change.

She quietly shut the door behind her and padded down the carpeted hallway towards the stairwell. There was a small telephone room near the end of the corridor, its walls papered in a pale-yellow damask that looked dark green in the dim light. The door was closed tonight and the interior dark. Lillie gave it a brief glance as she hurried by.

She was almost at the end of the corridor when she felt someone grab her from behind and place a hand over her mouth. Attempting a muffled scream, she was pulled back down the hallway and into the telephone room, where she got a startling whiff of a scent she recognized.

"Shh..." the man whispered in her ear and she remained perfectly still as he removed his hand from her mouth and released his hold. She turned to face him.

"A bit dramatic, don't you think," she scowled at Daniel in the darkness of the room. It wasn't a large space so she was closer to him than she would normally have found herself.

"I thought you might scream. I came to your door but there were voices inside...have you got company?" he probed, gently, while attempting to step back and to give her a little more space. He bumped into the back wall.

"Yes, Stefanie is here. She got away earlier this evening...of course she is a complete mess. I am going for supplies. Jack is there, and he is going to see about stitching up her wounds."

Daniel nodded but remained silent.

Her eyes were adjusting to the shadows and she took him in —pressed, dark merino trousers, finely crafted leather shoes, a shirt of the palest ivory and softly striped in dove grey, the beginning of a shadow across his granite jawline. He had slung his light coat, also woven of the finest summer-weight wool, over the back of the only chair in the room. The scent she had smelled before was stronger now that they were in a small space with the door closed: woody tobacco layered with something sweeter, jasmine, perhaps, or linden. She liked it.

"You should go...back to America. Please, I couldn't bear it if they came for you. As it is, I am lying to Jack, and Harry—and Petters, now that I think of it."

"Don't do that for me." He reached out as though to touch her but then dropped his hand. "But I'll go, if that's what you want."

Did she want that? She hardly knew anymore.

"Good. But before you get settled in on the ship back to America, give me your take on this—if I am correct in assuming the duke may not, in fact, be dead after all, wouldn't it also follow that that would take some planning and expertise? After all, it is a pretty elaborate undertaking. There would be a string of agencies needing to be either in on it or have the wool professionally pulled over their eyes. The police department in Newquay for starters, the coroner's office, his family..."

Daniel's eyes had taken on an intense darkness she couldn't quite read. "Or, he would need a family member to lie when they were identifying the body. It could be as simple as that."

"The duchess," she replied, with gravity.

"Who have you discussed this with?" he asked.

"Well, you, of course. And Harry and Rumple know, obviously."

"I see." He gave her a look of dissatisfaction. "And will Harry tell your fiancé?"

She wondered why he didn't refer to him as Jack.

"I don't know. I hope not—at least not yet. Normally I would say that my friendship with Harry is quite separate from my relationship with Jack, although he does sometimes believe that Jack's assistance would be beneficial to me—whether or not I agree with that. But, when all is said and done, I trust Harry."

"And you don't trust your fiancé?" he said it so quietly she had to strain to hear him.

"I do, yes, but it isn't about trust really. It's more about what he would need to do for his job, as an agent in the field. That is why I must remain steadfast in my role as a journalist to maintain confidentiality."

A flicker of a smile flashed so quickly across his face that she almost missed it entirely.

"What?" she asked him, frowning.

"It's just that you trust *me*, that's all." His reluctance to admit anything was palpable, but here he was seemingly entirely honest.

"There is one benefit in confiding in a man on the run from the law—he won't likely be blabbing anything around to anyone. Incidentally, should you not get going? Having you here makes me nervous for you. The police just need one tip-off to make your life, and mine, a living hell. For your own safety, you should leave. And if I don't return with some ice and a needle soon they are going to send out a search party."

"You want me to leave right this instant?" He raised a mocking eyebrow and again Lillie found his carved face, his long and lean frame, his complete composure attractive. "I shouldn't think there is a ship in the middle of the night," he finished neatly, watching her carefully for a moment.

"If you are at the ticket office early you will be sure to get passage."

"I'm willing to wager they aren't open at this hour, but yes, alright, you win. I'll leave you." He hesitated, apparently considering. "For now, anyway."

"Leave for good. I mean it. Get on a train and a boat and get back to America. By morning this place will be swarming with police and investigators—I can't protect you."

"Of course not, and I don't expect you to." He stared down at her, his grey eyes tender, something she rarely saw.

She opened the door and stepped into the hallway, thinking he would follow. She took one step forward but he swiftly pulled her back and let the door close behind them again. The two of them stood there, staring at each other. She in her night-clothes, him with his coat slung over his shoulder, held dangling on his index finger. The air between them electrified. She wanted to ask him if he would leave immediately and what the logistics of leaving England were for him? Where were his bags? Questions swirled through her mind, put there mostly by her nervousness, and her desire to take charge of something that she clearly had no control over.

"I guess this is it then." Lillie held out her hand, feeling ridiculous and Daniel gave her a hard look.

"A handshake? After the time we've just had, I should think that is a little...*formal*."

"Do you ever wonder..." She eyed him warily, "...if you hadn't..."

"Killed people."

"Right. And I wasn't..."

"Promised."

She gave him an exasperated look. "It isn't India and I'm not part of a caste."

"You understand the general inflection."

"And besides," she carried on. "It isn't written in stone that I should marry Jack."

"Only written on your finger." He pointed to the engagement ring she was wearing and she absently turned it in thought.

"Listen," he said finally, "I often wonder that if I had taken a different path somewhere along the way and led a life—an admirable life—instead of being part of a criminal existence for as long as I was, then perhaps you might have seen me as someone you could fall in love with. As it is, I can't be that person. Not now, anyway. I can change, and I am trying, but it doesn't erase my past."

"Ah, but if you had taken that different path I may never have met you." She raised her eyebrows in argument.

"Ever the philosopher." He reached out and brushed his fingers across her arm. They lingered there, over her wound which was healing nicely, and she felt the warmth of his hand. He was holding his breath. "I don't know when or if I will see you again." He trailed his fingers down her arm, looking as though he realized even as he did it that he shouldn't. He pulled them away quickly.

"No, I suppose not."

"So..." He drew out the word, apparently searching for some courage. The air between them tensed.

He moved forward and in one easy motion gathered her up in his arms letting his coat fall to the floor. He leaned in and kissed her as though she were the only woman he would ever truly love—which couldn't possibly be true—long, and urgently, and she felt her body fold into his while he pressed her back firmly into the door behind her, all the while wondering why she didn't resist him? She could feel every inch of him, the buckle of his belt, the buttons on his shirt, the temperature of his skin, through her thin silk robe. For just a moment—breathing in his scent and feeling the roughness of his cheek—she encircled his neck with her arms and felt as though they were one person. It was intoxicating. When they finally parted, he placed her back on the ground with more gentleness than she'd thought he was capable of, and slowly picked up his coat.

"It's nothing," he lied, trying to soothe her conscience. "All me. Nothing to do with you. I would say I'm sorry, but that would hardly be truthful." His grey eyes searched hers before he let them drop, hiding them from her. Just for a moment he seemed to lean in, and she felt herself draw forward, then he raised his eyes, deadened them, and took a step back.

With seeming reluctance he pushed open the door and started towards the stairs, pulling on his coat as he walked. He didn't look back. She supposed he didn't need to. She knew he loved her. Completely. Entirely. Without bias or restraint.

Two men loved her. And it was absolute misery.

42

LILLIE

"I think I am pregnant." Stefanie was on her knees in the bathroom, clutching the bowl of the toilet as she threw up into it. "In fact, I'm sure I am."

Lillie was holding a cloth to the back of her neck as the girl retched, again and again, her body vibrating. Lillie feared she would pull the stitches Jack had so neatly sewn into her legs just a few hours ago.

Neither of them had slept much—Lillie had tossed and turned, the memory of Daniel's body pushed against hers in the telephone room occupying her tormented mind, while the sound of Stefanie moving around on the sofa, trying to get comfortable with her wounded legs, made the night longer than either of them would have liked. Only now was the sun finally rising, and Lillie found herself grateful for the start of the day. She welcomed any interruption from her own thoughts.

Eventually, Stefanie stood up and wiped her mouth. "I'm sorry," she apologized, hoarsely. "It's better now."

"Please, don't be. You have been through a tremendous upheaval. Are you sure you aren't just coming down with something? Flu, perhaps? Why don't we take you to the hospital, just to be sure? We should have done it last night anyway."

"No, please."

"The hotel doctor, then. And I insist," Lillie added, before Stefanie could protest again. She handed a fresh cloth to the girl and left the bathroom to call the front desk.

She had no sooner pulled on some clothes and tidied up the room than there was a tap at the door. Stefanie was seated on the sofa as Lillie led the doctor into the room. She looked absolutely done in.

"This is Dr Heming, Stefanie." She turned to the doctor. "Please go ahead and use the bedroom for your examination." Lillie pointed to the open door and nodded at Stefanie who rose slowly.

When doctor and patient had sequestered themselves inside the other room, Lillie quietly made a few phone calls. The first was to the police department. The detective on duty the previous day was no longer there, but she was able to leave a message with his assistant that Stefanie was safe. The man told her they would send a couple of officers over that morning to question her and provide some general security in case anyone came looking for her. In the light of day, all the nervousness over who they could trust seemed to have dissipated somewhat, she reflected. The next call she made was to Jack.

"Good morning," he said softly, hearing her voice. "You certainly are up early."

"Stefanie is in with the doctor and neither of us slept very well."

"I will be right over, give me half an hour to get there." Jack hung up abruptly and Lillie pushed aside her guilty feelings—hearing his voice brought the memories of the previous evening even closer and she felt the pit in her stomach deepen.

By this time the doctor had finished his examination,

reopened the bedroom door, and was packing up his bag. Lillie joined Stefanie who was still lying on the bed.

"I have redressed her wounds," he said to her, and Lillie noted the new bandages. "The stitching looks good but those wounds need to stay covered. She will need to see me again in a few days so I can remove them. In the meantime, young lady, please look after yourself." He gave her a good-natured but stern look, which was rich coming from a doctor who looked barely older than she was, and made his way from the room. "I can see myself out," he assured them from the doorway.

Lillie heard the door open and close and turned her attention back to Stefanie who was staring at the ceiling of the bedroom.

"So?" Lillie asked, cautiously.

Stefanie sat up. "I am. Pregnant, that is. Well, I knew I was, didn't I? I hardly know why I am surprised." She twisted her long, white hair around her finger.

"I see. And did he say how far along you are?"

"A few months. It's hard to be exact."

"The duke?" Lillie asked, getting straight to the point. She didn't know if Stefanie had spent time with Alek recently or not, but if she was already a couple of months gone, then it couldn't have been his.

"Yes," she confirmed absently, looking as though she were a million miles away. "He would have made a good father, actually." She smiled at this, her eyes welling. "Even though..."

Lillie let this sit for a moment. "The file you gave the hotel clerk to give to me. There were some things in there, I'm not sure how much of it you saw?"

"I sorted through it but there wasn't much time. The bank statements were copies, of course, but they clearly showed the amount of money that seeped out of that branch and was diverted to accounts overseas. There was some internal theft going on. Those statements prove it."

"Yes," Lillie confirmed. "I assume the duke was responsible for that?"

Stefanie nodded. "It would seem so, and looking back at it, I should have realized what he was doing—or rather, what he had *me* doing for him—I was so stupidly naive."

"There were also pictures of grifters—petty criminals who had gone missing. Did you see those?"

"Yes, and the man in all those file clippings was the very same man who was visiting the duke at the Headland the morning he died."

This was news. "I didn't realize Charlie Linton was at the house that morning, and I don't think the police knew that either. Why was he there?"

"I'm not sure. They were quite private about their discussions, and I left to go diving so I didn't hear much of anything."

"Is it possible this Linton fellow is the one who shot the duke?"

"I don't think so. I was chased to the edge of the cliff and shot at by someone else entirely. I am sure whoever came for me was the same person who shot the duke. He is dead, Lillie. I saw him. That horrible person shot him." She appeared to be thinking about something. "No," she finished, firmly. "I know what I saw."

"Just consider this: What if this Linton fellow was the man who was shot—it's possible that the killer might have confused the two of them and shot the wrong man. Or the duke may not have even been in the room at the time and the killer just shot someone he *thought* was the duke. They are nearly identical!"

"I know they are. I wondered at the time if he was a long-lost brother, perhaps even a twin—it was a bizarre moment, seeing them side-by-side. But this Linton fellow, he was odd, I mean really strange and absolutely nothing like the duke. I didn't even want to be in the house with him, which is why I left and went to the cliffs."

"How far away were you when you saw the shooting?"

"A few hundred feet, certainly, possibly more."

"Stefanie, I wonder if the duke isn't still alive? And if he is alive it would mean someone else is in on it. The duchess, in all probability. Perhaps the shooter missed him and they substituted Linton's body for the duke's. It would explain why the duchess seems so shifty when she is questioned."

Stefanie seemed to mull this over. "Presumably the stolen money would have angered someone fiercely. But to kill for it? It's all a bit drastic, isn't it?"

"I think the money belongs to a man who could quite easily kill for it. It's American mob money and I can tell you, these people are hardly law-abiding."

"Which also makes sense, the men who kidnapped me were Americans, I'm sure of it. They questioned me on the funds, although what little information I had wasn't really very helpful. I presume they still think the duke is dead?"

"I'm not sure, but it's likely. Especially if they used all their resources to find and kidnap you."

"It does anger me, if this is the case. It would mean that the duke has hung both me and poor Angus out to dry. So much for love and devotion. I suppose money caps all." She sighed. "I should like to go back to Sweden when this is all over. My aunt and I are basically strangers, I seem to anger her for some unfathomable reason. I can't go back to work at the bank. I am alone and pregnant in a country that has never felt like home."

"What about Alek?"

Stefanie gave a short, cynical laugh. "Alek is completely dominated by his wife and her family. Unless he suddenly grows a backbone, I don't think we can be together."

Lillie wondered if she should tell Stefanie about Alek's whistleblowing but decided it wasn't her place. "You never know, he may very well be tired of his life here in London. He was completely distraught when you went missing."

There was a brief knock on the door and Lillie left Stefanie in the bedroom to answer it.

On the threshold stood a freshly showered and shaved Jack. "I took the liberty of calling Alek," he announced, walking into the room. He turned to face her. "He is downstairs waiting for us."

"I would have thought you might have asked Stefanie if she wanted that before you went ahead and did it."

He looked confused. "They are in love, are they not?"

"She's pregnant! And he is married!" Lillie whispered, sharply. "I don't think it's a good time, do you?"

"Shouldn't he know he has a baby on the way?"

"It isn't his!"

A dawning look crossed Jack's handsome face. How could an intelligence officer be so obtuse, she wondered? "Oh, I see. Well, that does present somewhat of an awkward problem." He scratched his chin. "Presumably she is going to have to tell him eventually."

"Yes, but after being kidnapped, getting injured during her escape, being up all night, vomiting all morning, and preparing for a police interrogation—I hardly think this is the right time."

"Perhaps you are right."

"Go down there immediately and tell him Stefanie is getting ready to receive the police. She can't see him this morning."

Jack began to protest but thought better of it.

When he had gone Lillie went back into the bedroom. Stefanie was standing at the mirror brushing her hair. The colour had come back into her face.

"I hope you are up for this," Lillie said gravely.

Stefanie put the brush down and turned to look at her. "Up for what?"

"I think we should go find the dead duke and his charming wife today."

43

FELIX PETTERS

Former Police Superintendent Felix Petters was picking at his eggs and overcooked sausages when the telephone in his immaculate kitchen rang. His adopted son, Jeremiah, had already left the house to deliver the morning papers on his twice-weekly route leaving Petters with the remains of the dishes, a scorched pan that would never come clean, and an unsettled feeling that perhaps he shouldn't have quit the police force after all. He placed a stack of porcelain in the sink to soak and reached across to answer it.

"Felix Petters here, good morning."

"Petters, its Detective Marley in Newquay. I have some information on those two men who were seen around the time of Angus Braithwaite's death. It seems not only were they staying at the hotel when Angus expired, but we have also found an eyewitness who saw two men matching the same description in the vicinity of the cottage fire that injured the missing girl's aunt."

"It seems they like Cornwall, detective."

"Enough to return twice in as many months," agreed Marley.

Even though he had been let go from the duchess's payroll, Petters couldn't help but be interested in what the detective had to say; he thoroughly disliked leaving a case undone, and anything he could glean would help Lillie.

"And now? Any leads on their whereabouts?"

"Well, that is where it gets interesting, actually, and I didn't want to get in touch before I knew for sure, but it seems they are professionals."

"Meaning?"

"Freelance mainly, some government work—quietly sanctioned, of course—and they do jobs for private citizens also. Wealthy ones mostly, as they don't come cheaply. Anyway, they've gone from here. We've asked around, the ticketing agent at the Newquay station not only remembered seeing them, but get this—they actually asked him how to get from Paddington Station to Chelsea. Seems they aren't from there and needed directions. Can you believe it?"

"Assassins, and not very bright ones at that." Petters stated, not wanting any misunderstanding.

"Mm," the detective confirmed.

"I suppose they really aren't our main concern though, are they? It's *who* hired them that is distressing."

"So the next question necessarily needs to be: why were they going to Chelsea?"

"To get paid, presumably."

"We believe so."

"But no sighting of who did the paying."

"Afraid not, but we'll keep looking."

"A great many people live in Chelsea." Petters added.

"Sure, but how many of them are connected with this case?"

"Only one that I know of."

"Exactly. Oh, and Felix, one more oddity, the missing girl's aunt checked herself out of the hospital and hasn't been seen since."

"Really? That's odd, isn't it...do you find that a little strange?"

"Very strange. We had an interview set up with her yesterday at the inn she was supposed to be staying at. Four o'clock came and went but she never turned up. I checked this morning and her room hasn't been touched. Could be nothing, maybe she has a boyfriend somewhere and chose to stay there instead...anyway, just keeping you apprised."

Petters hung up and stared into the soapy water of his sink. Then he picked up the phone again and asked the operator for Brown's Hotel, London.

44

LILLIE

The hotel lobby wasn't nearly as quiet that late morning as it had been when she had fetched the medical supplies for Stefanie's stitches the previous evening. A small queue had formed around the reception desk; those checking out were mingling with early arrivers. A fresh-faced porter circled with tiny glasses of cucumber water and a silver tray of ripe figs, attempting to keep the waiting guests happy. Lillie's mouth watered.

She had telephoned the police inspector to let him know Stefanie was under the weather and wouldn't be in any shape for him to conduct his questioning this morning. She could hear his annoyance over the receiver as surely as if he had been standing before her. It was a lie, to be sure, but sometimes these things were necessary. The very last thing the two of them wanted was to spend a long day being questioned when they had work to do. Jack had left the hotel with a disgruntled Alek in tow, and said he would see her after work.

Lillie hurried by the front desk and wondered if she should check her messages—seeing the queue grow larger and larger, she decided she would do it later. Harry was already in the breakfast room when she entered. He put his newspaper down and pulled out a chair for her. The table was laden with iced scones, sugared jam, and fresh fruit.

"Have some mango," Harry urged, pushing a bowl of glistening yellow slices towards her. "I don't miss the War years, I can tell you that with certainty. Fruit from the Empire and the end of sugar rationing has made me a happy man—and safe, fresh milk to boot, no more sniffing to see if it's gone off. I shall die happy if I never see another can of tinned milk." He poured her a cup of tea and topped it up with the milk.

"Harry, I haven't much time."

"Nonsense. One must always make time for breakfast."

"Stefanie and I are going to undertake a reconnaissance mission of the duke's townhouse today. I just wanted to let you know where we were going. If he is alive, I'm certain he will be in and out of that townhouse. He still has his things there, and I believe they only listed it with the estate agent as a cover."

"Ah, I see. If I were to fake my death, I could imagine sneaking back into the Tynesmore kitchens for a little bite here and there. It isn't unreasonable to assume he might be there. After all, where else does a dead man who isn't dead hide?"

"They do have a home in Oxford, but if he is making arrangements to disappear forever, I can't imagine he could do it from there."

"Unless he's already gone."

"But surely he would take his accomplice? The last I heard, the duchess was still in Oxford. Say, why don't you give her a jingle today? Just to see if she is still in residence—let's make sure."

"I shall. Incidentally, should Stefanie not be giving up the location of her kidnappers to the police this morning?"

"If she knew it, then yes, but she hasn't a clue where she was being held. All she knows is that is was a great deal east of here, and in an area with warehouses. It isn't much to go on."

"They will be coming for her, you know. Until they are caught and behind bars she is a target for those scoundrels. Especially with the duke still dead, in a manner of speaking. This whole situation is terribly confusing." He picked up a plate. "Banana? From Peru. Where is Peru, anyway, I can't imagine its part of the Commonwealth..."

"No, thank you."

"No to the banana, or no to Peru being a Commonwealth country?"

"No to the banana—honestly Harry, I haven't time..."

"I'll come with you then."

"No. I need you here. If the police come looking for Stefanie you need to ward them off. Tell them she is sick and can't be disturbed."

"Be careful, my dear. You really should consider taking some muscle."

Lillie thought of Daniel. It would have been nice to have him along, but by now he was surely boarding a ship in Southhampton.

"We will be fine. Let me know how you make out with the duchess." Lillie stood and, after some reconsideration, pocketed the Peruvian banana. "See you later."

∿

By dusk they were inside.

The duke's townhouse held the claustrophobic air of a building that hadn't been lived in. The last slanted rays of the sun illuminated a few magnificent spider webs and the first hint of a melancholy, blanketing dust.

Perhaps she had been wrong about the duke. Maybe he *was* dead after all.

They had waited, the two of them, and watched the building for the past six hours, taking breaks one by one to fetch tea, or a quick bite to eat, leaving their posts by a back street, never walking down the main road for fear of running into the duke or duchess coming or going.

When the dark began to creep, they made a decision that wasn't taken lightly, especially with a pregnant girl in tow. They were going to break into the house. They had wandered around the back of the magnificent Georgian townhouse and planned their entry while standing in a formal garden staring up at the darkened facade and sneaking hurried glances at the neighbouring buildings. Their eventual choice was a small window to the left of the kitchen door which was partially hidden by the foliage of a rather large, sweet chestnut tree that was overdue for a trim.

Stefanie nudged her arm. "Look," she had whispered, pointing to two metal containers by the door. "Milk jugs. Someone has been here recently—otherwise they surely would have been picked up by now."

Lillie had nodded, wrapping her arm with her scarf and swiftly breaking the window with her elbow. It was now or never, and they had both winced in surprise at the sound it made. Finding the latch to the door, they had made their way through the darkened kitchen and up the narrow stairs to the main floor.

Now they stood in the foyer watching the sun go down through two tall windows on either side of the front door. There was a long console table in the entrance, its surface stacked with mail and two large Queen Anne lamps, their burnished brass reflecting what little light they still had from outside. A couple of Louis XVI armchairs were placed on either side of it. The house had the feeling that all empty houses had. Eerily still. Inanimate and undisturbed, as though it were holding its breath and awaiting the arrival of its patron so it could come to life again.

Lillie thought briefly of the empty milk jugs.

They padded around quietly, first through the drawing room, its space a museum to the heavy furnishings of generational heirlooms—the type very few care to outfit their homes with, but find difficulty parting with all the same. The long, heavy drapes were drawn, covering an entire wall of the room and thrusting it into a suffocating darkness. They moved on to the study, then the dining room, circling an enormous Edwardian mahogany table and its Victorian balloon back chairs, sixteen in total. There was a small, galley-style servers pantry through which they passed, what little light they still had glinted off silver serving pieces piled high on either side of its narrow corridor. Beyond this were the stairs they had come up from the kitchen and the doors to a smaller sitting room, which was furnished in a more delicate style from the larger drawing room. Its walls were papered in a floral spray, the colour of which Lillie couldn't make out in the darkness. The furniture consisted of a delicate George III writing desk with three small drawers and a burnished leather top, two elegant wingback chairs and a small linen settee. Two tall, narrow windows faced the now darkened garden. The room smelled faintly of a woman's perfume.

The floorpan of the house was nearly circular. Each room connecting to another, and then connecting to another, so one could move freely through it without having to go back. They moved silently through the sitting room and emerged into a small corridor with a water closet on the right and a cloak cupboard on the left. Eventually finding themselves back in the foyer, they stopped to regroup. To the left was a grand spiral staircase which took them to the third floor. The suspended silence of the entry was punctuated by the ticking of a large Gustavian clock at the base of the staircase, the home's only nod to Scandinavian design. It looked strangely out of place.

Stefanie motioned to the stairs. "We are here, we might as well go up and have a look..."

She looked as though she were about to say something further but stopped mid-sentence, cocking her head in the direction of the kitchen stairs. Lillie thought she heard the soft squeak of a loose floorboard and she held a finger to her lips. Even in the darkness they felt exposed.

Barely audible, even to her, Lillie whispered, "Someone is here."

Stefanie nodded her agreement.

Someone was in the house with them. Someone unannounced and here *they* were, unwelcome intruders.

Stefanie silently moved towards the drawing room, and Lillie hurried behind. They moved to the heavily draped windows and ducked in behind the heavy damask drapes. It was as good a place as any.

They could hear the footfalls now, nearly silent against the emptiness of the air. They had reached the top of the stairs and were moving through the house, methodically, slowly, each agonizing step a moment closer to their being discovered.

With dread, Lillie thought of the broken kitchen window. And then she held her breath.

45

FELIX PETTERS

F elix Petters, his feet impeccably shod in polished dress shoes, sped along the London pavement, careful to avoid any cracks or rubbish. His pace was brisk. Not knowing the city particularly well he had made a directional error getting off the bus and was now backtracking. He was further from the duke's townhouse than he would have liked.

His brief conversation that morning with Lillie had resulted in a frustrating start to the day. Not only had he been unable to get the kitchen cleaned and put back in order after Jeremiah had left for his paper round, but he had had to arrange for a neighbour to be at home for him when he got back, something he didn't generally like to do unless it was absolutely necessary. But the call from the Newquay detective had bothered him. They were dealing with professional assassins and it was reasonable to assume that Stefanie, and now Lillie, were credible targets. It was this knowledge that caused Petters to catch the very next train out of Oxford.

He passed a Chinese-run laundry with an adjacent apothecary, a host of bustling restaurants, and the darkened windows of a public library at quite a clip before he reached the street he was looking for. The sky was inky now and its blackness had taken the heat of the day with it—the creeping twilight across a clear sky revealed a smattering of tiny stars and constellations. He glanced up as he waited to cross, thinking how insignificant he and those around him were compared to the vast canvas of the universe. A whiff of tobacco lingered on the air, along with the headiness of damp. Summer was coming to a close and he felt the usual ardent anticipation of an impending autumn.

Petters picked his way across the intersection and hurried down the side street, past wilting hornbeams, white Georgian houses, and an occasional open park devoid of lingerers. As he neared the duke's townhouse, he noticed the streets changed somewhat. The buildings became cleaner and grander, their front greenery more manicured. Iron fences shone black under the light of the moon, their elegant spindles a deterrent to errant boxwood.

He spotted the address he was looking for and turned to face the front door. Petters stared up at a house in darkness.

A chill passed over him. He noticed a flutter of drapes inside, but other than that, he couldn't make out a thing.

46

LILLIE

They stayed there, the two of them, crushed against the drapes until Lillie felt a creeping heat and moved to give the two of them some more space. It felt like they had been there for an eternity but it couldn't have been more than ten minutes at most. There hadn't been a sound from the rest of the house.

Perhaps the intruder had left? Or was he standing at the threshold of the drawing room, observing their minute movements behind the curtains, waiting patiently for them to reveal themselves? It was an unnerving sensation.

She weighed their options. Stay, and be found, eventually— putting them on the back foot. Or creep out and risk being seen, possibly injured, and maybe even killed. Neither seemed particularly attractive and even less so with a pregnant girl in tow. But could she leave Stefanie here alone?

Deciding she didn't have much choice, she whispered into the darkness. "Stay here, I won't be long." She would do a quick reconnaissance and come back for her.

"I don't think so," Stefanie replied. "Where you go, I go."

Lillie admired the girl's conviction, especially in the face of her own dwindling confidence.

"Right, let's go then."

The two of them moved silently across the room, choosing the carpet over the wood floor when possible, and towards the open drawing room door. The hallway was dark but the moon lit the space enough to show them their surroundings. The library was ahead of them, and to their right the dining room. Both were empty. Lillie didn't want to stand out in the open like they were now, so she moved towards the library to regroup.

As she did she heard an unmistakable click. From the staircase came a recognizable voice and she heard Stefanie suddenly catch her breath.

"I have been following your column, Miss Mead. I daresay you may be just as good a detective as a journalist."

Lillie spun to face the voice. Staring dumbfounded at the woman before her, she cursed herself for misreading the situation entirely.

"Apparently not," she replied, willing herself to calm. "For I was quite expecting someone else here this evening."

The gun was levelled at Stefanie's chest and Lillie had no doubt that should the woman decide to take a shot, it was unlikely she would miss. She felt the blood race through her veins, her heart beat quickened. She would need to keep her talking.

"Auntie Clara? What are you doing?" Stefanie's voice conveyed all the bewilderment Lillie also felt.

"What do you think? I came to finish what I started."

"You mean you...it was you that morning on the cliffs? You shot the duke?"

"Aye."

"But why? Why would you do that?" Stefanie's voice was frantic now and Lillie feared not only for their safety, but felt sick at the prospect of this deranged woman taking the life on an unborn child right along with them.

"Isn't it obvious?" The gun wobbled a little as she spoke and Lillie feared the woman might accidentally discharge it. "You wander into that bank and become the favoured one, the *adored* one. I got you that job. He hired you because of me, because he loved *me!*" Her voice rose hysterically and it reverberated off the the walls. Looking at her in her crazed state, her hair a mess, her eyes red-rimmed, her lips drawn back in a snarl, Lillie wondered what the duke would have ever seen in the likes of her. Lillie thought she could hear voices coming from below but without a view to the kitchen stairs she couldn't be sure of anything. She kept an eye on the gun and strained to listen.

Stefanie was pleading with her aunt. "I didn't know, Auntie, please...how could I have known about you and the duke? You never said."

"As if I would," the woman retorted, sharply.

"If I had known, I never would have..." She trailed off at the sound of voices in the dining room.

Clara followed her line of vision as a man came around the corner and, seeing the situation before him, stopped abruptly. Clara sucked in her breath sharply in astonishment, and Lillie realized the woman might have been thinking she had seen a ghost. Before her stood Charlie Linton, but not the Charlie Linton from the newspaper clippings. This Charlie Linton was dressed in a dinner jacket, his thinning hair was coiffed back in a negligible wave, his face was clean-shaven and his eyes sparkled. He was the duke's twin in every way imaginable.

It took him a moment to regroup. He glanced around at Lillie and Stephanie then settled his eyes back on Clara and her gun.

"Now, now. Why don't you put that down?" he soothed. "This isn't going to solve anything, is it? It's only going to land you in a great deal of trouble." He had a lovely, calm way about him and Lillie prayed it would be enough to defuse the situation.

Clara had begun to recover from her initial shock and see Linton for who he was. Perhaps it was the voice, or the mannerisms, but with the realization that she wasn't seeing a dead man came the recovery of control—she was still the one holding the gun.

"I'm already in trouble." Her voice shook and Lillie hoped she was a woman capable of second thoughts. "I killed him, and if I don't kill all of you and leave this country tonight, I'm done for."

"Please don't, Auntie, please," Stefanie pleaded.

What happened next so astonished Lillie that she felt as though she were in a dream. Linton abruptly rushed forward towards Clara and the staircase. Clara fired, narrowly missing him and instead hitting the large lamp on the console table by the door. It shattered spectacularly and the pieces rained to the floor with a clatter. In almost the same instant there was an enormous crash and the front door was flung open to reveal a surprised but at-the-ready Felix Petters. He stood on the threshold, gun drawn, eyes set on Clara.

Through all the chaos none of them saw a woman creep around the corner from the corridor that housed the water closet and the coat cupboard. The duchess now stood below Clara's perch on the stairs and, unbeknownst to Stefanie's aunt, drew a small pistol and aimed it.

She fired once, startling them all. Then again, and then a third time. All three bullets hit their target. As if in a surreal dream, Clara stared down at the swath of blood oozing across the front of her dress. She wobbled precariously on the step, and as though in slow motion, crashed through the bannister and fell to the ground. There was a sickening thud and Stefanie let out a startled cry of anguish.

"Drop it," came from the voice in the doorway. Petters spoke in a tone that can only come from reliable police training. He levelled his pistol at the duchess's chest, with the intention to kill.

The duchess looked at him in defeat. She hesitated for only a moment, and then she slowly raised her hands.

47

LILLIE

"Perhaps she should have had a career on the stage," Stefanie said grimly. She was still sitting on the bottom stair in the duke and duchess's townhouse staring at the upturned face of a woman who had, quite handily, deceived them all. Charlie Linton, the man whose resemblance to the duke was eerily disturbing, sat near her. Aunt Clara's skin had assumed the ashen hue of death and Lillie wished the police would finish up and take the body to the morgue.

"A woman who can play the villain will always be in a theatre troupe's employ," Harry solemnly summed up. Lillie shot him a withering glance, which he, as usual, failed to comprehend. He continued with oblivion. "Shall I escort you two back to the hotel? It looks as though things are finishing here and one hardly needs to be present for the packing up."

Harry had arrived with Rumple only minutes after Petters had crashed through the front door, and had immediately busied himself with calling the police, instructing Rumple to make tea in the downstairs kitchen, and comforting Stefanie, while they waited for officers to arrive. Rumple now quietly handed Lillie a second cup, then glided away and back down the stairs to the kitchen.

Stefanie was momentarily distracted by two police officers who were coming out of the drawing room. They stopped briefly to discuss something with the small group of police who were now set up in the library.

"I am terribly sorry for telling your aunt where you had gone," Harry said abruptly. "When she showed up at the hotel this afternoon I just assumed that being family meant she wanted to help you. I hardly imagined she wanted to kill you." Harry stared at the body.

"Yes, well, nor did I. I knew the figure on the cliffs that day seemed familiar, but she was completely shrouded in a scarf and hat. I thought it was a man, actually. But there was something in the stance, the way the figure stood...I should have clued in on it."

"And the duke never told you of their affair?" Lillie asked.

"I had no idea. There wasn't ever any discussion. He made me feel as though I was the only woman he had ever cheated with. You never really know a person, do you?"

Lillie thought about this. No, she supposed, thinking of her own private dealings with Daniel—something she hadn't told anyone other than Harry about. And then there was Jack's constant subterfuge. How much of anyone do any of us really know, she wondered?

The duchess had been taken to the station only moments before. Through her tears, she had been remarkably forthcoming about everything—she loved Charlie Linton, she had told them. She always had. The three of them had grown up together in Oxfordshire. Linton had gone to South Africa a few years after the duke and duchess were married, but by then he and the duchess had already begun what was to become a tumultuous and torrid affair lasting over twenty years.

In 1900, she told them—while Charlie silently listened as
though the conversation was about someone else—the British
forces had their backs to the wall and the Boers were gaining
the upper hand. Linton had gone, along with thousands of
other British troops, in a hastily organized contingent to fight
the Boers. He hadn't come back the same man, and his relationship with both her and his twin brother, the duke, had changed
—what he had seen at war meant he was a different man—but
they picked up where they had left off, he and the duchess, and
they had continued their affair.

Even when Linton had turned to drugs and alcohol to curb
the memory of war, the duchess hadn't lost touch. Her intention was to be with him. The money she and the duke
conspired to steal from the American mob was part of a long-
term plan for both of them. She was to finally be with Linton,
and the duke had planned to whisk Stefanie away to the West
Indies and then, eventually, to Canada. They had discussed
their futures and were in agreement that neither of them were
in love with each other.

"And Angus?" Lillie had asked her while the duchess sat on
one of the balloon- backed dining chairs, an officer on each
side.

"He knew," she sighed. "Unbeknownst to me, he knew, and
he was blackmailing the duke."

She hadn't admitted to killing him, but Lillie supposed that
would come out in the interrogation at the station. No doubt
the two men staying in Cornwall, upon her hire, were the ones
to put a bullet in his chest.

"And the fire? At Clara's cottage?"

The duchess had sat stone-faced, staring ahead. Eventually she replied. "I thought she knew," she said, with gravity. "I
thought she had evidence of what we were doing. The duke
was such a terrible thief, he talked—to his mistresses, to his
associates at the bank. He could hardly keep a secret and I

didn't want to leave town and have a trail of evidence behind me to trip us up. I sent a couple of hired men in to sort through her things, to see if there was anything to lead the police or the mob back to me. It was unfortunate she came home early. She put up quite a argument and they—well, they panicked, I suppose. The place was ransacked, they had knocked her unconscious, and in all their thuggish wisdom they decided setting fire to the place was as a good a decision as any." She had looked around at them. "Obviously, it wasn't."

A police car had sat idling at the curb, and the officers had removed the woman from the dining room, careful to not let her linger where Charlie Linton had sat on the stair in the foyer, watching as his fragile world fell apart.

He spoke quietly now. "I didn't know about it all, she never said..."

Harry replied, "No, well, I suppose the loss of one's fortune is hardly dinner conversation."

"I was estranged from my family after South Africa, I suppose they didn't think I needed to be privy to financial matters. I'm sorry for that now, perhaps I could have stopped all this before it went this way."

Stefanie nodded absently, no doubt thinking the same thing.

Lillie continued. "Originally I thought Alek must have been involved, but it seems his troubles were quite separate from those of the bank's. I feel badly for misjudging him."

"No, he isn't a bad man. Just a tremendously weak one," Stefanie sighed, then appeared to remember Harry's offer of a lift home. "If you think it is alright for us to leave, I would like that." She looked to Felix Petters who was leaning against a well-trimmed wall and speaking to one of the uniformed police officers and the lead investigator who, rather oddly, was dressed in tails. By the looks of it the poor man had been attending a formal function prior to the emergency call. He held his top hat in his hands.

He turned to them. "Yes, go ahead. If I need anything else I know where to find you. Ah...Mr Linton, would you please accompany me to the station." He motioned to Lillie and stepped out of earshot. "Miss Mead, if you wouldn't mind, it would be better for the investigation if this matter wasn't reported in tomorrow's newspaper."

Lillie nodded her agreement. "I'll give it some time. You will, however, grant me an exclusive when the time comes?"

"Reporters," he stated bluntly. "Always pushing for something."

"Rather like law enforcement," she retorted, amiably. Then added. "Thank you for responding so quickly."

He made a tip of his imaginary hat. "The Met, at your service."

Lillie turned to Harry and Stefanie. "Let's go then."

The three of them stepped carefully around the police, the body on the floor to which Stefanie gave a last mournful glimpse, and the crowd of neighbours who were now gathering behind the police tape at the door. The night was cool and the streetlights were on, casting the scene in an amber glow. If it weren't for all the onlookers and police, it could have been any ordinary evening in Chelsea.

As they walked towards the car at the curb, Lillie saw a man standing alone a few yards to their left, in a shadowed area devoid of onlookers. She couldn't see his face but the body was stamped on her memory—the leanness, the buckle on his trousers, the pearled buttons on his dress shirt, the long taut arms wrapped around her. She didn't need to see any of these things to know it was him.

She paused, her head turned, and watched him.

"Hurry up," Harry scolded, holding the car door open for

her. Stefanie was already inside and Rumple was at the wheel. He, too, had noticed what she was looking at.

"Coming ..." she answered, but she hardly wanted to tear her eyes away. The man in the shadows nodded once to her, then turned into the darkness. She watched as it swallowed him up.

Rumple started the engine.

48

LILLIE

TWO WEEKS LATER

"What I don't understand is how you could stay away for years, and let me believe you were dead?" She wondered how they had got here, again, onto this particular subject matter.

Outside the car window, the Oxfordshire landscape was clinging to the last vestiges of summer. It wouldn't be long before the cool mornings gave way to burning leaves and dewy ground. Lillie wished she could change course and rope the conversation back to the weather, or the article, or even his work.

"Tell me truthfully, was there someone else?" She surprised herself saying it out loud. Had she thought it before? Was that what kept her from jumping in with both feet, bullets be damned?

She remembered the moment in the hotel in London when she watched as he flirted with the hotel attendant. The way he leaned in across the gleaming counter and made the woman laugh, the way that she should interpret it as more than friendly. She felt instantly sick. Was it possible the Jack she knew could be someone else entirely. That the man she loved could lie to her? That perhaps his authenticity didn't run the whole way through?

She wasn't surprised when he didn't answer right away. *Had* there been someone else during the war years that kept him from her? An interlude, a romance, someone he worked with, perhaps? She thought of the closeness she had experienced with a former assassin, of all people. A man with a tormented past and a shaky future. A man she thought about more than she should. She was completely aware of her own hypocrisy.

Jack turned his head to look at her briefly before settling his eyes back on the road. "It was a very different time, but nothing has ever been more important than my love for you."

It sounded suspiciously like he was sidestepping a direct question, she thought with frustration. Why couldn't he just be honest with her? Or maybe she was just being paranoid. She took to staring out the window and dropped the line of questioning. What good did any of this meddling do now? They were soon to be married and all she was doing was rocking the boat.

They exited the main road and turned through a large set of iron and stone gates and headed up a lengthy crushed stone drive. A long, slow, late afternoon breeze blew across the Tynesmore gardens and whispered through the leafy branches of a row of ancient oaks lining the gravel courtyard. Jack pulled the Lagonda up in front of Harry's house and Lillie hopped out before he could come around and open her door. The stones crunched beneath her feet and pushed against the soles of her shoes as she ducked her head back into the car.

Jack frowned at her. "You really should wait until I open your door."

"Pish." She laughed at him, hoping it sounded convincingly light-hearted. Although even riddled with angst and guilt, her relief at being back in Oxford was growing by the minute. This place empowered her with a lightness of being she had never really found anywhere else, regardless of how complicated her life had become. She wondered how her cottage had fared in her absence and looked forward to finally going home to it that evening. She would putter in the garden until dusk, she decided, planning how next year she might eke out a little space to put in a row of runner beans amongst the primroses and hydrangeas. Perhaps she might even add some tomato plants on the south side of the house, provided she could keep the deer away. She wondered at her ability to compartmentalize her life.

"I'll just drop the car off in Harry's garage and see if his man can't figure out what that pinging sound is."

"Tea is in the garden so come directly there." Lillie gave the door a push to close, and hurried around the side of the house.

They had only just arrived back from London, although it felt a million miles away now, and she wished she had had time to change into a sundress. The filth of the city clung to her. She had stopped briefly in town in order to hand her article in to the newspaper. It would print tomorrow and her boss, Jeremy Winston, had been pleased to see her. She wondered if he wasn't often a little *too* pleased to see her and she had been grateful Jack had chosen to stay in the car.

Jeremy had perused her work quickly while she stood in his office, trying not to look impatient.

"Won't you stay for little while?" he had asked her, not looking up from the page, his glasses perched on the end of his nose in a delicate balancing act. She watched his eyes skim the page like two little tadpoles moving in unison across the water.

"I really can't. I want to say goodbye to Stefanie. She is staying over at Harry's place and she leaves for Sweden tomorrow. Before she goes I would like to get a follow-up interview done, now that things have settled. You never know, we might want it for the next issue." She was reaching and they both knew it. The final story was all but written and would print a few days after the one she had just handed to Winston. Her real intent was to get out of the office so she could think about things.

"I see." Jeremy tried, with futility, to mask his disappointment. He turned and placed her article on the desktop. "Well written, as always, and a follow up would be nice. I don't want too much blame placed on the institutional apparatus of the bank, if at all possible. The work of a few shouldn't condemn the many." He caught the look of annoyance on her face and attempted to appease her. "Just something to be mindful of," he finished awkwardly.

How nice it would be to run her own newspaper and not walk a constant tightrope. But Lillie nodded her agreement anyway, glancing at the clock over his shoulder. Two thirty. She twitched, wanting to wrap this up.

"Well," she began, "I'll be in first thing tomorrow to write up the rest of my notes."

Jeremy opened his mouth, as though he wanted to say something else, then seemed to decide against it. Lillie took the opportunity to pick up her bag where she had left it next to the door and hurriedly said her goodbyes.

Now, forty minutes later, she stood on Harry's flagstone patio overlooking a manicured but still very English-looking garden. She admired how the wildness of lavender wove its way between trimmed boxwood hedging and encircled the trunks of great, bulbous Portuguese laurels.

Stefanie was already seated at a round table that had been draped in a tasteful chintz tablecloth, it's voluminous cabbage roses painted fantastically in lavenders and robin's-egg blue to match a late summer sky. She had her hands rested over her growing belly, its little mound foreshadowing a new life that wouldn't be long in making its debut. Her long hair was plaited and fell forward across her shoulder as she bent her head forward to whisper something to her unborn baby. Lillie hated to interrupt and wondered if she shouldn't perhaps backtrack and pop into the house instead. Before she could decide, Harry, oblivious to the tender moment, emerged from the French doors flanked by Constance, his absurdly large wolfhound, and, surprisingly, Alek.

"Ah! There you are," he called to her. Constance trotted over to give her a welcoming sniff before settling down on the lawn, great paws outstretched. The dog immediately set to work grooming something off one of her front legs. "Come, sit, we have been anxiously waiting for you. How was the venue?"

Harry had suggested Lillie and Jack investigate a rather large, but immaculately kept hotel on the outskirts of Oxford as a possible location to hold their wedding breakfast after the church service. They had stopped there on their way into town before her meeting with Jeremy.

"Yes, quite nice actually." Lillie said hello to Stefanie and shook Alek's hand as she took her seat. "But what wouldn't be nice on a day like today. I wonder if it isn't a little large, almost cavernous in its immenseness. I did rather hope for a more intimate affair, less of the pomp and less of the ceremony."

Harry eyed her warily. "My dear, it is a *wedding*, after all."

"I know." She avoided his gaze and placed her napkin on her lap, attempting to smooth the starched crease. "But it needn't be a state affair."

"I see," Harry said quietly. "Perhaps then you might reconsider taking me up on my offer of hosting your reception here, at Tynesmore?" He leaned in closer and murmured conspiratorially. "At least then if you back out at the last moment you shan't be out of pocket for the rental."

"Harry, the last time you had a wedding here at Tynesmore it was your own and it was hardly lacking in the pomp department. I seem to remember an abominable French organizer who made everyone uncomfortable, a hot air balloon the size of Kensington Palace, and enough flowers to sink a Napoleonic battleship."

"The French have never been known for their sea-going prowess, that much is certainly true," Harry replied.

"I think it would be appealing to have a small wedding reception," Stefanie put in. "Something in the spring, or summer, in a little garden somewhere overlooking the ocean. I always thought Cornwall would make a lovely wedding spot."

Lillie smiled her thanks and attempted to divert the conversation. "Will you miss it?"

"Yes, and no," Stefanie replied nostalgically. "Without my aunt it doesn't really make sense to go back there. And while I do love the scenery, to say nothing of the diving cliffs, there are so many troubled memories now. And I can't go back to work for the bank, not with everything that has happened. I am looking forward to going home to Sweden."

"Sweden," Harry repeated, reaching across for the teapot and setting to work pouring each of them a cup. "A place I have never had the privilege of travelling to. Perhaps we shall come visit."

"That would be nice." She smiled at them. "Just don't come in the winter." She glanced around the table. "Alek is coming with me. We've been thinking of opening a tea shop there. My friend Anneka tells me there is a lovely old place for lease on the high street, I could fix it up a bit, a lick of paint here and there, and I don't need much of a kitchen."

Alek smiled at Stefanie across the table.

"A tea shop?" Lillie asked with surprise, choosing to sidestep the question of Alek's extraction from his miserable marriage. She knew from what little Jack had told her that thanks to Alek's information, his wife and her father were up on arms trafficking charges. She didn't expect the case to be settled any time soon and this certainly would have made it much easier for Alek to leave his wife.

"Ah, so that is what you were doing in my kitchen?" Harry laughed.

Stefanie smiled. She had taken Harry up on his generous offer of a room at Tynesmore until she could decide on her ulti-mate destination. They had arrived a few days ago while Lillie had stayed in London to tie up things with her article and the investigation. It had taken a few days for the police to grant her the exclusive interview they had promised, and Lillie had tried to see the duchess in custody but had been denied. No doubt her trial would be long and complicated. The source of the missing money, Flegenheimst and his American cronies, seemed to have vanished into thin air. Back to America, no doubt, to carry on with whatever nefarious activities had made them that fortune.

"Try it." Stefanie motioned to their cups and Lillie stirred a little milk into hers and raised it to her lips. It was deliciously fruity, with a subtle hint of peach. Quite unusual for tea.

"I call this one *Peach Jam*, although I think it needs a little tweaking yet."

"It's so unexpected! And in England, no less. If you ever tire of being in Sweden, you would always do well in America."

"Do you think so?" Stefanie seemed pleased. "I have quite a few of them now; creams, herbals, blacks and even some white teas. It's coming up with names for them all that is challenging. Yesterday I made a *Summer Abroad*: citrus and lavender with a black base; quite good actually. I used to make them with my aunt, but it was more for fun than anything."

"Perhaps you might serve them at your wedding?" Harry interjected.

"Capital idea," came a voice from behind Lillie. Jack strode onto the patio and said his hellos. "And about time we started seriously discussing this wedding of ours." His dark hair was ruffled from the breeze and he had the top button of his soft blue dress shirt unbuttoned, his jacket he discarded onto the back of an empty chair. As he shook hands with Alek and Harry, Lillie noticed a smear of oil from the car across his cuff. It was difficult not to find him remarkably handsome.

"Anything new on the duchess?" Harry asked, pouring him a cup of tea and passing around a plate of coloured madeleines. Lillie pinched a pink one then, rethinking her decision, also added a yellow one to her plate. "I still feel tremendously dull-witted for not seeing through it all."

Jack swallowed a gulp of tea. "Not really, no. She's still in custody and will be for some time. We have yet to find the two men associated with Angus's death and the cottage fire. I wonder if the Home Office may not have enough to go on. From what I hear, there isn't much evidence—which is to be expected when you drop a couple of professionals into the mix."

The table remained silent for a short time and then conversation invariably turned to other things. Harry was heading to the station later that evening to collect Primrose. She had been away for over a month and he was excited for her return. In true Harry fashion, he had planned a dinner as grand as anything seen in the dining halls of Buckingham Palace.

"I should think she will just want a bath and a glass of wine," Lillie warned him. Jack was mulling out loud over when he should return to London, and Stefanie and Alek went back to discussing her new business venture. They imagined the tea shop would have tall ceilings and high windows, they would paint it peony pink and hang a brass sign with its name over the door. They debated for a time on its naming and Harry piped up throwing in his suggestions, none of which seemed at all suitable for a tea house.

As the haze of the afternoon flooded the fields around them, even the birds grew drowsy with the heat thereby silencing their twitters. Lillie got up and stretched out her arms. It was time to go.

"I am sorry to dash off and leave you all but I need to get home. I can imagine the layer of dust accumulating and I would think my poor, parched garden is in need of a good water. Jack?" She looked down at her husband-to-be with a mixture of emotions.

She loved him, of that she was sure. What was less clear was how she would feel being married to him; his strange, dangerous and nomadic life. And the constant nagging fear that he could disappear at any moment. But even deeper was something else. Something less tangible and less conscious. A burrowing sense of something she had buried, pushed down to unreachable depths. The truthful recognition of what had really happened to him during the war. What had really caused him to disappear and let them all believe he was dead? It was the job, of course it was. But no regular human being could go along with that, could they? No normal person could willingly watch their friends and family believe they had expired. Which meant Jack was far from normal. He was extraordinary. And she wasn't sure she could be married to *extraordinary*. For with it came a dark realization that he would do whatever it took to continue in his occupation as an intelligence officer. She sighed. The world of spies and informants was one she little understood.

Jack stood up, mistaking her sigh for impatience. They said their thanks and goodbyes.

"I can't thank you enough," Stefanie said softly, her eyes filling. "You never gave up on me."

As they pulled away from Tynesmore in the Lagonda, Lillie breathed in the fresh Oxford air. Jack reached one hand off the steering wheel and found her hand. "A late September wedding, then?" he asked, tentatively. When she didn't immediately answer he filled in the silence. "Or October. October can be beautiful in England. Or would you like to go abroad? That's an option as well…if you like…"

She squeezed his hand. It was all she could manage at the moment.

EPILOGUE

The cottage breathed its smoke into the twilight, a long, curling stream of grey escaping the chimney and diffusing its way towards the emerging stars. A cricket chirped, and then another in answer, and another after that, until a chorus erupted in the thicket bordering the rolling fields beyond and cascading on through the night air to be punctuated only by a passing car on the distant high street or a runaway hound.

He waited.

Through the cottage windows he could make out shadows, the odd flash of colour from her dress—French blue—as she puttered between what looked to be the kitchen and the sitting room. He had never been inside, but imagined it now from his place under the great canopy of an ancient walnut tree.

It would be tidy, of course, and comforting. There would be chintz fabric, but only the very faded type—cotton in all likelihood, or linen, in blues or greens, possibly even yellow. Fresh. Like she was. Her furniture would be delicately worn, with a fine chair or two here and there—Louis XV perhaps, or Chippendale—juxtaposed with a farmhouse salt-scrubbed table.

Something dinner could be laid upon without worrying about spills.

Upstairs would be small and cramped, warm in the evenings, and smelling like her. Rose or lavender linen water splashed across her bed covers. A clawfoot tub littered with water droplets from her bath, a half-empty cup of tea forgotten beside it. He looked up at the leaded windows and imagined her there, wrapped in a towel, her wet hair piled upon her head while she rubbed milk cream over her bare skin.

She would be reading a book by now, downstairs by the fire, or writing her weekly column—her pen scratching quickly across the surface of her paper, futilely trying to keep pace with her thoughts. The early September evenings had turned cold, the last rush of summer now gone, the leaves beginning to turn and rustle beneath his feet.

Was she alone?

He wondered what she would have for dinner. Something simple—a green salad from her garden and some toast and eggs. Supper for one. Poached pears for dessert, dribbled with cassis syrup, and then an early night. He imagined himself crawling into her bed, wrapping them both in her lavender sheets and feeling the autumn breeze blow through her open window, billowing the curtains over their entwined bodies, cooling their skin, her hair in his face.

He was taking a chance still being here in England, a country where he was still a wanted criminal. Law enforcement wouldn't care less that he was a changed man; rehabilitated and making amends, sorry for his past sins. But he had a good cover this time—his papers false but impeccable. Getting caught was something that happened to people who weren't smart or prepared enough to undertake their said mission.

He wondered if she had decided on a wedding date? It wasn't fair of him to be here, muddling her mind. Perhaps he should go—slide back into the darkness of anonymity and forget she existed.

If only he could, both their lives would be the easier for it.

He edged himself from under the tree and began to walk towards her front door. The gate creaked on its hinges as he opened it and he left it ajar not wanting to alert her.

He still hadn't decided.

His footfalls on the cobblestone path fell as though he were a hesitant child creeping downstairs after dark for extra dessert, expecting a lashing.

He raised one trembling hand to knock.

Did he dare?

The eventual sound of his knuckles on the door echoed quietly throughout her little yard and splashed across the darkness.

Even the crickets held their breath.

ABOUT THE AUTHOR

Lisa Zumpano is the author of the Lillie Mead Historical Mystery Series.
She resides in Vancouver, Canada.

JOIN THE READERS GROUP
It's the best way to get up-to-date details of new releases, special offers and news.

You will receive a free digital copy of:
The Harry Green Guide on How to Throw a 'Roaring' Party 1920's Style

See details through my website at lisazumpano.com

Connecting with readers is my favourite part of being an author.
I'll look forward to seeing you there.

Made in the USA
Las Vegas, NV
08 June 2022